Guide Me Home

"Connie Cortright creates wonderful, rich characters and sets them in a little written about time period, the 1920s. *Guide Me Home* brings the Jazz Age to life in crisp detail. At points, you'll want to cheer; at others, you'll be moved to tears. All in all, a great debut novel, one you'll want to pick up and not put down until you reach the end."

–Liz Tolsma, Author of *Snow on the Tulips*, 2014 Carol Award finalist

"Connie Cortright's novel of a young schoolteacher's first year in a small, Lutheran school sensitively captured for this reader both Emma's dutiful nature and prairie upbringing, as well as the tempting and glamorous 1920s world in which she lives with its shimmering chandeliers, men on the make, and lakefront mansions."

–Lorna Wiedmann, Ph. D.

Grace Alone Series

Book 1

The heartwarming story of *Guide Me Home* begins the Grace Alone Series, the saga of three sisters facing times of change and challenge in the 1920s, 1930s, and 1940s.

Guide Me Home

CONNIE CORTRIGHT

Scripture quotations are taken from the King James Version of the Bible.

http://www.conniecortright.com

Published by Milk Door Publications

Edited by Liz Tolsma / The Write Direction Editing

Cover design by Lisa Hainline / Lionsgate Book Design

Printed by CreateSpace, An Amazon.com Company

Available from Amazon.com and other book stores

ISBN: 978-0-9968441-0-9

Dedication

To my loving husband, HB, whose wit and patience saw me through this project from beginning to the end. Without your input and insight into the hero's character, this book would not exist. Also, to my mother and father who have believed in me from the very beginning, ten years ago.

AUTHOR'S NOTE

Guide Me Home is the story of a Lutheran parochial school teacher in the Roaring Twenties. In Wisconsin and the Midwest at this time in addition to public schools, Roman Catholic parishes and Lutheran parishes commonly operated elementary schools for their respective church's children.

Our heroine, Miss Emma Ehlke, is not a "Lutheran nun," but a young, single woman who was trained for her profession in a teacher's college run by her Lutheran denomination. Her training was similar to the normal school colleges, which trained public school teachers, but she was also taught to teach religion to her students.

New teachers like Emma were assigned to teach at a Lutheran grade school upon graduation from college. Typically, a school board chosen from among the men of the congregation governed Lutheran schools. The Lutheran school was an endeavor that involved the entire congregation.

Since virtually all the children attending Emma's school were from the congregation's families, Emma would be expected to hold devotions, teach Bible stories, and also hymnody. Older students would receive instruction in Martin Luther's *Small Catechism* by the pastor in preparation for reception into the congregation as young, "confirmed" adults. New adult converts to Lutheranism also had to study the doctrines of their new faith by the same method.

In the story, Pastor Hannemann lives in a "parsonage," a supplied home situated next to the church. Married male teachers usually lived in "teacherages" owned by the congregation. Young, unmarried teachers like Emma were usually boarded with a church family.

CHAPTER 1

"I'm here to talk to you about my son." A piercing voice shot across the classroom.

Emma Ehlke dropped her pen, splattering ink over the neatly organized stack of lesson plans. The whole morning's work stained in a second. The verbal ambush made Emma's eyes dart in the direction of the sound as her heart slammed against her ribs.

A stout, middle-aged woman with speckled gray hair stood in the doorway with her hands on her hips. By the pinched look on her round red face, Emma wondered if she'd just bitten into a lemon.

"Mrs. Ethel Piggott. You met me at church." Her prominent chin preceding her, the woman marched purposefully toward Emma, her long skirt swishing around her ankles.

Emma recovered herself. A calming breath. A smoothing back of her hair to steady her hands. Glasses deliberately removed and placed on her desk. She stood and walked to the edge of the raised platform.

To make a good impression was paramount in her mind as a new teacher. Mrs. Piggott. She ransacked her brain to remember a student with that name. She lifted the hem of her skirt to step down. "I'm Miss—."

"You don't have to tell me who you are." The woman crossed her arms. "I can't believe you don't remember me. My husband, Meyer, or *Mr.* Piggott to you, is the school board chairman." Her voice crackled with arrogance.

Emma stepped off the platform and walked between two rows of wooden desks bolted to the floor. With her clammy palm outstretched in greeting, the heels of Emma's lace-up shoes clicked as she crossed the creaky floor to meet the woman midway. "I beg your pardon. It's just that I've made the acquaintance of so many people since Sunday it's hard to remember everyone's name."

Major lapse not remembering this lady.

She'd spent the last three days filling her head with lesson plans, textbooks, and names of children. Less than a week remained to get prepared for school's opening. Surely, um, Mrs. Piggly should understand that under the circumstances it was hard to think straight, much less remember everyone from church.

Shaking Emma's hand, Mrs. P. snorted. "Not surprising. Since you're a first-year teacher, I wanted to come in this week to make sure you start the year off on the right foot." An animated nod caused her wide-brimmed hat with outsized orange flowers to teeter precariously on her head. Raising a gloved hand, she set the straw bonnet back in place.

The woman's pungently sweet perfume invaded Emma's nostrils. She held her breath while resolving to stay calm. She couldn't let a parent upset her before school even started. Disarm her with politeness. "Thank you for your—"

Mrs. P. charged on, her raspy voice grating like fingernails scraping against a chalkboard. "My son, Karl, is in your third grade and you should know he's a very special boy and will need extra time and care from you."

Just what she needed. A student who required special consideration. A project. Impossible with so many children in her room. "Thank you so much for coming to see me. It'll help to know these things ahead of time." What else could she say?

"You have to understand he is our youngest child. Karl came along quite a few years after our Betty. He has a married sister with a baby, so he's already an uncle. Betty and her husband live up north in Wisconsin, but still come home to visit often. He struggles to get our attention when the baby is around." Peering over her glasses, she cleared her throat. "To an amateur like you, he may seem naughty."

Emma clenched her fists. Amateur! How could Mrs. Piggery possibly consider her an amateur? Question her ability that way? She had her teaching degree where this mother probably hadn't even finished high school. Her pulse raced. "I understand your concern for Karl. It's good to hear about his circumstances." She breathed out slowly, but her stomach flipped so many times it might as well join a circus.

"Well, that's why I'm here this morning to tell you, so you go about things the right way."

Emma forced a smile onto her face. If only she could hide her anger in front of this, this parent. The gall of this Piggotty woman to come in here and call her an amateur. She swallowed. "It'll help me deal with any problems with him coming up early in the school year."

"Problems? Problems with Karl?" Mrs. Piggott's nostrils flared as she spoke. "If he gets the attention he deserves, you won't have any problems with him. He only needs to be understood. Just make sure *you* realize it." Her teeth bit off each word in staccato fashion. "He. Doesn't. Cause. Problems."

Was she scolding her? Emma tried to stifle a gasp, but failed miserably. What now? No course in college had taught her how to deal with situations like this. As her heart pounded in her ears, she hid her clenched hands behind her back. "Ma'am, you must understand I have forty students in four grades in this room."

Mrs. Piggery just kept clucking. "Just make sure you give him proper attention, and he'll be the wonderful student he's always been."

Her mind racing, Emma let out her breath. Her blood pressure must have doubled by now. Weighing each word before speaking, she obviously couldn't say what was on the tip of her tongue. "I assure you I will give each student as much attention as possible, fairly and equitably. However, at the end of each day, I will need to teach all the subjects the school board requires at St. John's."

"I was afraid you'd say that." Mrs. P. planted herself within inches of Emma's face, her stale breath filling the space between them. "I've been trying to tell Mr. Dietz we need a third classroom in our school. Now, here we are in the same old situation." Her icy stare reinforced the cold words she spoke. "Mr. Piggott tried to persuade the board at my urging, but they wouldn't listen to him. If we must have just the two classrooms, we really should have a new male teacher. At least he would know how to handle the children better."

Male teacher? Emma opened her mouth but didn't have time to respond.

"We have you, so we'll have to do the best we can." Mrs. P. bowed her head and exhaled before continuing. "You ask around. I know how to deal with children after raising my own. If you need advice, you know whom to call. Good day. Oh, yes, and welcome to Racine." The tornado left the room as suddenly as she had entered it.

Emma stood frozen in place in the silence after the storm, her mind reeling. She couldn't think straight. Falling onto a student desk, she put her head in her hands. How could parents prefer a male teacher for first graders? It didn't make any sense. What should she have said to this woman?

She let out a breath and forced herself off the desk. Emma couldn't believe she would have to face these sentiments in a parochial school. Shouldn't she be able to assume all of the parents loved God and their children as much as she did? After all, they all belonged to the same Lutheran church. Piggy wasn't very loving as far as Emma could see. How could Mrs. P. question her capabilities even before she had taught one day? Amateur?

She'd better find Mr. Dietz. The principal should be able to advise her on how to deal with Karl in light of what his mother had said. All the parents couldn't be like her, could they? She hurried across the hall to find the principal. Not in his room. She searched the other rooms downstairs. He was not in sight. Shaking her head, she slumped her shoulders.

If only Ma were closer. She'd always been someone Emma could confide in, but she was miles away. Probably canning tomatoes in a hot kitchen. As the oldest daughter in the family, Emma should be there to help her. Not this year.

She wasn't feeling guilty about it, though. She'd wanted to escape from farm life in the small Wisconsin town of Juneau. No way would she get caught like the rest of her schoolmates, marrying farmers, having babies, and working hard their entire lives.

But right now city life didn't look so appealing. Not if teaching meant facing mothers like Mrs. Piggeldy very often. This wasn't how she'd pictured the school year would start. What had she gotten herself into?

Blinking away threatening tears, Emma sighed. Was she homesick already? She snapped upright at the suggestion. Of course not. She couldn't feel sorry for herself right now. No time for that.

Even so, she sure would like to talk to someone. If nothing else, she had to get some facts and get Mrs. What's-her-name off her chest.

Would Pastor Hannemann be in his office? He'd picked her up at the train station five days ago, but she really didn't know him very well. Still, she'd often confided in Pastor Vogel at home while growing up, so maybe he could help. At least he was close by since the Pastor's house was next to the school.

Grabbing her gloves before leaving her room, she marched down the steps and out the door. As she strode across the lawn to the parsonage, her ankle-length skirt wrapped around her legs, threatening to trip her. Pausing to smooth her chignon, she knocked on his door.

***

Pastor Nils Hannemann placed his pen on the desk and closed his Bible. He glanced out his office window and stared at the church wall twenty feet away. There were advantages living in the house next to the church, but the view out the window was not one of them.

His eyes returned to the blank pages sitting in front of him. Writing sermons on a regular basis was harder than he had thought. Since he'd graduated from the seminary in May, he'd discovered the reality of the task. After running short of time the first few weeks, he had begun his sermons a bit earlier, so he wouldn't get caught up in the Saturday night cram routine.

Nils surveyed his books arrayed around him like a general surveying his troops. Fidgeting, he reshuffled his books on his desk. Somehow this made him feel more in command to do sermonic battle with his text.

At least he wasn't working in the fields back home. His heart had never been in farm work. Pa probably knew that before he did. His brothers seemed to thrive on caring for the animals and harvesting the crops, but for him doing the chores was a boring and repetitive task.

From a very young age, old Pastor Schroeder had encouraged him to think about going to the seminary and becoming a pastor. Maybe Pa had put him up to it in the first place. Nils smiled at the thought.

The ticking clock reminded him time was fleeting. Thursday already. He picked up his pen determined to set out his outline of St. Paul's words to Timothy. Propping his elbow on his desk, he rested his chin in the palm of his hand. He had to keep going, or he'd never finish.

A knock at the door brought him to a halt. Not what he needed right now. But he had no choice. Time to find out who needed his help at this hour. With a sigh, he pushed back his chair and straightened his tie. The sermon—and battle—would have to wait.

Nils opened the door before the knock repeated. "Ah, Miss Ehlke. What can I do for you?"

"Pastor, do you have a few minutes?" She stood on his doorstep, her brow wrinkling. Tall and willowy with high cheekbones on her oval face, her normally creamy skin could have rivaled the pink sunset of yesterday. Her lips pinched into a thin line, her brown eyes glared at him. She smiled, but at best, the smile appeared forced, her usual bright spirit hidden behind a dark cloud at the moment.

"Why, of course, Miss Ehlke. Come in, come in. Has something happened?" Would he even be able to help her? After going to an all-male high school, college, and the seminary, he was a bit over his head about how to handle women. What if she needed to talk about something womanish?

Nils opened the door wide and motioned for her to enter. They turned toward the left and walked into his study, a faint touch of her pleasing scent reaching him. He shook his head to clear it. He reflexively refused to attend to it.

The unfinished sermon glared at him, but he turned his back on it and perched on the edge of his desk. At the moment, his new teacher was more important.

After sitting and removing her gloves, she gazed up at him. In the ensuing silence, a light breeze blew in the window rustling the curtain. Tucking strands of her brown hair behind her ear, she leaned forward before beginning her tale. "Pastor, a certain Mrs. Piggery, um, Piggott barged into my room . . ."

After that initial outburst, she took a deep breath before managing to relate to him what had transpired earlier. She started to worry her gloves, twisting them this way and that. "I haven't even started teaching yet and already . . ." Her voice rose with each syllable out of her mouth and then trailed off to a whisper. "She didn't even give me a chance to prove to myself, or the congregation, that I'll be a good teacher. She called me an 'amateur.'"

He reached toward her, palms out. "Miss Ehlke, slow down."

How could he help her understand what he had had to learn himself in a very short time, namely that dealing with people's personalities was a challenging part of ministry? He smiled. "You and I, we'll always encounter people like that, even teaching in our Lutheran school."

She clasped her hands on her lap. "But I . . . I know . . . I'll be a good teacher. I went through three years of college. I've had all the courses. Why would she think she knows more than I do about teaching?"

Visions flew through his mind of her standing at the train station all by herself, ready to face the classroom, no, the world. He'd picked her up and driven her home on Saturday. She'd held her head high that day, her jaw set in determination, even though it quivered with uncertainty. Now she'd experienced reality—how people could treat her even in a Christian setting.

Like him, she'd been assigned to their congregation after graduation. He'd walked into this totally new life in June. New church. New city. New people. New job. Not an easy thing to do.

She'd probably experience all the same things in the next couple of weeks. But now she faced an irrational parent on top of it. What would come next?

His mind raced, searching for the right words. "People sometimes say things before they think. We both have to learn to be polite to them, but then not dwell on what was said."

She perched on the edge of her chair. "Does this fix it? What do I do in the meantime? How do I deal with her son in my classroom on Monday? Sounds to me like she's expecting preferential treatment for him."

Nils sighed. If only he felt more adequate to address her situation. He was new at this, too. He didn't have all the answers. She surely was spunky. Too spunky?

Maybe he'd have to talk to the pastor at the church in Kenosha for advice. What was his name? Yes. Berg. He was older and had more experience with faculty. Still, an effort should be made to answer Miss Ehlke.

"You're only starting out. Taking one day at a time is your best plan for now." Sheesh! That was "deep" but the best he could come up with.

Leaning against the back of the chair, she sighed. "Maybe after my first day she'd have something to criticize, but at least she should give me a chance."

"With God's help, you'll do fine." Nils folded his arms. "He needs to be our focus in our daily lives. We're in His hands. He says in Matthew: 'I am with you always—"

" —even unto the end of the world,'" she finished. "That passage was a great comfort for me in college."

"Um, yes." Nils blinked. Guess she knows her Bible. "He's more important than what any parent says to you. Remember God will guide you in your classroom, also."

"Yes, of course, you're right." She sighed as her eyes locked onto him. Her shoulders dropped as if she was finally relaxing.

"You're doing His work by teaching His little ones. He won't let you down." He paused to let it sink in and to gauge her reaction.

Miss Ehlke nodded. "I've been doing so much planning this week to make everything perfect for school that I forgot about Him."

"You can trust God to help you. You'll get through the day just fine."

A slow smile spread over her face. "Thank you, Pastor."

Nils let out a slow breath. "By the way, since we'll be working together, please feel free to call me Neil. I prefer that to my given name. Nils is hard for some people to pronounce."

"And please call me Emma." Her smile blossomed.

Finding her smile enchanting, Neil crossed one ankle over the other. "Now, back to Mrs. Piggott."

"She surprised me. I never even prayed when she barged into my room. She got me so flustered." Emma looked at her hands fidgeting in her lap. "I could have used God's help figuring out what to say to her."

"Sometimes she's a bit powerful and insensitive. I'm sure she didn't mean to insult you." He cleared his throat. "Her husband is chairman of the school board."

"She made that quite clear."

"The Piggotts are an important part of our congregation. We have to be very careful on how we deal with them in church, and especially in school. I've heard Mrs. Piggott keeps herself very informed with what's happening in Karl's classroom." Neil pushed himself upright and walked around the desk.

"She'll be watching and critiquing my every move then." She tucked a few stray strands of hair into the bun on the back of her head.

"Well, let's hope not. I'll give her husband a word of caution, but enough about that today." Neil sat in his chair, the usual irritating squeak filling the silence. "Try to put her words out of your mind for now. Concentrate on getting ready for Monday and don't worry about anything else." He smiled to put her at ease.

"That sounds easy to do, but . . ." She shook her head.

"In fact, you've worked so hard this week already." He shuffled through a stack of papers and pulled out a single sheet. "By Saturday night, you'll need some time off. The school board is sponsoring an ice-cream social in the church basement."

"Ice-cream social?"

He glanced down at the paper in his hand. "The whole congregation comes together on the last Saturday of the summer. I imagine the kids enjoy seeing their pals again, and teachers can meet the new parents."

Her face went blank. "Do *all* the parents come?"

"Not sure. I've never been to one before."

"How will I remember everyone's name at the same time? I didn't remember many from last Sunday—not even Mrs. P.'s until today, that is."

"There is one name you'll never forget."

Her lips turned up in a half-smile. "I wish I could have met Mrs. Piggott at the social. She couldn't have climbed down my throat like she did."

"You're probably right there." Laughing, he laid the paper on his desk. "Tell you what. I'll ask the committee to make sure there are name tags for folks to pin on so we don't have to remember all the names that night."

She nodded. "That would be a relief. Actually, the ice-cream social sounds like a perfect way to spend a Saturday evening. I haven't had ice cream in ages. We didn't get it at home much. Only on special occasions."

"Same here. We didn't own our own ice-cream maker so we had to borrow one from the neighbor."

"It's so much work to crank the handle for such a long time."

"Guess that makes it a special treat. Hope you'll come."

"I wouldn't miss it."

"I'm hoping to meet some members myself. Several families still haven't attended church since I came in June. I'll need the name tags, too." Good chance for him to get better acquainted with her, also.

Emma nodded and stood up. "Well, I'm so glad you were home. Thanks so much for your help."

"You're very welcome." He walked her to the door and swung it open for her. "Come by anytime you want to talk. My door is always open."

He watched her walk down the sidewalk toward home. Was she ready for her new role in their church? She had quite an attitude—possibly not the correct one. If only St. Paul had written Third Timothy and explained how to deal with teachers and parents. And women!

Well, back to the books. Glancing out the window instead, Neil sighed. Maybe Emma wasn't an amateur, but she was a novice. He hoped she'd find how to deal with challenges soon, just as he had. In any case, the school of experience was about to open.

CHAPTER 2

Freddie Neumann jerked his watch out of his pocket. "Good thing we're almost home, Jules. Ma would shoot me if I were late." Stuffing it away, he glanced at his friend.

"Stop your worrying. We're not late." Jules pulled his 1922 Dodge sedan next to the curb in front of Freddie's house. "I gotta scram. Say hi to your ma from me."

Freddie hopped out of the car and flicked a wave at Jules as exhaust fumes filled his nostrils. Glancing down the street, he spotted a young woman approaching, her ankle-length skirt swaying this way and that to the rhythm of her hips. Tendrils of brown hair framed her oval face. What a doll. If only he could introduce himself to her.

Wait a minute. He recognized her. The new teacher from next door. He couldn't pass up an opportunity like this.

He sauntered toward the sidewalk just in time to intercept her. "Hi, I'm Freddie Neumann. You're the new teacher at St. John's School, aren't you?"

Her eyes widened as she stepped back. "Emma Ehlke." Her voice not much more than a whisper, she retreated a few more steps. "How . . . how did you know?"

"We're members at the church." He smiled at her.

She narrowed her eyes. "I don't recall meeting you on Sunday, but I met so many people that day. I'm sure I don't remember everyone."

"Actually, I wasn't in church last Sunday. I was enjoying the swell weather with my buddy, Julian." He crossed his arms. He would be in church next Sunday for sure. If it meant getting on her good side, he wouldn't miss again. "My mother, Agnes, was there, though. Maybe you remember meeting her."

"Like I said, I met so many people. It's hard to recollect them all." A flush crept across her cheeks.

"Saw you in the Muellers' backyard that afternoon, so guess we'll be neighbors." Freddie pointed to her house next door. Very convenient for him. He could hook up with her whenever he wanted. Since he didn't have a car to get about, that would be perfect.

The change was immediate. Her smile lighting up her face, she stood tall. "We were playing croquet with the principal's family and Pastor after lunch."

"Yup. Looked like you were having fun." Her hair had been down, flowing around her shoulders. That's what had caught his attention. He grinned.

The rosy color edged higher on her face. "I'm so glad we'll be neighbors. It'll be nice to see a friendly face in church next Sunday."

"I'll be there. You can count on that." He'd have a good reason to go now. "But you'll see me at the ice-cream social first. You must have heard about it."

"Only a while ago. Pastor invited me. Sounds like fun." Emma's eyes twinkled as she gave a shrug with one shoulder. "I also need to meet more of my students and their parents."

"Make sure you save some time for me, as well." Why had he done that? He hadn't been to a social for years—not since his school days. Was he that desperate to get on her good side?

"Absolutely. We can have an ice-cream-eating contest." She nodded once and laughed. "Just teasing."

"I'll bring my friend Julian and his girlfriend Vivienne. You need to meet them." No backing out now. What if they wouldn't come with him?

"O.K. That would be perfect. I haven't met too many people my age."

"Swell, we'll introduce you to life in Racine." And get to know you a whole lot better. But he couldn't say that out loud. He needed a new dame in his life since he'd broken up with Peggy last month.

She nodded. "Terrific. I'll see you Saturday at church then." She waved before ambling up the drive toward her house.

He watched as she retreated. No doubt about it. He wanted to know her better. Ma had told him she was a country gal. He'd make sure she got a city education. He couldn't wipe the smile off his face.

Now he had to persuade Jules and Vivi to go along with his scheme. Not an easy task. This was going to be interesting. He'd have to tell them it was a matter of life and death. He jumped up the porch steps in two strides.

Marching into the kitchen, he headed for the cookie jar. "Hi, Ma." He stuffed a gingersnap into his mouth and turned to his mother. "You've met the new teacher, haven't you?"

"Of course I've met her. I told you last Sunday. If you'd come to church with me and Pa, you'd have met her, too. You didn't have to go fishing with Jules." She turned back to the stove to stir the contents of the pot. The tantalizing smell of beef stew filled the kitchen.

"I just met her outside." He reached for another cookie.

She slapped his hand. "Friedrich Wilhelm Heinrich Neumann, stay out of that cookie jar!" He towered over her, but she poked him repeatedly in the middle of his chest. "Just because you're twenty-three doesn't mean you have to act like a ten-year-old, stealing cookies an hour before supper." Her hand stopped in midair. "You met her just now?"

He struggled to keep his tone soft. "Yup. We had a nice chat." Ma treated him like a kid too often these days. He needed to live on his own very soon. That's why he needed Jules—and his car.

"Who introduced her to you?"

He shrugged. "I just walked up and introduced myself."

Ma gasped. "Men and women don't talk to each other until they've been introduced. What must she have thought?"

"Ma, that's the old standard. It doesn't have to be like that nowadays. It's nineteen twenty-six. Things have changed."

"Well, I don't like all the changes." She waved her hand dismissively. "Don't try to distract me. You could have been at church to meet her properly. Besides fishing is no excuse at all for missing church."

"O.K., O.K., Ma." He leaned against the sink. He didn't need this right now.

"Freddie, we have not raised you all these years to think that way about God's house. It's important to worship and praise God for all the wonderful things He does for us. Your father and I have told you so many times through the years, but you still don't understand or believe it."

His eyes roamed next door. "You may be right. I think I'll start going to church more often now."

Ma's head snapped up. "Does your decision have anything to do with Miss Ehlke? She seemed very sweet when I met her last Sunday. You should get to know her better." She turned back to the stove.

"Exactly what I plan to do." Not a hard decision to make.

A smile spread across Ma's face. "If Miss Ehlke is the reason you'll start going to church again, I won't complain. You need a good influence in your life." She patted him on the shoulder as she made her way into the living room. "Gotta tell Pa the good news."

***

Emma headed toward her new home. The broad front porch, surrounding the two-story white Victorian house, invited her to relax after her long day at school. If only she had time. She skipped up the steps and opened the front door. She'd been here only a few days, but this house was home to her now, at least for the year.

She entered the living room with its lovely dark blue floral wallpaper gracing the walls and a rug covering the wood floor. The settee and matching chair added to the homey atmosphere, as well as the pungent scent from the red roses sitting on top of the piano. The aroma reminded her of Ma's flowerbed on the farm. She smiled as she walked up the steps to her room.

After removing her hat and gloves, she flopped on her bed and gazed at the electric light bulb hanging from the ceiling. So nice to live in a house with electricity. So much better than home. A breeze fluttered the curtains bringing in the scent of newly mown grass.

This was the type of room she had only dreamed about before. The sky-blue gingham curtains, covering the gabled window, complemented the patterned counterpane on the bed. A blue oval braided rug covered most of the wood floor. She sighed. Her feet would appreciate that in winter.

She couldn't ask for a better place to find room and board. It didn't mean she didn't miss Ma and Pa, though. They all had shed tears at the station in Beaver Dam when her parents had unloaded her trunk from the wagon. She crossed her arms as a pain raced through her chest. When Pa had pressed his small Bible into her hand, she had almost decided not to get on the train.

She'd been gone less than a week. How long would it be before the pain disappeared? Every year at college she'd gone through the same thing for a couple weeks, but this was different. Now the responsibilities of teaching a classroom full of children rested on her shoulders. She had no one to pick her up if she failed.

Shaking her head, she stood up. That didn't mean she wanted to live on a farm all her life. She was here to find out what real life was like. She'd just have to face this new reality. The ache would subside in time. It always did.

What a day. She rolled her aching shoulders—too much tension. Mrs. P.'s visit loomed in her mind. She might as well forget working for the rest of the day. Her head was ready to explode.

Running next door to talk to Pastor had certainly helped. Had he minded her barging into his home without an invitation, especially when he was working? She should have asked herself the question before she knocked on his door. She hoped he didn't think ill of her because she had been in such a state when she had arrived. She needed his counsel about Mrs. um, Piggery, but even more, about her first day of school.

Thank you, God, for having Pastor remind me to trust you. I can't stand in front of a classroom of students without Your help. Be with me as I do Your work here at St. John's.

Slipping off her skirt and blouse, she reached behind the door and grabbed the housedress hanging on the hook. The best part of the day, oddly, was talking to Freddie. At first she'd been horrified by his brazenness. Would any man in Juneau talk to a strange woman without being introduced? Maybe this happened often in the city. At least he belonged to the same church, so no problem. She could trust him then.

Freddie might be someone she could relate to on a personal level. Other than the children in her class, she'd be dealing with Mr. Dietz and the parents most often. Obviously, she'd have to act professionally with them. She needed someone to relax and have fun with.

She fastened the last button on her dress. She couldn't let her hair down in front of Pastor either. Even though they were the same age, he was still a pastor. She obviously couldn't talk to him unless she had a problem. Maybe she'd even worn out her welcome bursting in on him today. She certainly couldn't call him by his first name either, no matter what he said.

Emma slipped her feet into her slippers. What she really needed was a friend her age. Freddie might be that new friend. And maybe there'd be a girl as well. Hadn't he mentioned his friend's girlfriend? Wouldn't it be wonderful to have someone to talk to besides Mrs. Mueller?

She'd been eager to leave the farm and experience life in a city. After all, Ma's magazine called it the Jazz Age. Things had to be exciting if it had a name like that. Every time she saw the colored pictures of beautiful women with short hair wearing flapper dresses, Emma's heart had beaten double time. Maybe Freddie would be her ticket to the excitement those women had. She couldn't wait until Saturday evening now.

Emma opened her door and headed out into the hallway. Mrs. Mueller no doubt needed help with supper.

A girlish giggle escaped from the room across the hall. Lizzie sat on the floor with paper dolls scattered around her. "Hello, Miss Ehlke. I'm pretending my Patty doll fell in the mud." She laughed again.

"Oh my. How will you clean her up?" Emma smiled at the little girl. Lizzie would be an asset to her fourth grade next week.

"I'll make a bathtub for her out of a shoe box."

"Good idea. I need to see if your ma needs help in the kitchen."

Emma hurried down the steps and headed toward the kitchen, passing through the dining room with its long oval table resting over a braided rug on the wooden floor. Every morning so far, the sun had shone on the sparkling china dishes behind the glass doors of the hutch. This room had class.

Entering the kitchen, she let the swinging door close behind her. "Can I help you with supper, Mrs. Mueller?"

"Since you'll be living with us for a while, I wish you'd call me Hilda." Mrs. Mueller's smile accented the two red Macintoshes that doubled as cheeks. The brown chignon, speckled with gray, pulled her hair well off her round face. With a plump body, she stood several inches shorter than Emma, but she had the same spirit that Ma had—always busy caring for her growing family.

"O.K. Then let me know how I can help."

"I picked the last of the beans from the garden this afternoon. Maybe you could wash and snip them for me." Hilda handed her an apron along with a large bag of green beans.

"Sounds good." As Emma tied the apron strings, she searched the bright kitchen. "Where's a bowl?"

Hilda pointed to the cupboard next to the wall. "They're in the last door."

Peering through the glass doors, Emma studied the contents of the cabinet, finding the bowls sitting on the top shelf. She poured the beans into the bowl and set it in the sink, turning on the tap. "It's so wonderful to have running water and electricity in the house. I still haven't gotten used to it. No need to pump water outside anymore."

Hilda laughed. "Exactly. We've only had it for about five years. What a blessing." She continued peeling potatoes. "How was your day today?"

"Not so great, I'm afraid." Emma snapped the beans in half. "One of the parents came into my room trying to educate me on how to run my classroom. It was rather upsetting."

Hilda's hands stilled as she glanced at Emma. "Sorry to hear that. Some people talk before they think. Causes lots of trouble sometimes."

Emma nodded. "Mr. Dietz wasn't around. The only person I could find to talk to was Pastor Hannemann."

Hilda's hands resumed their work on the spuds. "Did you have a nice chat with him?"

Emma didn't hesitate. "Yes. He was very helpful. I hope I didn't disturb him too much. He had books spread out all over his desk. He looked busy."

"I'm sure he was glad to talk to you." Hilda picked up another potato. "You two should get along well with so much in common. He's just a little older than you are, and you both graduated last spring."

"I know. He told me he's only been here a couple months, so he's just meeting the members of the congregation, also."

"In fact, his family runs a farm way up north in Wisconsin. I can't remember the town, but you're both from the same background." Hilda placed her peeled potato in the pot.

Emma turned toward her. "I didn't know that."

Farmers' sons were usually needed to run the farm when they got older. Why would he be a pastor then?

Chapter 3

Emma peeked around the wide pillars planted throughout the church basement. Tables were scattered around the room, filled with boys and girls of all ages enjoying ice cream. The noise level alone was enough to make her head ache.

"Miss Ehlke, the yummy ice cream is over here." Lizzie Mueller pointed to the table set up close to the kitchen serving-window. "What is your favorite flavor?"

"Vanilla, of course, but I'm not hungry right now. Why don't you and your ma go on ahead of me?" Smiling, Emma tugged on Lizzie's pigtail.

Hilda held out her hand toward her daughter. "Let's go, little one."

"O.K." They headed in the direction of the food.

With the hairs on the back of her neck rising, Emma stood in the doorway. How would she ever manage to remember the names of all these people? Taking a deep breath, she stiffened her spine and stood tall. If she had to face forty children on Monday morning, she could do this.

The chatter filling the room attested to the fact that these people knew each other, but she was the total stranger. She swallowed. They'd soon be her friends since they were all members of the congregation. She just had to have the courage to meet them.

"Ah, Miss Ehlke."

Wearing his usual dark suit and white shirt, Pastor walked toward her. His dark brown hair was neatly split in the middle and combed to either side. He never had a hair out of place as far as Emma could see, except for one untamed curl in the middle of his forehead. As she looked at him, the curl melded with the line of his nose to form a question mark framed by the angles of his cheeks and strong chin. He arched his eyebrows, which made the question mark rise as if to herald a question.

"I've been wondering where you were. Here's your name tag, but everyone will pretty much remember your name."

Sighing, Emma nodded. "I know. It's the names of everyone else that I'm worried about." She pinned her name to her white shirtwaist.

"They all have theirs on also, so you shouldn't be so shy. Remember that a couple months ago I faced the same challenge that you are facing." Pastor looked at her name tag. "You put that on a bit crooked."

She glanced down to see her upside down name. Was it really cockeyed? Or was he just picky? She turned it a fraction of an inch.

He smiled at her tag, not making eye contact. "Much better. Let me introduce you to some people."

***

"Hey, it'll be jake." Freddie winced. If only it would be fine. Persuading Jules to go to the church social was tougher than he thought. Wind whipped through the open windows of Julian's automobile.

Vivi brushed black hair out of her eyes. "Of course, it will be O.K."

"Aw, baloney!" Jules took one hand off the steering wheel and slapped it down again. "Level with me. Are you really going to take us to an ice-cream social?"

Freddie sat forward in the back seat to be heard above the rushing wind. "We have to go, Jules. I told her I'd be there." Trees flew past his window. How could he get Jules to agree?

"I haven't been to church for years. I think the last time was for some Christmas program when I was six years old." Jules scanned the road right and left as he stopped at an intersection. "I never want to be caught dead in a church again—well, maybe dead, but that would be the only way."

Freddie laughed as he rubbed his neck. "Don't worry, Buddy. It's not in church. It's in the basement."

Vivi scowled at Jules. "Julian. That is very bad. You should not say that about going to the church. Church is good for you. I went every Sunday when I was the little girl in France."

With color rising on his cheeks matching his curly russet hair, Jules stared out the front window. "Baby, get off my case. I've never seen you step foot inside a church since I've known you, so you better not preach to me. I don't want to hear it."

Freddie patted him on the shoulder. "Let's not get all balled up about it. We're only talking about a dish of ice cream."

"Enough of the talk, you two." Vivi folded her arms. "This is not tricky. We go eat the ice cream and we leave soon, eh? Not make it into the problem."

Scowling, Jules's eyes connected with Freddie's in the mirror. "This dame must really be something if you are dragging us there with you." He shook his head.

Freddie blew out his breath. "Jules, I'm telling you, she's the cat's meow. You should've seen her long brown hair on Sunday. Like it was just begging me to bury my hands in it." Inhaling sharply, his hands mimicked the motion in the air. "Course, I was looking at her out of my kitchen window." He shrugged and sighed.

Vivi put her arm along the back of the seat, peering at Freddie. "I am looking forward to meeting the doll that has finally turned the head of Monsieur Freddie Neumann." She laughed. "I never thought the day to come when Freddie would be, ah, the smitten."

Jules glanced over his shoulder at Freddie. "I'm still not convinced. How well do you know her?"

"I don't really know her much at all. Ma heard from Mrs. Mueller that Emma's a farm girl from Juneau, so I'm sure she's a kid in many ways." Smiling, Freddie pointed to himself with his thumbs. "I've taken it upon myself to show her the ropes."

Vivi shook her finger at him. "Maybe I should warn her about you, Monsieur Freddie."

"But I thought we were going to go dancing tonight." Jules shook his head.

"Ice cream now, the dancing is next weekend." Vivi laid her hand on his arm.

Freddie slumped against the back seat. It was a good thing Vivi had influence over her boyfriend. Otherwise, he might not have been able to convince Jules to go.

His stomach scratched at his insides. Was he actually getting nervous? He had lots of experience with other dames, "flappers" to many people. Emma was different. He'd have to be careful with what he said and how he said it. Somehow the thought of having a crush on a parochial school teacher was a bit daunting. The pastor and principal would be watching what she did and whom she did it with. Would he be up to the challenge?

When they arrived at the red brick church, several people poured out of the door, already on their way home. The three friends strolled across the churchyard and down the basement steps. The large musty room resembled an abandoned battlefield with bowls sitting here and there along with puddles of formerly frozen ice cream dotting the floor. The remaining children bounced from one friend to another, giggling, while parents clustered around the occupied tables.

Spotting Emma, Freddie smiled and waved.

Returning his smile, she hurried across the floor. "You're late. I thought you decided not to come." Slender fingers tucked some straying hair behind her ear.

Freddie pulled out his watch from his vest pocket and checked the time. "We planned it that way. We didn't want to talk to you when you were busy with all the parents and kiddos." He shrugged as he surveyed the room. "Now most of them are getting ready to leave, so we can have you to ourselves."

Smiling, she slid him a glance. "My, that was thoughtful."

Freddie turned and pointed toward Jules and Vivi. "By the way, this is Julian Meyer and Vivienne Cohen. Jules works with me, and Vivi is his girlfriend." He nodded toward Emma. "This is Emma Ehlke, the new teach, my neighbor."

Emma reached out her hand. "I'm happy to meet both of you. Freddie told me he was bringing some friends along tonight."

Jules mumbled under his breath. "Wasn't my idea."

Freddie glared at him. If only he didn't start all over again with his protests. Trying to distract Emma, he pointed at his friend. "We work on an assembly line at a tractor factory. Case New Holland tractors."

"That sounds interesting."

Jules harrumphed. "Not really."

Glaring at Jules, Vivi grasped Emma's hand in both of hers. "I am glad to meet you, Emma."

"I haven't met any folks my age since I just moved here last week." With twinkling eyes, Emma put her hand on Vivi's arm. "I'm hoping we can get to know each other."

Vivi hugged her with one arm. "It will be the thrill to have another girl with me when I go out with these two fellows. I am always, how do you say, outnumbered when I am with them. Now it will be two against two." She nudged Jules with her shoulder. "Maybe we do girl stuff once in awhile."

"Sheesh." Jules shook his head. "Don't get any funny ideas just because there are two of you."

Freddie pointed to the table filled with ice cream and toppings. "How about some ice cream before it's all melted?" He walked toward the table, grabbed an empty bowl and headed for the chocolate. "Then maybe we can show you around a little, Emma, give you the dime tour."

Smiling, Emma reached for the container of vanilla. "Sounds good to me. I've met more than my share of parents for one night. I'm ready to leave."

Freddie nodded toward Jules. "We could take a drive down to Kenosha and show her the sights." He sprinkled some nuts on his ice cream. "Have you been down to Kenosha yet?"

Emma added the strawberry topping to her bowl. "No, Mr. Dietz showed me around Racine the day after I arrived. Other than that, I haven't been anywhere besides church and school." She turned toward Freddie. "I'd love to see what Kenosha is like."

Vivi put a cherry on top of her ice cream. "That is the swell idea."

***

Neil shifted from one foot to the other. His legs hurt after standing on the cement floor for an hour. He looked around for a chair. Glancing up, he spotted Mrs. Piggott strutting toward him. Sitting would have to wait. "Hello, it's so nice to see you this evening."

"Yes, what a lovely social. I've seen so many of the school mothers here tonight. It's good to have time to chat with them." She set her empty bowl on the table.

"I'm glad Mr. Dietz and Miss Ehlke were both able to come tonight." Neil stifled the urge to bring up her visit to Emma's classroom.

"Yes, I stopped in for a chat with Miss Ehlke this week."

"Oh?" He bit his tongue. It would be better to let her tell him her side of the story. He stacked the empty bowls on the table and placed the spoons adjacent to the stack. Wiping up a drop of melted ice cream, he glanced at her.

"I wanted to offer her my advice when it came to handling children in a classroom since she's not a mother yet." She moved her clutch bag from one hand to the other.

"I'm sure she appreciated any advice you gave her." How else could he respond? He'd have to follow his own advice to Emma and handle the school board chairman's wife with care. He couldn't very well tell her what he really thought. "Since women teachers can't be married, none of them have experience raising children."

"Exactly. That's why I've been urging my husband to request a male teacher for the lower grades. We might find someone experienced that way."

"Ah, here comes Mr. Dietz now. You can share your thoughts with him." Neil beckoned to the principal. Maybe she'd tell Mr. Dietz herself. Then he could fill in the details of Emma's conversation later.

Robert Dietz strode across the basement joining the small group. Shorter and stouter than Neil, the principal nonetheless had an air of authority about him with his wide shoulders and muscular build. He might have been mistaken for an army general, dressed differently. However, his blue suit and buttoned-down vest confirmed his status.

"Mr. Dietz, I was just telling Pastor that I think the congregation should get a male teacher in the lower grades, as well as the upper. Maybe we could find one with some child-rearing experience that way."

Neil cleared his throat. At least she spoke her mind, so he wouldn't have to tell tales.

"Ah, Mrs. Piggott, you know the school board has discussed this already. We're probably going to add another classroom next year, so we'll need another teacher on staff. A male teacher would be an excellent idea for the middle grades, leaving Miss Ehlke in the lower grades."

"I went to visit her room on Thursday to offer her my counsel and help."

Robert's eyebrows jumped up, attesting to his surprise. He stood with his arms folded behind his back. "Oh?"

"I told her my idea of having a male teacher. She didn't seem to agree with me about that. I can't understand why." Looking across the room, Mrs. Piggott shrugged. "My Meyer is signaling that it's time to go. I'll talk to you later. Good night, Mr. Dietz. Pastor." She nodded toward both men.

"So Emma didn't tell you about her visit from Mrs. Piggott?" Neil watched the latter waddle across the room toward the stairs.

"No, I'm surprised she didn't." Robert stroked his chin. "Of course, I was out at the end of the week making home visits. Maybe she couldn't catch me."

Robert's wife Caroline brought two-year-old Alice to him. "Can you hold her while I help clean up?"

"Sure." He scooped Alice into his arms and ran his hand down her yellow curls. The smile on his face broadcast his love for his daughter.

Neil's gut clenched. Would he ever find the love of a wife? Would his arms embrace a daughter? So many of his buddies from seminary days had gotten married since graduation. He'd never been blessed like they had been.

Maybe it had something to do with the fact that Ma had died in childbirth when he was ten years old. He'd grown up fast after that. He smiled. At least, he knew his way around a kitchen, but he sure didn't know how to interact with women. He'd had so little contact with the fairer sex since then. They often puzzled him. Shaking his head, he forced himself back to the conversation.

Robert continued. "Mrs. Piggott can be so —"

"Difficult?" Neil saw Emma walk across the room toward three young people. Straightening a chair at the table, he turned back toward Robert.

"Exactly. I hope Emma survived Mrs. Piggott's 'counsel and help'." Smiling, Robert shifted Alice to his other arm.

Picking up a napkin from the floor, Neil glanced at the group of four again. "I reminded her that God was on her side. However, I'm a bit concerned that she's very naïve for her age. Shouldn't she have expected a parent to offer suggestions to her? Parents can be very opinionated when it comes to their children. "

"True, but you must admit that Mrs. Piggott isn't the usual parent. I should say something to her before school on Monday." Robert turned in the direction Neil was staring. "What are you so interested in over there?"

The four were helping themselves at the ice cream table. "Who are those young people with Emma? The man with blond hair looks familiar, but I couldn't put a name to his face." Should he know him? He'd been trying to learn the names of church members, but couldn't recall him.

"The blond-haired one is the only one I know." Robert squinted in their direction. "His name is Freddie Neumann, a neighbor to the Muellers. He and his parents, Agnes and Oscar, belong to St. John's." He set Alice on the floor. "You might remember them."

Nodding, Neil pushed a chair close to the table. "I remember them, but I didn't know they were neighbors to the Muellers."

"Yup, it means they're neighbors to Emma, as well."

"Hmmm, that might be good for her. She'll have someone her age to chat with then." Neil noticed Emma talking to Mrs. Mueller before she joined the other three heading toward the steps.

"I'm not exactly sure if living next door to Freddie is a good or bad thing at this point." Robert joined Neil in watching the four disappear out the door. "He hasn't been at church for a long time. He was confirmed here, but his attendance is so sporadic lately. Maybe a friendship with Emma will bring him back to church regularly."

"Let's hope it works that way." Neil focused on Robert again. "I'll have to talk to Freddie soon to encourage him." He mentally made a note of this for later. "I certainly hope they don't influence Emma to go the other way."

***

Freddie smiled and extended his elbow toward Emma. "We'll be going in Jules's jalopy tonight." As if they had a choice.

Smiling, Emma hooked her fingertips around his arm.

"What do you mean 'tonight'?" Jules opened the car door for Vivi. "We always take my car because you don't have one." He helped her into the front seat.

"I know that, but Emma didn't have to find out now." The four joined in a laugh as Freddie helped her into the back seat. He continued to grin.

"I've worked long and hard at the factory to save enough money for a car like this." Jules rubbed his hand along the dashboard. "I'm very proud of my jalopy." He started the car and pulled out of the parking lot.

"Yes, we know, Julian." Vivi ran her hand up his arm. "You talk about your auto very often."

A couple miles south of church, they left the city streets and ventured onto the dirt road. Jules shouted to be heard above the noise of the engine. "I know it wasn't in the best shape when I bought it, but now it's all spiffed up. Besides, I have to have a car." He smiled at Vivi. "How could I take you places otherwise?"

Vivi blushed and laughed. "True. And I love your jalopy." She gave Jules a peck on the cheek.

Jules made eye contact in the mirror with Freddie. "Besides, if you're going to hang around with a gal again, my jalopy will surely be used for some great times ahead."

Heat rose up Freddie's neck. "Thanks a lot, Jules." He slid a glance in Emma's direction to see if she was blushing, too. Instead her smile lit up the evening.

"Hey, my pleasure, Bud."

The next couple hours flew by. Jules, Vivi, and Freddie had a grand time showing Emma all the sights of Kenosha. They drove through the downtown area, pointing out the three movie theaters, the ritzy ballroom where they would go dancing, and the best ice cream parlors. Of course they drove down by Lake Michigan to see the park.

What about showing her their favorite speakeasy? Freddie shook his head. Probably a bad idea to take a parochial school teacher into an illegal speakeasy. It wouldn't make a very good first impression. Better wait until later to share this side of him with her.

They headed back toward Racine, the car headlights illuminating the way. Emma leaned against the back seat, the wind tossing her hair. "I had a great time tonight. When I was home on the farm, my wish was to have a night on the town like this."

Freddie stifled the urge to grasp her hand. Not yet. Slow down. "Your wish is my command." He bowed his head toward her.

As the car approached the street where they lived, Emma leaned toward Vivi. "Do you know I haven't once thought about school since we left the church social?" She patted Vivi on the shoulder. "You all were just what I needed tonight."

Vivi turned to smile at Emma. "I had the grand time, too. I am glad we helped you forget the teaching for a bit."

"I'll help you forget teaching any time you'd like." Freddie winked at her.

She brushed her hair behind her ear as she glanced at him. "Thanks so much for suggesting this."

The car jerked to a halt in front of the Muellers' house. After the guys threw open the doors and hopped out, Freddie whispered to Jules, "Isn't she something else?"

"Yes, indeed. Some gal." Jules slapped him on the back.

Freddie ran around the car to offer his assistance to Emma. When she emerged, he closed the door. "I'll see you two later. Thanks for driving tonight, Jules." He watched as they pulled away from the curb.

With his hands behind his back, Freddie ambled up the Muellers' driveway with Emma at his side. The dark sky twinkled with glittery stars as the cool night air surrounded them. Freddie stopped at the porch steps. "Thanks for going with us tonight. I had loads of fun." The first night of many, he hoped.

"Thank you so much for inviting me. It was nice to get away for a while." Emma looked up at him. "I'll see you in church tomorrow."

She trotted up the steps and turned to wave before opening the door.

"Sure." Freddie closed his eyes. Close one. He'd almost forgotten about church tomorrow. Now he couldn't sleep in. He crossed the lawn bordering the two houses and hopped up his steps. This was the first girl who had inspired him to attend church. Maybe it could help him get on her good side.

Chapter 4

Sunday afternoon Emma swayed listlessly on the porch swing, her mind full of one thing. School. Tomorrow would be her first day. Her shoulders ached with tension. She'd done everything she could think of. Lesson plans completed. Books ready to hand out. Chalk boards shiny. Floor spotless. Still, who knew what tomorrow would bring? She smoothed the wrinkles out of her floral print skirt.

Her stomach rolled with the undulating swing. How was she supposed to handle forty kids at once? Would she even remember all their names? How would she teach all the subjects for four grades in one day? So many questions.

She'd had all the teaching courses, but when it came right down to it, college classes were much different than standing in front of children. Her heart raced. Calm down. *O Lord, help me get through the first day.* The twittering birds in the trees soothed her frazzled nerves. She could do this.

She'd helped her five younger siblings with homework while still at home. She'd even been the right-hand man to her teacher in the one-room school, but standing in front of forty children was a whole different ball game. She rubbed her hand over her roiling abdomen. One day at a time.

Out of the corner of her eye, she noticed Jules's car pull up in front of the house next door. Freddie skipped down the porch steps toward Jules and Vivi. After several minutes they spotted her and sauntered across the front yard and up the drive.

Freddie gave her a brief salute, his blue eyes teasing her. "Hey, Teach!"

Emma winced at the greeting, a reminder of tomorrow.

"You busy? Scoot over and we'll join you." He bounced up the steps.

"I'd love some company. I'm sure it would be all right with the Muellers." Emma moved over, and Vivi sat beside her on the swing.

Freddie leaned against the porch railing with one ankle crossed over the other. He looked as relaxed as a cat. "Jules and Vivi came to hang out for a bit. Thought you'd like to join us, seeing you're sitting here alone."

Emma needed a diversion. "O.K. I need to think of something else besides school."

Vivi patted her hand. "You will do fine. On the first day, all kids are too scared of the new teacher to make the trouble."

Jules joined Freddie by the railing.

Emma merely smiled and pushed the glider back with her feet to set it in motion. The sweet smell of roses floated in the slow-moving air as they swayed back and forth.

"Hmmm. We talk about something else, O.K?" Vivi tapped her chin.

Emma brushed her hair behind her ear and nodded. "I like your accent. Are you from a different country? Why did you come? How did you end up here?"

"Wait. That is many questions to answer, but I will try. I am from France."

"I've never met anyone who wasn't born here in America. Tell me, please."

"O.K., but it is the long story, *ma amie*." Vivi squinted her eyes and tilted her head toward Emma. "Are you sure you want to be hearing it?"

Emma smiled and nodded. "Sure I'm sure. I like to hear people's stories—we have all afternoon."

"I am from a little town called St. Luc near the Ardennes. I met the American soldier. Alan Cohen." The swing swayed and stopped. "I was very young and, um, naïve. I thought he was very gallant and handsome and exotic. When he asked me to marry him . . ." Vivi studied her hands in her lap.

Emma pushed with her feet to start swinging again. "Please, please don't stop."

"Ah, I was so desperate to get away from the war, you see, that I told Alan I was sixteen years old, when really I was only fifteen."

Gasping, Emma placed her hand on Vivi's. "I had no idea, and you were so young. I can't imagine what it must have been like."

Emma glanced at the guys. Jules's face almost matched the color of the white house. Did he know this story?

"*Oui*, lots of girls did that. I guess living close to the war made us grow up fast." Vivi twisted her hands in her lap. "He married me—August before the war was over." The rat-tat-tatting of a woodpecker on a nearby tree imitated the sound of guns.

"Alan put me on a boat to America." Vivi stared toward the street. "I had the terrible trip here. I did not speak the English except for few words. But I arrived finally in Kenosha and managed to find his house, his parents' house."

Emma's hand flew to her chest. "How—without knowing English?"

"That turned out to be the easy part. The Cohens, Alan's mother and his papa—they did not like it much, what Alan and I had done."

"Why?" Emma hung on every word. "Because you were so young, or not American?"

Vivi clucked her tongue. "No, nothing like that. It was because I be not Jewish." Vivi's weak smile didn't reach her eyes. "Then, we got word Alan was killed in the battle a week before the Armistice."

"Oh, no!" Emma put her hand on Vivi's arm. "That's terrible. I'm so sorry." To go through all that at such a young age.

Freddie ran his fingers through his blond hair. "Hey, come on now. We didn't come over here to get Emma depressed before her first day of school." He pushed off the railing. "I think we should go over to my house and do something. Croquet anyone?" he said, faking an English accent.

Emma shook her head. "I'm not very good at croquet."

"Nah! You were playing last Sunday, Teach, so I know you can do it."

It didn't mean she enjoyed it that much. "Not very well."

Would these new friends poke fun at her as her classmates did during grade school? Her heart sped up as her eyes roved between Freddie and Jules. She'd never enjoyed playing sporting games since. Too embarrassing.

Jules nodded his agreement. "I'm game."

"It sounds like the fun." Vivi jumped up.

Outvoted, Emma followed Vivi across the porch.

As Freddie and Jules headed down the steps toward Freddie's house, they became involved in a conversation about baseball. In the hot sun, Emma and Vivi followed at a slower pace. The shadows of the tall trees played games on the sidewalk as the leaves blew in the breeze. No need to hurry on such a beautiful summer day.

"Tell me the rest. What happened to you after, after Alan, you know?"

"I tell you quickly since the guys are talking right now." Vivi smiled. "It did not take too long before the Cohens asked me to leave their house. At least, I had learned my English a bit in the months I lived with them. I got the job as the hairdresser in Kenosha since I knew the spiffy French hairstyles. I have been on my own since the time."

"Oh, Vivi, what a hard life you've had." Emma linked arms with her as they walked. "I'm twenty—only a little younger than you, but this is the first time I've been away from home besides college. I can't imagine doing what you did when I was fifteen or sixteen. I was still going to high school at that age."

"Ah, *c'est la vie!* You do what you have to do when life deals out the cards." Vivi shrugged. "That is all behind, so now we enjoy the nice sunny day." She patted Emma's arm. "Time to go play the croquet."

As they hit the ball from one wicket to the next, Emma laughed so hard her side hurt. Somehow every other shot went the wrong direction. And no one, not even the guys, taunted her about how badly she played. They had great fun chasing the balls across the lawn. She had no time to dwell on the upcoming school day.

Later that evening after she had written a letter to her family, she had a chance to think about her new friends. Of course, she'd had friends in college, close friends she could confide in. She missed all the girls terribly, but she had never before had any friends that were men. This was a new experience for her.

Most of all, she'd never had a friend like Vivienne before either. Vivi, with her short black bobbed hair and red lipstick, wore skirts shorter than anything Emma owned. Who knew, maybe she even wore rayon stockings.

Did Vivi even believe in God? Everyone in Emma's life, up until now, shared her faith. To Emma, that was normal. God was so important to her and her family. Now she had a chance to become friends with someone who maybe didn't know what God and faith were all about. How might God use her in the months ahead?

***

A ray of sunlight streaming through her window, Emma woke from a deep sleep. Her eyes flew open as she heard someone calling from downstairs. Oh, no! Monday morning and she wasn't up yet. She threw back the sheets and tore out of bed. Not a way to start her career.

Hilda called to Lizzie, interrupting Emma's thoughts. Better hurry. She needed to be there plenty early on the first day of school.

Minutes later, she pulled her brown striped skirt over her tan blouse and buttoned it in the back. Stepping into her high-laced shoes, she fastened them quickly with her buttonhook. As she stood up, she ran a hand down her skirt. No wrinkles today. The mirror on the back of her bedroom door agreed with her. All set.

Walking down the steps, she heard the Mueller household scurrying around the kitchen. The tantalizing smell of Hilda's hot cakes called to her as she stepped through the swinging door.

"Lizzie, make sure you comb your hair and brush your teeth. You can't be late for school." Hilda spotted Emma as she entered the room. "Ah, good morning. Have a seat. Your breakfast will be ready in a minute."

"Thank you." She pulled out the chair and sat down. "I was afraid of oversleeping this morning. The bed was so comfortable."

The pan of sausages sizzled as Hilda stirred them with her wooden spoon. "I'm glad you had a good night's sleep before your first day as a teacher."

Emma's stomach rose to her throat. Flapjacks and sausages didn't appeal to her anymore. "I'm not very hungry this morning. One pancake will do me just fine." She smiled at Hilda but was sure she didn't convince her. She'd choke down the food to show her appreciation.

Hilda packed a lunch for her, as well as Lizzie. One less thing to think about. The idea of eating a lunch at school out of a lunch pail brought back lots of memories. How many had she eaten over the years? Now she would be doing it as the teacher in the classroom.

After breakfast, Emma left for school early. The weather was sunny and not too hot. A good start to the day. God would help her get through this.

She went over the many plans she'd made for today. Her class would join the rest of the school in church for an opening service. How would she squeeze in all the classes after that? An impossible task. She would probably be worn out when the four o'clock bell rang.

By the time she reached school, she convinced herself she was prepared for her day. Children headed toward the school from different directions. They were here already. *Father in heaven, be with me today. Guide and guard the children on their way to school.* She had no more time to be nervous. Her first day was about to begin.

She didn't stop and take a break until she collapsed in her chair after the children left for home late in the afternoon. Papers were scattered all over her desk. The blackboard was smudged with white chalk after getting erased so many times. Were the children as exhausted as she was? She groaned. All this work to do for tomorrow. She turned when she heard a knock on her classroom door.

Mr. Dietz walked into her room. "How'd it go? Tired?" He sat on one of the student desks.

Elbows propped on her desk, Emma braced her chin on her open palms. "I am. My legs and feet are screaming at me. I stood all day." Dust motes floated in the air as the sun streamed through the open window.

He nodded. "Hmm. That happens every year on the first week of school. Take heart. By the end of the week you'll be used to it."

"My throat feels like I've marched through the desert." She put up her hand to rub her neck. Had she ever been this bushed?

Mr. Dietz laughed. "By next week you'll be a pro. The aches and pains will be gone."

"Besides being tired, my day went O.K. I even remember the names of most of my students." Her shoulders relaxed for the first time.

"Speaking of your students, I hear you had a visit from Mrs. Piggott last week." Mr. Dietz crossed his arms.

"Let me put it this way, I had no problem remembering Karl at all today. His mother made sure of that. But I'd have to say he behaved himself." Emma flipped through the papers on her desk. She had to face all this work yet tonight.

Mr. Dietz nodded. "Children are usually well behaved when school starts. Give 'em three weeks. Anyway, his mother had a chat with me on Saturday evening. I'm betting she came off a wee bit insulting, reminding you about having no teaching experience."

"She didn't mince words." Emma offered a wry smile.

"Pay her no mind. She was trying to make the point she's made through her husband ever since the vacancy came up." Mr. Dietz changed his voice, imitating the rhythm and tenor of Mrs. Piggott. "What we need is a male teacher. A man might be married and have children of his own already." He sighed. "Anyway, she often talks before thinking. Hope it didn't get you too upset."

"It gave me a chance to talk to Pastor. He helped get me over my first-day jitters." Letting out her breath, she sat up straighter. "On a brighter note, I'm really going to enjoy having Lizzie as my student. She's such a smart girl."

"What grade is she in now?"

"She's in fourth grade. She strikes me as if she'll be my best student. And my little helper." Picking up her pen, warmth spread through her chest. "And then there are my first graders. They were so cute and sweet. I don't think I'll have any trouble with them."

He stood up. "I'd better let you get busy again. Lots of work to do myself." He waved as he exited her room.

Her legs throbbed as she stared at the pile of student papers. *Lord, continue to help me with this work.* But she was surprised to find herself looking forward to tomorrow.

***

After supper, Freddie perched on the top step of the porch, his elbows resting on his knees. He heard the Muellers' screen door slam and watched Emma descend the steps. He trotted down the sidewalk to intercept her. "Hey, Teach! How was your first day?"

"Oh, my! Hello, *Mr.* Neumann. *Miss Teacher* is fine, but *Emma* is so tired tonight." She smiled. "Actually, I feel like I've been teaching for weeks instead of one day." Her shoulders drooped.

"You won't catch me trying it. I'm not that brave. Anyway, how'd it go?"

"Pretty well. You know, I think I'm going to enjoy it." She perked up, her cheeks turning rosy. "By the end of the day, I could remember all their names." Her eyes sparkled.

Freddie leaned against the neighbor's fence. "So, if you're so tired, how come you're going back to school?"

"No rest for the wicked, or at least, for teachers. I have to go back to get ready for tomorrow." Emma edged away from the fence. "I have so many classes to plan out, I'm sure I'll be working every night after supper."

"Man. I suppose that's part of being a new teacher." Freddie grinned as he fell in step beside her. The birds sang their evening songs as they walked. "Just make sure you keep Friday night open so the four of us can go out to help you relax."

"We'll see. I may want to put my feet up by then."

Freddie pouted with an exaggerated expression. "Not going to happen."

Emma laughed. "Don't worry. I'll be ready by Friday, but you'll probably have to pinch me to keep me awake."

"Dancing. Yep. We'll just have to plan on something like dancing. That'll keep you awake." Freddie arched his eyebrows. "I'm sure Jules and Vivi could be persuaded. You should see Vivi. She's a natural when it comes to the new dances."

"Oh, that's not me. I never learned the new steps." Emma shook her head. "I know how to polka, waltz, and two-step." She counted on her fingers. "Beyond that, I'm lost."

"Don't worry." Freddie bumped his shoulder into hers. "When it comes to dancing, I'm the teacher."

They finished the two-block walk down the street and approached the red brick school. Freddie whistled as he bounded up the stairs. Looking behind him, he said, "Been ages since I was in this place. Let me see your room, Teach."

"I suppose so. But I warn you, there's not much to see."

"That's O.K. I just want to see."

She shrugged and unlocked the door. They entered the school and stood in the vestibule midway between the two levels of the building with steps going up and several more going down to the lower level.

"Yup, this brings back memories. Smell that chalk dust." He shivered. Too familiar for him.

Emma nodded toward the upper floor. "My room is on the left. The upper grade room is to the right." She then pointed toward the lower level. "The room on the left downstairs now is a place for the congregation to hold meetings, and the other is used currently for the lunchroom."

"Still the same, just like when I went here. Back then, though, we had Miss Wolfgram. She was . . ." Freddie clucked and walked up the steps ahead of her.

"I'm glad the children have the luxury of bathrooms inside the building, not outside as I did. We had an outhouse when I went to the country school." She reached her room and switched on the lights.

"That would have been cold in the winter." He smiled and surveyed the crowded room. "So many desks. How many students?"

"Forty."

He whistled. "Wow. No wonder you're exhausted." He headed for the door. "I'll let you get back to work again. Don't forget about Friday."

"Don't worry, I won't. It'll probably be the only thing that keeps me going until then." She waved as he skipped down the steps.

With a smile on his face, he walked outside. He certainly wouldn't forget either.

CHAPTER 5

Emma reached for her ankle-length navy skirt hanging on a hook in the closet. Getting dressed for the dance wasn't easy. What should she wear with it? She shrugged. Not too many choices. Slipping her arms into her long-sleeved white shirtwaist, she picked up her watch. Almost six-thirty. She'd better hurry.

Freddie had said he'd be there by seven, but she wanted to be ready early. At least the navy pinstripes in the blouse matched her skirt. Before buttoning her shirt, she pulled her long flowing hair from under the collar. Tucking the tail of her blouse into her waistband, she glanced in the mirror to see if her skirt was straight.

When she had finished getting ready, she hurried outside to wait for him. Ah, the swing. Pushing back with her feet, the weight of the past week fell off her shoulders. Time to forget about school. The twitter of the birds kept her company while the sweet smell of the rose bushes filled the air. What a perfect way to relax.

She'd been looking forward to this evening all week. Freddie had mentioned it every night when he walked her back to school. As if she could forget. The moment had finally come.

Hearing a door slam, she glanced toward Freddie's house and spotted him strolling across the lawn.

"So, *Miss* Teach, how do you feel after your first week?" He loped up the stairs and leaned against the porch railing.

She smiled. "Well, *Mr.* Neumann, having lived through an exhausting week, I'm really not feeling too tired. I'm looking forward to getting away from it all for a bit."

"Ready to do some hopping tonight?" He did a jig right on the porch.

"I've been thinking about it a lot, I can tell you that." Truth be told, learning a few new steps gave her the jitters. Could she do them well enough? Would she trip over her own feet? "I'll do my best to keep up with you."

Freddie nodded. "Tonight I insist you forget school and think only about having a great time. I know Vivi is looking forward to seeing you." He flicked a glance over his shoulder and pointed toward the approaching car. "Here they come now."

Emma waved at Vivi as the car pulled to a stop in front of the house. Freddie motioned to her to precede him down the stairs, and then opened the car door. What a gentleman. He climbed into the back seat after her, and they headed toward Kenosha.

After exchanging greetings, Vivi turned in her seat. "Tell me about your first week of the teaching."

So much for getting away from work. Emma smiled. "It went pretty well, considering. The children were so eager to learn everything, especially the first graders. They're learning the sounds of the alphabet. They'll be starting to read short words soon. It's so much fun to teach them, like little sponges, soaking up my every word. Yesterday, they were even bringing me flowers and pictures."

"*Oui*, already they love you then." Vivi grinned. "I did so too for my first teacher."

"I think the third and fourth graders are still waiting and watching. Wait until the first person is naughty, then we'll see what they do. I'll have to be an ogre the first time." They all joined Emma in a chuckle. "At least they were all good this week."

Tall fields of dark green corn stalks lined both sides of the gravel road as the car sped between them. The wind and dust whipped in the side windows, blowing Emma's curly hair into a tangled mass. Reaching into her purse, she retrieved a hankie and covered her mouth, trying to prevent the dust from choking her.

"How it is possible to handle the forty children at the same time?" Vivi pressed a hand against her chest. "I would run out of the room in less than two minutes, screaming."

Emma laughed out loud. "So far, it hasn't been a problem. The whispering little girls were the biggest nuisance I had this week. And that's not much of a problem. I'm sure things will change when they get to know me better." She might run out screaming herself in a couple weeks.

Jules broke into the conversation. "Hey, enough shop talk for tonight. We're going to paint the town, so let's concentrate on that." He took his eyes off the road and peeked over his shoulder at Emma. "Freddie told us you don't know how to do the Charleston yet. We'll have to remedy that." A rare smile lit up his eyes.

Jitters bombarded Emma. "When I was growing up, we did lots of dancing at weddings and such, but it was all old-fashioned dances." Emma glanced from Jules to Vivi. "I love dancing, so I hope I'll catch on quickly." If only.

"Well, I'm the teacher tonight." Freddie pointed his thumbs at his chest.

"What are you going to teach me?" Emma coughed as dust enveloped the car from a passing motorist.

"I'm a pro at the Charleston and the Black Bottom. Those will be easy with me to help you." Freddie laid his arm along the back of the seat.

"Don't forget about the Collegiate and the Raccoon." Jules eyed Freddie in the mirror.

Freddie tapped him on the back of the head. "We're still learning those, so I didn't mention them."

Vivi waved her hand dismissively. "Emma, not to worry about those new dances. When you hear the jazz, your feet will start the tapping. We will be showing you a couple of new steps. That is all."

Freddie's eyes turned to Emma. "Hey, we're just going to have a good time."

"Ab-so-lute-ly." Vivi turned to look into the back seat. "This was the long week for me. I need the night out on the town."

***

When Emma and her friends reached the Grand Ballroom in Kenosha, they found a place to park and tumbled out of the jalopy. The sun settled on the horizon as a choir of frogs tuned up for their nightly chorus.

Vivi stepped out of the car, allowing Emma to observe what she was wearing—a light blue sleeveless dress hanging straight down to a dropped waistline, ending with a midcalf-length skirt. Her matching hat was helmetlike. Emma sucked in her breath. "Vivi, I really love your dress. I'm going to have to go shopping soon to find something more stylish." She ran her hand down her plain skirt.

"That is the grand idea." Vivi's eyes sparkled. "I think we go do the shopping trip to find you the nifty dress for the dancing nights." Vivi linked her arm with Emma as they walked.

"If we wait until after payday, I'll happily go shopping with you." Emma smiled. Might take more than one paycheck.

"We have much of the time to make the plan, then."

"I'm sure you'd know the best stores for deals. I'll depend on your expert advice." Emma stepped lightly along. Just what she'd dreamed about. Vivi would be the perfect one to show her how to look like the fancy women in the fashion magazines.

"I do know a couple of the dress shops."

"I love your hat, too. It looks so chic." Emma closed her eyes and saw herself wearing such a bonnet over shorter hair with a drop-waist dress. How fashionable she would look. A smile tugged her lips as she looked down to see where she was walking.

Vivi squeezed her arm. "Thank you. It is the cloche hat. Yes, all the rage with the short bobbed haircuts." She patted her hair. "It keeps the hair where I want it while we are driving the car in the wind."

Jules grabbed Vivi's hand. "Come on, baby. No more girl talk now. Let's get a wiggle on so we can dance. The jazzy music is calling our names." Jules tapped his foot to the distant beat of a drum.

After paying the fifty-cent entry fee, they entered the ballroom. A musty odor like day-old beer permeated the crowded room. Emma swallowed to rid herself of the claustrophobic feeling that pressed down on her.

The walls, covered in dark wood paneling, were interspersed with several large windows. In the fading twilight, the room appeared almost too dark, the wall sconces not bright enough to chase away the shadows. A large crystal globe hung suspended from the center of the ceiling. Maybe this would light up later, brightening the room.

It was much larger than the one back home—the Pavilion at Beaver Dam. The seams of the wood floor were almost invisible, worn off by many happy feet.

On the far end of the dance floor, a three-piece band on the stage performed a waltz. Was that why the lights were so dim?

Freddie grabbed Emma's hand as they reached the dance floor. "Perfect tune for us, 'Let Me Call You Sweetheart.' You said you know how to waltz, so let's give it a whirl."

He spun her into his arms and led her into the crowd. Gazing up at him, she matched his steps to the lilting 1-2-3, 1-2-3 beat of the music. She'd previously danced with other men, mostly her father and cousins, but this was different. She'd never been so close to Freddie. The sensation of his hand on her back spread warmth up and down her spine. Her cheeks burned.

She blinked several times. What should she say? "Is it always this dark in here, or will that large globe in the middle of the ceiling light up?" Good one, Emma. Such an intelligent comment.

Freddie tipped his head back and chuckled. "You're cute when you're blushing."

The heat on her cheeks intensified. Coughing twice, she cleared her throat, finding it as dry as a creek bed in August.

"You don't have to be embarrassed just because I have my arm around you." His eyes twinkled. "By the way, you're a terrific hoofer."

"Hoofer?" Finally her voice returned.

"Yeah, dancer. You never heard that before?"

"No."

"You have lots to learn, Em. But, to answer your question, that is a crystal chandelier." He pulled her closer. "Later, it will turn on, rotating to light up the dance floor."

As they spun in circles, Emma peered up at Freddie. If only she hadn't mentioned the light in the first place. There must be other things that people talk about while dancing. He probably thought she was a hick from the country. "Oh."

Freddie smiled down at her. "I think the lights are low during the waltzes to get everyone in the right mood. Is it working?"

Emma nodded, following Freddie's lead around the floor. It was working, indeed. She had the impression she was floating on a cloud. She wasn't even sure if her feet were touching the floor anymore. If only the music would go on and on. Even after it stopped, Freddie kept his hand on her back. Emma's stomach quivered deep inside. Was it Freddie's closeness, or something she had eaten for dinner?

An instant later, the music changed to a faster tempo, a different beat than she'd ever heard before. Time to figure out a new dance step. She scanned the crowd for Vivi and Jules. Could she watch Vivi for a little while? That sure would be helpful. Freddie tugged her hand and led her onto the floor again. Guess not.

"This is the Charleston, Em." He spoke next to her ear trying to be heard over the music. "Watch me to learn the steps."

Her eyes glued to Freddie's feet, memorizing their movements. His feet took him back and forward with legs kicking out sometimes and knees crossing at other times. Would she ever figure all of this out? He grabbed her hand to bring her into the rhythm with him. After a couple attempts, she finally caught on. Before the song ended, relief flowed over her as she kicked up her heels with everyone else.

Several hours later, after Emma had attempted more new dances, she paused to catch her breath. "I thought I was exhausted before we came." She drew in deep breaths, trying to get her heart to slow down. "I actually feel more wide awake than I have in a couple days."

Freddie smiled at her. "Attagirl! You just needed a night out. Are you sure you never learned any of these dances before?"

"No, no, not until tonight." Emma grinned.

"You looked like a pro to me, a real hoofer." They both chuckled. "You could compete with Vivi any day." He grasped her hand to exit the floor. "Someday we'll have to go to a dance marathon and see who lasts longer, Vivi or you."

"A dance marathon?" Emma fanned her face. "Something else new?"

"Yeah, a couple years ago they started to have them up in Milwaukee. We've never had one here yet, but I'd drive up just to see how long we'd last in the contest." Freddie winked at her. "I've heard of people dancing more than thirty-six hours in some places. It's becoming all the rage in larger cities."

The music switched to a slow tempo when the band began playing "When Irish Eyes Are Smiling."

"Not sure if you're Irish, but it's time for the crystal chandelier to do its magic." Freddie swung her into his arms. "The last dance for the night is under the glittering lights. Isn't this nice?"

Flecks of rainbow-colored lights flashed around the room, bouncing off the dancers as they floated to the waltz rhythm. Emma relaxed with her hand on Freddie's shoulder. "Mmm-hmm, I wish it would never stop."

She swayed to the music with Freddie's hand on her back. This evening was more than she could ever have imagined. It was thrilling to learn the new dances with him, but these slower waltzes were something else. Very special. Her heart was warming up to Freddie and his wonderful smile. If only this night could last forever.

As the music ceased and the room once again grew silent, Freddie interrupted Emma's musing. "That's the end. Are you ready to find Vivi and Jules and head home?"

"I don't feel tired anymore, but I guess so." Emma put her hand on his arm. "Thanks for bringing me tonight, Freddie. I had a great time."

"I'm so glad you did. I did too." He clasped her hand and headed across the room.

As the four friends drove back to Racine, they had a lively discussion about the evening. Jules and Vivi told Emma they were impressed with how well she had caught on to all the different steps. They were already trying to figure out when they could get together for the next dance. Because the conversation in the car never slowed down, they arrived home in record time. They called out their goodnights while Emma and Freddie got out of Jules's car.

Freddie slammed the car door and walked beside Emma toward the porch steps. She hesitated. What would Freddie do now? They'd had a nice evening, but she'd never been on a real date before.

What was expected of a girl afterward? Would Freddie try to kiss her? Should she kiss him back? She studied her gloved hands. "Thank you so much again for the wonderful time. I don't know how I'll be able to concentrate on my schoolwork tomorrow."

"We wanted to paint the town, and I guess we succeeded." Freddie grinned.

When they reached her door, he turned toward her. Grasping her shoulders, he stepped closer. An inch away. She could feel his breath on her lips. She closed her eyes. He kissed her with a gentle touch. Before she had a chance to react, he turned and trotted toward his house.

Blinking, Emma touched her lips. Her first kiss. She let out her breath and sighed. The perfect ending to a perfect night. She walked into the Muellers' house and up the stairs. She was about to shut her door when eighteen-year-old Mary barged into her room.

"You're home late. Didn't you hear me calling your name? You forgot to turn out the light downstairs when you came up."

Snapping back to reality, Emma stared at her bed and dresser. How had she gotten all the way up the stairs? "Oh. I'm sorry. I didn't hear you."

"Are you sure you're feeling all right?" Mary settled on the foot of Emma's bed. "Lizzie was asking where you were tonight. You know how pesky little sisters are."

"Hmmm." Emma blinked twice.

"What happened to you? You have this dreamy look in your eyes." Mary tilted her head and grinned. "Does this have something to do with Freddie and the dance?" She wagged her finger at Emma. "Tell me what happened tonight. I want all the details."

For the next hour Emma described the events of the evening. Mary, who had never been on a date either, asked all the right questions to get the tidbits out of her. She was reluctant to tell Mary about the kiss. In the end Mary didn't ask about the end of the night, so she managed to avoid the subject altogether. The dance had definitely been the highlight of her week. Could things possibly get any better?

CHAPTER 6

Standing at the church door before the Sunday service, Neil greeted his parishioners, his black preaching gown flapping in the breeze against his neatly pressed pants. He watched Emma hurry up the church sidewalk with liveliness in her step. The twitter of the birds complemented her pleasant smile while the breeze ruffled the hair peeking out from under her hat. So, the dreaded First Week must have proceeded differently than expected. A good sign, and a relief.

She bounced up the steps. "Good morning, Pastor."

Shaking her hand, Neil returned her smile. "Miss Ehlke, you look as though you survived your first week of teaching and then some. How was it?"

He'd planned to visit her on Friday after school. If only the Fitzmeyers hadn't come. But when duty called, he didn't have a choice.

"Not bad, not bad at all. One week down and only thirty-five more to go." The smile broadened at this. She brushed a few stray hairs behind her ear. "No seriously, it went quite well. Really quite well."

"I'm pleased. Hmm. I really don't have time to talk now before church, but I'd like to hear more after the service." He gave her a half-smile. "Will you be around later?"

"Of course. I'll be heading over to my classroom after church. I still have a couple things to do for tomorrow. Please pop in if you want." She walked into the sanctuary and looked one way then the other before sitting with the Muellers.

After the service, Neil searched briefly for Emma, but she must have slipped past him as he again stood at the church door. After the last parishioner had grasped his hand with well wishes for the day, he headed over to school. She sat at her desk bent over a stack of papers.

He removed his fedora and knocked on the doorframe. "Am I disturbing you?"

Laying her glasses on the desk, she shook her head. "No, no. Please. I need a break from all these arithmetic papers. So many to correct every day."

"I'm sorry I didn't have a chance to check in with you during your first week. I've been so busy all week." Neil sat on a student desk, his hat sitting next to him. "But anyway, tell me how things are going. Any problems with the Piggott boy? Or was he a solid citizen this past week?"

A grin lit up her face as she toyed with her glasses lying in front of her. "No. Karl was a very good student this week. As I said, my first week went well for me."

"Splendid." Just what he wanted to hear. "I prayed that they'd be good at the start of the year. Sets the right tone as the year starts to chug forward." Chug? He winced a little at his own choice of words.

She took no notice, but merely nodded. "Contrary to my worst fears, the children behaved very well, but I'm sure something will happen sooner or later." Her eyes twinkling, she pointed toward some crayon drawings pinned up on the wall. "I received several pictures from the first graders to hang on the wall, so I think they like me."

Smart kids. They couldn't be attracted to her smile as he was, though. Grinning, Neil straightened the rim of his fedora. "I noticed you were here all day yesterday. I do hope you aren't working too many long hours. You'll wear yourself out fast."

That at least was experience speaking. During his first two months in Racine, Neil had never taken a day off. That didn't last long. At least on the farm, rainy days forced Pa and the boys to take some time off. No rainy days in the parish.

Now, however, taking some time off was mandatory for him. "Make sure you take some time to relax once in a while."

"You don't have to worry, Pastor. I have an ally who helps me do just that. Freddie Neumann talks to me almost every day. You know Freddie, don't you?" She glanced at him with her sparkly eyes.

He hesitated. "Of course, I mean, I've met him. I know he lives next door to the Muellers."

He wasn't in church many Sundays, though. But Neil couldn't bring that up. He propped one leg over the other knee.

"He walks me back to school after supper. It's my time to talk about other things." She shuffled through the papers on her desk.

Every day? "I'm glad you have a friend outside of school."

Did he really mean it? She needed an outlet, but Freddie?

"Yes. It was so great. Friday night he took me to Kenosha dancing with his friends. We had a fantastic time."

Dancing? His heart pounding, Neil's eyes widened. Probably Freddie's idea. He hoped not Emma's, at least. Whatever the case, it was a bad idea. And he supposed he would have to say so. How? His mind drew a blank, wordless.

"They taught me all the new dances I never learned in Juneau when I was growing up." Her wide eyes glowed. "It was just the thing after the first Friday of school."

What? His heart raced, but his words came out halting and slow. "You went dancing? To modern music?" He shook his head and plunged forward. "Miss Ehlke, I'm sorry, but that's not a good idea, not at all."

Neil's sweaty palms stuck to the desktop. He didn't want to appear as if he were jumping down her throat, but this was a serious blunder. He swallowed to prevent angry words from flying out of his mouth. As a pastor, he couldn't lose his temper in front of her.

While many of his parishioners were probably O.K. with dancing at something like a wedding, he was sure "modern music," jazz, was different. And despite the plain double standard, none of them would accept dancing on the part of their pastor or teacher. Not even a polka. At weddings, he was expected to say the prayer and leave before any dancing began. Pastors and teachers just could not do that. Period.

As if a switch had been thrown, Emma's color drained from her face. Her smile straightened to a stern line and her eyes glinted, brows furrowing.

He took a quick breath. "Emma, you have to understand the situation for both of us here at St. John's." He wiped his hands on his pants, taking the time to explain. "Look. You are a parochial school teacher working in a congregation."

She tsked. "Yes?"

"You have to see that you are living in a fishbowl—as if you were being watched all the time. They're watching all of us—you, me, Mr. Dietz. " This was not going well. He just wasn't explaining things as he should. He folded his hands around his knee to stop them from shaking.

This was the part of the ministry that he disliked the most. He loved preaching and doing the liturgy in the worship services, but counseling people really took it out of him. *Lord, help me to say the right words to her.*

"A fishbowl?"

"Let me make it clear." He looked down for a second. "Many members of our church would be very offended if they knew one of their teachers danced to jazz music last Friday night."

"What do you mean? I really don't understand how it is anyone's business what I do on my own time?" Her face turning red, Emma blew out a breath. She spoke slowly enunciating each word. "I . . . we didn't do anything wrong."

"Now don't misunderstand me, Emma." He held up his hands, palms out. "I'm not saying all dancing is a sin." He didn't want to give her the wrong impression so he chose the words carefully. "Some types of dances are not bad, but the modern ones are—"

She interrupted him. "Freddie took me so I could relax after my first week of school." Her eyes glaring, she crossed her arms on her desk. "We had a wonderful time."

"What I'm trying to say . . ." If only he could get his point across. Once again, his inexperience with females was frustrating him. "You have to consider what other people think of things you do, not giving the wrong impression to members of our congregation, especially to the parents of your students. It's part of the ministry." He hesitated before continuing. "Did you ask yourself, 'What would Ethel Piggott think if she could see me dancing'?"

The ticking clock beat out the time as seconds slipped by. Emma's eyes widened as she gasped. "What? Of course I didn't think about her." Her red cheeks would have rivaled a fire engine. "That was the purpose of going dancing. To forget about school." Every word was clipped.

"I'm sure it's true, but you are still part of the congregation when you are out having fun. Did you see anyone from church?"

"No one I recognized anyway." She bit down on her lip.

"I'm not trying to be hard, but maybe next time you'll think about this before you do something like that. I really need to stress to you how important it is to be aware of your actions now that you are a teacher. I hope you understand I'm only saying this for your good." Neil stood up. Had he gotten the message through to her? Somehow he doubted it.

She blew out a breath. "Thank you for the, the um . . . *talk*. I'll remember what you said, and be more careful next time." She concentrated on the papers in front of her.

Neil retrieved his hat and headed toward the door. "Enough said for now. Have a good day in school tomorrow." He tipped his hat before placing it on his head. Had he helped or hurt the situation? Time would tell.

***

Emma packed up and headed home, her heart racing as she marched along. How could she correct any more papers? She couldn't even think straight. Why would Pastor think that Mrs. Piggott's opinion was more important than what she wanted to do in her spare time? Was he justified with his criticism of her? What was so wrong about just having fun? Was this how it was going to be?

Almost everyone in her church at Juneau loved to dance. How come church members in Racine would be so upset about dancing if people back home weren't? What would Freddie think about all of this?

She had to calm down before she got home. She took a deep breath and shook her head to rid it of the swirling questions. She ambled along the last block, letting the warm sunshine seep into her bones.

Walking up the back steps of the house, she let herself in the kitchen door. "I'm sorry I'm late for dinner." Would Hilda be able to tell she had been upset?

Hilda hustled around the kitchen between the stove and the table. "I was wondering if you'd get home in time." She drained the boiling water from the potato kettle into the sink. "We're about ready to sit down."

Emma removed her hat and gloves. "Can I help with anything?" If only her cheeks didn't feel so warm. Did they give her away?

"Oh, thanks. Please stir the gravy for me. It hasn't boiled yet." She pointed to the lone pot still sitting on the burner. "I was late myself. Agnes Neumann stopped me when I was coming up the driveway."

"Freddie's mother?" Her pulse back to normal, Emma stirred the kettle's contents in continuous circles.

"Yeah. She said Freddie was gone this morning before his folks got out of bed. She's worried about his church attendance." Hilda threw a glance at Emma. "She says he misses more Sundays than he goes."

No wonder she couldn't find him at church this morning. At least this was a different topic to worry about. What should she say? She peered at the swirling brown liquid as she stirred. "I'm sorry to hear that." Maybe she could encourage him to attend more often.

***

Freddie strolled across the lawn and knocked on Emma's door. When Mr. Mueller called her name, she walked down the hallway toward him, wiping her hands on a towel. "Em, it's such a swell day. Jules and Vivi are coming. We're going to take a ride in his jalopy down to North Beach Park. Wanna come?"

Curly brown hair framed her face as she smiled. "Sure. I'm finished with the dishes, so now's a good time. Give me a second to get my things."

"Perfect," he drawled, leaning against the pillar on the porch.

She returned with her hat set in place and her gloves on her hands. "Freddie, I searched for you in church this morning." Walking down the steps, she slanted a glance at him before studying her feet. "I was hoping to sit with you, but I never saw you." Her eyes returned to meet his. "Where were you?"

The chirping birds filled the silence. He swallowed. Why did she have to bring up the topic of church? This morning he'd forgotten about his resolve to go to church every week. When he remembered what day it was, he and Jules were sitting in a boat waiting for a fish to bite. Too late.

He shrugged. "I . . . I was tied up trying to help Jules with something. He called me early and said it would only take a couple minutes. When I saw the clock, I knew I made a mess of it. Too late to make it to church. I didn't think it was good manners to come in late." He blinked. He was telling her the truth, just not all of it. That was all he wanted to admit.

Emma narrowed her eyes and tilted her head. "I guess we'd better tell Jules not to call you on a Sunday morning from now on. He'll have to wait till you're out of church to pester you."

"Now there's a thought." He stared down the street.

Clearing her throat, she shifted from one foot to the other as they stood on the lawn. "I couldn't concentrate this morning anyway, so I might as well have not gone either." After a short pause, she continued, "Can we chat about something else before Jules and Vivi get here?"

"Sure. Something eating you?" His breath caught in his throat. Now what?

"After church, Pastor came to my room to talk to me about school. I told him all about it, and then told him we went dancing on Friday night." She rubbed her forehead and rushed on, not giving him a chance to respond. "He got pretty upset when I told him about the dance."

Freddie let out a breath as his shoulders relaxed. Her tirade was against Pastor, not him. What should his reaction be? "You're pulling my leg."

She shook her head. "Uh-uh. He said because I'm a teacher in a church school, I shouldn't go to a dance. He said some of the people in the congregation would be offended if they found out. Can you believe that? We didn't do anything wrong."

Can't ruin the afternoon by having her upset. "And how. We just went out to have a night on the town. It was all on the up and up. I . . . we . . . didn't do anything askance." He touched her arm.

"I know most of the members of my congregation in Juneau dance at weddings often—and have a good time." Her voice rose a decibel. "What's the difference between my church at home and the church here? We went dancing on Friday to have some fun." She appeared to have run a mile, her cheeks a bright pink.

"Look, you don't want to get into a sticky situation. Maybe we should ask ourselves what kind of music they dance to in Juneau?" Freddie answered his own question before she could take a breath. "I've seen people from church do the waltz and polka at weddings, but I've never heard any jazz there."

Her shoulders sagged. "Hmm. Never thought of that. Maybe you're right. I've never seen any of those new dances at a wedding either."

"I wonder if there's some unwritten rule against the more modern dances and music." The silence drove home the point. "Maybe Pastor Hannemann was only objecting to you learning the modern dances."

Her eyes tightened as if she had a battle raging in her mind. "Perhaps." Emma shot him a glance. "'I'd never have thought I needed to worry about what people would think of those dances." Her voice a mere whisper. "Maybe Pastor was right."

"Ab-so-lute-ly." He shrugged. "Let's not worry about it. We'll just have to be more careful when we paint the town."

Emma frowned and studied the grass. "Maybe." She didn't sound convinced.

He folded his hands behind his back. "We'll have to go to a dance hall farther away from Racine so no one finds out you were hoofing, that's all. Milwaukee is far enough, and they have lots of dance joints. Then you won't be in hot water."

"I'll have to think about this for a while." She brushed her hair behind her ear.

He flicked a glance over his shoulder at the sound of an approaching car. "Well, you'll have to do your thinking later." He pointed down the road. "Here comes Jules now. Let's not give them an earful today. We'll ponder it another time."

He let out the breath he had been holding. No more discussion about this for now. He had his work cut out for him. How could he talk her into dancing without her conscience bothering her?

Chapter 7

As she hurried to school the next day, Emma pulled her scarf over her head, preventing water from pouring down the collar of her coat. The rain lessened with each step she took. What had happened to the beautiful weather they'd had the day before? Did this portend a bad day ahead?

Her hair was pulled back into a chignon and a raincoat covered her navy skirt and white blouse. If only her skirt weren't wrinkled beyond repair when she arrived.

Thank goodness it wasn't the first day. With a week under her belt, she didn't feel so nervous. At least she knew the children's names and a little about the personalities in her classroom. Now she could begin teaching in earnest.

She was thankful the rain stopped as she walked past the parsonage before turning up the sidewalk toward school. Could she manage to avoid Pastor Hannemann for a couple days? Well, not really avoid him, but at least not go looking for him. She trotted up the steps.

What should she say to Pastor about the dancing issue? Freddie's idea from yesterday still screamed in her mind. Go to a dance in Milwaukee? Would that work? Wouldn't that be almost like telling a lie?

She'd be upset if she couldn't go dancing anymore, but she didn't want to make a major mistake in her new congregation by doing something unacceptable. Teaching was more important than that any day. She shrugged. Too late now to do anything about it. Time to concentrate on the children.

"Miss Ehlke, Miss Ehlke."

Emma turned as a little girl with blond braids ran toward her. What was her name again? First grader. Carla? No. Karen? No. She sits with Elsie. Clara. Clara Krueger. She smiled as she reached out toward the girl. That was close. "Hello, Clara. How are you today?"

"I brung you a rose from Ma's garden." Clara placed a pink flower into Emma's outstretched hand. "Careful so you don't stick yourself with the pointy things."

"You *brought* me a rose. How beautiful." The flower's scent reached Emma's nose before she brought it close to her face. "It smells wonderful. Thank you so much."

The smile on Clara's face told Emma what she needed to know. This student, at least, liked her new teacher.

"The bell will ring soon. You can go play with the rest of the children until then, but stay off the wet grass." Emma pointed toward the playground.

"Yes, Miss Ehlke." Clara spun around and skipped away.

The smile stayed on Emma's face as she climbed the stairs to her room. Her nose wrinkled when she smelled the musty odor permeating her classroom. Fresh air was a necessity in here. She threw the windows open to let in the rain-washed breezes. The room needed as much cool air as possible before so many little bodies heated it up.

She found a small glass on a shelf and filled it with water. It should work to keep the rose alive as long as possible. The flower sat prominently on her desk by the time the morning bell rang.

The children trooped into the room, placed their lunchboxes in the cloakroom, and took their seats, two per desk. When Emma read the morning devotion to them, Clara's eyes grew as large as saucers. Ah. The rose. Clara needed to know how special the gift was to her teacher. Smiling, Emma nodded in her direction before starting the Bible story.

Just before lunchtime, Pastor burst into the room. So much for avoiding him. She couldn't very well steer clear of him if he barged into her room. Why would he barge in like that? His wide eyes told her she'd better put petty thoughts aside.

He strode toward her and stopped mere inches away. His face ashen, he gasped for breath before whispering. "Just got a phone call. Funnel cloud on the edge of town."

Emma's eyes flew to the window. She hadn't noticed the thick darkness now enveloping them. Her heart beat double time. All the children were in *her* care. *God help us all to stay safe.*

"Get them down to the lunchroom and take shelter under the tables. I'll tell Mr. Dietz." He disappeared as fast as he'd come. Any thought about being upset with their conversation yesterday disappeared with him.

Taking a slow breath, Emma tried to mask her fear in front of the students. "There's a storm coming, children. We need to go downstairs."

Clara asked with raised hand. "Should we take our books along?"

Was she serious? Of course, children couldn't comprehend something as terrible as a tornado. "No, don't worry about your books just now." Her hands shaking, Emma clasped them together. "Before we go down, let's pray and ask God to be with us." She bowed her head. "Heavenly Father, be with all of us, and our families, as this storm comes to our city. Keep us safe in Your care. Amen."

Forty Amens echoed hers. She took a steadying breath.

"File down the steps and head for the lunchroom. Lizzie, lead the way."

As the children walked out the door and down the steps, Emma encouraged the first graders to hurry. She closed all the windows and followed the last one down the stairs. Across the hall, the older children marched in single file on the same route.

Pastor stood on the landing, his navy suit taut across his broad shoulders. He directed them down the second set of steps and into the room on the right. His brown eyes connected with Emma's over the heads of the children. Her heart settled into an even rhythm with his calming look.

Emma hurried the smallest ones into the large room already filled with students. While the wind shook the high basement windows, Mr. Dietz showed the children where to sit on the floor.

She located her class crowded under the rows of tables, huddled closest to the inside wall. Out of the corner of her eye she glimpsed Karl Piggott and Eddie Vorpagel causing a ruckus. This was not a good time for her boys to act up.

Pointing at the two boys, Emma beckoned with her finger. "Karl and Eddie, you may go sit across the room with Mr. Dietz's class." She didn't want to deal with them when she had several of her youngest children quietly whimpering.

Her hands still shaking, she approached the principal as he talked to Pastor. "I sent two of my boys over to your side of the room since they were pushing each other in the middle of this. I have too many little girls close to tears to manage Karl Piggott and his friend right now."

All three gazed across the room as the principal pointed toward the younger children sitting among his eighth graders. He motioned to the older ones as they towered over the third-grade boys. "You won't have to worry about them anymore. My eighth graders will keep them in hand."

"Thanks." Emma glanced at Pastor. "Any news? Will the tornado reach us?"

Pastor swiveled his head in her direction. "We'll just stay here until the storm passes. And pray hard." The sound of the wind roared outside. Rain beat on the small windows high on the walls.

Mr. Dietz nodded. "That's your department, Pastor."

Emma pointed toward her class. "I have to check on them."

Pastor followed her. "I'll help you out."

She strolled among her second graders, ruffling some of the girls' hair, murmuring calm words to them. As her eyes roamed around the room, she spotted Pastor squatting on the floor with his arm around Clara, wiping tears off her cheeks with his white handkerchief. Pastor had his arm around a first grader? He cared enough to pay attention to the little girl?

Emma couldn't have imagined her pastor doing this to her when she was six years old. She wouldn't mind a caring arm around her shoulder right about now. Emma straightened her shoulders. No time for that.

Forcing herself to take a slow breath, she approached the principal. "Mr. Dietz, do you mind if we sing some songs? I think that will quiet them down."

Nodding, Mr. Dietz kept his eyes on his students. "Whatever helps."

Emma retraced her steps toward her students. If only she could run and hide in her mother's apron like she did as a child when it stormed. Thinking back, she could still smell the cinnamon and sugar in it. She shook her head to bring her back to the present. Now, she was the adult the children depended on. She squeezed her eyes shut for a brief moment.

Clapping her hands, she surveyed the room. "Children, let's sing a song about Jesus. He'll help us through this storm." She jumped as thunder crashed outside. Several children screeched. *Lord, let this help them.*

Closing her eyes, she opened her mouth to sing:

What a friend we have in Jesus,
All our sins and griefs to bear!

She slid Pastor a glance and saw him winking at her. Winking? Now? He opened his mouth and harmonized his bass voice with hers. A smile tugging at her lip, she couldn't think straight.

What a privilege to carry
Everything to God in prayer!

What was the reason she been upset with him yesterday? She couldn't remember so it must not have been important.

As she continued to sing, she heard others around her join in. Little girls' voices blended with hers.

Oh, what peace we often forfeit,
Oh, what needless pain we bear,
All because we do not carry
Everything to God in prayer!

By the time they finished the verse, the littlest children were shouting the melody. The next time they sang the verse, the volume of the music overpowered the sound of the storm outside, as loud as it was.

Twenty minutes later, they all emerged from the lower level to gather their lunches from the classrooms. After the children returned downstairs with their lunchboxes, Pastor and Mr. Dietz inspected the damage outside. Emma waited patiently with the students to hear the report.

Pastor announced to the entire school. "God be praised. No major damage outside for our school or church property. Several branches are down, but everything else is fine."

Surveying the entire room, Mr. Dietz instructed all the children. "At noon recess, we'll all do our part by picking up branches and leaves and piling them in back of church for the men to deal with."

Emma's eyes filled with tears as a weight lifted off her shoulders. She blinked back the threatening tears and smiled. She'd be happy to spend time outside picking up debris. God had spared them from the worst of the squall.

***

After supper Emma walked back toward the school as the sun approached the western horizon, filling the sky with purple and pinkish hues. A beautiful ending to a day that had started out so unsettled. She spotted Freddie coming down his porch steps as she passed his house. "Hi, Freddie."

He trotted down the sidewalk toward her. "Yoho! Quite a storm we had today, huh?"

She stopped in front of his house. "And how. We're so blessed that the tornado dissipated before it reached school." She hoped it hadn't hit the farm either. It would be days before she got a letter from Ma.

He nodded. "That's what I heard. The factory across the street from us had part of the roof torn off, so it was a close one."

"I'm heading back to school, as usual." She turned to stroll down the sidewalk past broken branches piled up at the curb.

He matched her steps. "Sorry I had to leave last night. I'd have really been in hot water with Ma if I hadn't come home to cut the lawn. I didn't mean to run out on you."

"Oh, don't worry about it." She waved his concern away. Sidestepping a frog that hopped in front of her, she glanced at him. "Remember, I grew up on a farm where doing chores was part of life."

He clasped his hands behind his back. "Did you and Vivi have a swell time walking by the lake? It was a terrific day yesterday."

"Oh, a lovely time." She smiled. "We never run out of things to chat about. We were discussing the latest fashions. How was the ball game?"

Freddie matched her smile. "Terrific. Well, um—We enjoyed ourselves more watching the game than walking in the sand." His eyes lit up. "You should have seen the home run that was smacked over the left field fence. Even Jules couldn't have hit one that far."

They walked in silence for a minute, the chirping crickets producing background music for them. "Freddie, I'd really rather finish the conversation we started yesterday about dancing."

His mouth opened and closed again as he stopped in midstride. "We're just about to school. I don't think we have time to talk about it now."

"I've thought more about it . . ." She paused and peered into his blue eyes. "I was really upset yesterday after Pastor Hannemann talked to me, but now I've calmed down. I'm rethinking what I said." Taking a step toward him, she took a deep breath. Was this the right decision? "If modern dancing will offend people, then I think I'd better not go anymore."

"Wait a . . ."

She put up her hands to prevent his words. "I don't want to make a big mistake here at my new congregation before I've even completed a month of teaching."

Freddie slipped his hands into his back pockets. He hesitated, but finally nodded. "Yeah, I guess it's a good idea for the time being. There are plenty of other things we can do on the weekends."

She smiled. "For now anyway."

At least he didn't seem upset.

"Don't work too late tonight." As they had reached the school, he waved. "I'll see you tomorrow night."

He turned and headed back down the street.

She skipped up the school steps and unlocked the door. Her shoulders relaxed. Good thing he agreed without a fuss. What would she have done otherwise? "Now what will I teach tomorrow?"

***

Neil filled a glass of water and glanced out the kitchen window. Emma and Freddie were standing on the school walkway talking. The setting sun glimmered on her light brown hair. A smile on her oval face lit up her eyes, bringing out her loveliness. Heat rose under his collar.

Freddie turned and strolled down the sidewalk, waving at her. Neil frowned. Why did he escort her back to school every evening? Neil didn't begrudge her time to relax in her busy schedule, but why Freddie?

He drank some water, quenching the burning within. Freddie hadn't been in church again yesterday. If his faith were strong, he'd be there every Sunday. The only time he'd come since June was the week after Emma came to town. What were Freddie's intentions toward her?

Setting the glass down, he leaned against the counter, rubbing his jaw. Why was he clenching his teeth so hard? No logical reason. The word "jealous" jumped into his head. Of course not. He wasn't jealous. Was he? He shook his head. Perhaps a bit. She had been spending so much time with Freddie. *Lord, forgive me.*

He swallowed. Freddie's blond hair and blue eyes probably attracted every girl in Racine. He looked as if he were the type of person to cozy up to a pretty girl like Emma just to get something out of her.

That's not the type of friend who would help her in her new role in the congregation. She needed someone who would encourage her to grow through a relationship. *Like me.* He let out his breath slowly. If only. She wasn't interested in him, though. Why would she be? After all, he was a pastor. Probably too dull.

Neil looked around his neat kitchen. Every plate and cup in his glass-fronted cabinets was stacked up as it should be. The crockery jars on the counter top were arranged from smallest to largest and lined up as straight as a row of corn in his Pa's field. However, this big house was awfully empty. He longed to fill it with his lifelong love. But who was this special woman? *God, you know. Give me patience until you reveal her to me.*

Emma's room light flickered on. He picked up the glass and drained it. She'd been on his mind ever since their conversation the day before. Why had he come down so hard on her when she brought up the dance? Yet it wasn't advisable for her to go dancing when she was a teacher in the congregation. Didn't they tell her that at college?

Whether they did or not, he couldn't stand by and see her exposed to gossip so early in the school year. When he was at the seminary, he'd heard of members leaving a congregation because of a church worker dancing. He didn't want that happening here at St. John's. However, he could have chosen better words.

Neil grabbed his hat, headed out the door and up the school steps. He'd better talk to her tonight. When he reached the top of the stairs, he stuck his head in her doorway. "I saw your light on." He entered her room. "Do you have a minute?"

Neil's eyes instinctively surveyed the neat and tidy room but froze when he spotted a partially empty row of books leaning catawampus against each other. Not good for the spines of those tilted books, besides being unsightly. His impulse was to go over there and straighten them. He thought better of it, even though the urge to do so almost drove him to distraction. He had only come for a quick conversation.

"Sure, Pastor." She removed her glasses and laid them on her desk, avoiding eye contact with him.

He tilted his head. "I thought you agreed to call me by my first name."

She shook her head and glanced up. "Oh, I could never do that. You're my pastor. But feel free to call me Emma." She nibbled on her lip.

He smiled and nodded. "O.K., but I need to talk to you."

"That's fine," she said, pushing her papers back on her desk. "I'll work on my Bible story lesson in a bit."

Removing his hat, he sat on a small desk. "I won't keep you long." Heat rose up his neck, but he willed it to stop there. "I wanted to thank you for keeping your head during the tornado scare today. That was a terrific idea to get the kids to sing hymns."

"I noticed that the little ones started to cry. Figured singing was a way to get their mind off their fear."

"It worked well. I'd have never thought of it." Of course, he couldn't really think straight at all with those big brown eyes staring at him.

"We did that at home with my younger brothers and sisters when they were scared of storms."

"I also came here to apologize to you."

"I don't understand." Her eyes widened. "You don't need to do that."

"Yes, I do." He studied his hat. "After I left yesterday, I felt terrible. If I hurt your feelings, I didn't mean to." He flicked a glance at her. "I'm sorry I spoke so brusquely to you about the dancing issue."

A tentative smile appeared on her face.

"Some people in our congregation are really touchy about certain things." He'd better be careful how this was stated.

She glanced at the pen in her hand. "I know. You were right about that. Mrs. Piggott would have been very upset to know I went dancing."

"She's the one I was thinking of. She wouldn't understand modern dancing at all." He shook his head.

"I don't want to do anything to cause a problem in the congregation. It's just hard for me to understand that what I do on my own time should be scrutinized."

"I know what you mean. Mrs. Piggott most likely wouldn't be upset if another church member went dancing, but because you're the church's teacher, it makes a difference. Pastors and teachers are held to a higher standard of Christian living. Doesn't seem as if it's right or fair sometimes, but that's the way it is." He shrugged. "I was trying to warn you about this so you'll be careful what you do around town."

"I'll remember that." She laid the pen on her desk. "Thank you so much for your concern."

"I don't want to keep you, so I'll say good night. Have a good day tomorrow." He waved on his way out the door.

Neil sighed as he hurried down the steps. He'd apologized for his tone of voice and still gotten the message across. At least, something was accomplished tonight. Heading toward the parsonage, he shook his head. He surely didn't want to deal with a teacher who was enamored of the "flapper" lifestyle.

Chapter 8

Leaving school, Freddie ambled down the sidewalk toward home. How could he persuade Emma to go dancing now? She'd decided to give it up to avoid trouble with Pastor, so now he was stuck with a problem.

He couldn't stay away from it entirely since he enjoyed dancing so much. Would he end up going without her? He'd never gotten serious with a gal like Emma before. Her inexperience and innocence attracted him. He liked that about her. It would be fun to show her a good time and introduce her to the world, yet he had to figure out how to deal with her strong sense of ethics. How would he be able to let her experience life without her conscience getting in the way? As he turned up his driveway, he nodded. He'd have to proceed with great caution.

Two hours later he leaned over the porch railing, rubbing his forehead. No good ideas yet. He'd have to consult Jules about it. He heard a clicking sound approaching from the left. In a matter of moments a woman emerged from the inky darkness, her skirt outlined by the dim light. Emma.

"Hi!" He hurried down the steps.

When she spotted him, she waved and waited for him under a streetlight. "Guess what just happened?"

What a beautiful smile. He slipped a hand into his pocket. "You got a raise?"

She laughed. "Very funny. After only one week of school. Yeah, sure."

He shook his head. "I can't possibly guess."

"Pastor Hannemann came into my classroom shortly after you left." Her hair bounced as she nodded. "He came in to apologize. Can you believe it?"

"What did he say?"

"He said he was sorry for the way he talked to me on Sunday." She took off her gloves.

"He was sorry?" This could be helpful.

"But he also said since some people in the congregation are so sensitive about modern dances, I should be careful what I do 'around town' as he put it." She shrugged.

"That's terrific news." If only he could leap for joy. Instead he remained frozen to the spot.

"Good news?" Her eyebrows knitted together. "I was glad to hear him apologize. I assured him I'd be more careful, but I told you before I don't want to offend church members."

"But he only mentioned the modern dances and what you do 'around town'. We'll just have to go up to Milwaukee when we want to dance next time."

"You really think so?" She frowned, giving her head a tiny shake.

"Sure. We'll be fine as long as we're careful as you promised." Would this work? "Take some time to think about it. I'm sure you'll agree with me in a couple weeks."

"Well, I'll see." She let out her breath. "He was so nice tonight. I think I misjudged him yesterday."

"I'm glad he apologized. I thought he shouldn't have come down so hard on you so close to the beginning of the school year." Maybe getting her dancing again wouldn't be such a challenge.

"Perhaps I should have apologized to him, as well," Emma said, smiling. "I was pretty upset with him."

"Aw, it's all behind us. I'm sure it's all jake—it'll be fine."

"Yeah, maybe you're right. I'd better head home now. See you later, Freddie." She waved as she walked away.

Emma didn't need to be any friendlier to Pastor Hannemann. Freddie didn't want a rival where she was concerned, but would Pastor really have a chance to win her from him? Nah.

Dancing wouldn't be a problem if he were patient. Maybe her talk with Pastor would actually help, easing Emma's conscience with this dancing business.

As she headed up the Muellers' drive, he watched her skirt sway with the rhythm of her steps. Freddie smiled. Now he could concentrate on more important things, like the swing of her hips.

***

The sun peeked through the window and penetrated Emma's dream, bringing her fully awake. School. She blinked and stretched her arms. Time to get up and ready. Eager to face the day, she jumped out of bed.

After eating a quick breakfast, she headed out the door. As she walked toward school, red and yellow leaves from vibrant maple trees fluttered here and there overhead. Fall was here already. Time was flying—a month of school almost gone. She'd have to think of an art project in the next couple weeks using the downed leaves. Memories tugged from her past, collecting leaves for her teacher in the one-room country school.

Which of her students would collect leaves for her? Of course, Lizzie Mueller came to mind since she lived with her family. She'd be the first to help with the leaves.

Who else? That first grader with the cute lisp, William Schmidt, was always so helpful.

Oh, and Anna Fitzmeyer in the second grade was as cute as a bug, but, boy, she might be a handful in the future with her red hair. Her temper hadn't shown itself in the classroom so far, although last Friday, she'd gotten angry with Sarah during lunchtime over a broken cookie. Emma had to do some fast talking to diffuse the situation, bringing Jesus' love into a conversation about a broken cookie, for goodness' sakes. At least the two girls skipped away holding hands after the heart-to-heart chat.

Then, of course, there was Karl Piggott. Goose bumps raced up her arm. Why did the thought of Karl do this to her? Not much trouble so far, besides the pushing match during the storm, but it was still early in the school year. It was a sure bet he wouldn't be interested in pretty leaves.

Her cheerfulness lasted until late morning after arithmetic. When the third graders headed back to their seats, the first graders walked toward the platform for reading. As Emma glanced down at her lesson plans to see what they would be studying, she heard a clunk and a high-pitched squeal. Her eyes searched the room to find the cause.

Six-year-old Clara lay on the floor in the aisle crying. Out of the corner of Emma's eye, she noticed a grinning Karl wink at Eddie. Several older boys in the back of the room snickered. Looking over the rim of her glasses, Emma glared at them as her insides quivered like a bowl of Jell-O.

She rushed to Clara's side. "Where does it hurt?"

"Mith Ehlke," lisped Willie. "I thaw Karl thtick out hith foot and trip Clara."

Was that the reason for the smile between Karl and Eddie? The goose bumps returned with a vengeance. She swiveled her eyes between Eddie and Karl and back to Clara. *Dear Lord, help me handle this in the best way possible.*

Clara pointed to her knee. Emma discreetly lifted her long skirt and peeked at the knee. It appeared red but was not bleeding. Rubbing it, she glanced up at Clara. "Is that better?"

She smiled with tears still rolling down her cheeks. "Yes, Miss Ehlke."

Not a soul in the classroom made a peep. Outside the noise of playing children filled the void. Could they hear her heart pounding in her chest? She took a deep breath. Now what? "Then you can join your class at the blackboard."

Now focus on Karl. Did he do it on purpose to cause problems? She removed her glasses and asked sternly, "Karl, did you trip Clara?" Better come down hard.

Karl shrugged his shoulders. "Yeah. It was an accident. Didn't mean to do it."

She put her hand around the back of his neck and pinched slowly. "Then why did I see you smile at Eddie when you slipped into your seat?"

"I dunno."

Her heart raced as his face turned red. Sure sounded like he was lying to her. But how to prove it? "She could have gotten badly injured in her fall."

Her hand continued to tighten its grip on the back of his neck. "It was Eddie's idea." Karl pointed over a couple rows to his compadre, whose eyes were glued to his desk.

Guess she didn't have to prove anything after Karl's confession. Now what? "Then I think you both should apologize to Clara."

"Sorry, Clara." The boys muttered, not looking directly at the girl.

That was an apology? Not in her book. She'd learned a thing or two about apologizing to her siblings while she was growing up. No apology was complete without tears at the very minimum. In Ma's book anyway. Emma nodded. If Ma's book was good enough for her generation, it would be good enough for Emma, too.

"You don't sound very sorry at all. I'd like both of you to stand in the front of the room so you think about how God wants us to treat each other. That way I can keep my eye on you while I'm teaching first grade. Karl, you can stand by the door and Eddie can stand by the windows, facing me." She removed her hand from Karl's neck and pointed toward the front of the room. "Then during recess you can write on the blackboard thirty times: I will not trip Clara again."

Groans went up from the two culprits as they slunk to their designated spots. That should make them sorry. Emma nodded as she walked back toward the front. Would it be the end of the incident? Fastening her glasses behind her ears, she stepped up onto the platform. Had she passed the test that the boys had given her?

"First graders, today we're going to learn some short-*a* words." Taking a calming breath, she turned to the blackboard, pointing to a column of words. "Let's sound out these words. What sound does the 'h' make?" She tried to concentrate on the task at hand as the chalk clicked on the writing surface.

She had a bomb waiting to explode in her classroom with Karl as the fuse, but she had to deal with each incident as it happened. She needed to take one day at a time with God's help. Would she be ready to diffuse trouble next time?

***

Emma pivoted toward her room after waving to the last student for the day. Climbing the stairs, she let out a slow breath. If only she could have time to sit at her desk and relax for a minute before getting back to work.

Before stepping into her classroom, she heard feet clomping up the stairway. Glancing over her shoulder, she spotted a heavyset woman in a gray coat heading her way. Oh, no. Mrs. Piggott. Not what she needed at this moment.

Her heart imitating the beat of Mrs. P.'s footsteps, she forced herself back into the hallway to meet Karl's mother. Smiling, she greeted her. "Good afternoon, Mrs. Piggott."

A scowl between her eyes as deep as the Grand Canyon, the woman stared at Emma. "Don't bother to 'good afternoon' me, Miss Ehlke. How can you wish me a good afternoon when you accuse my son of tripping a first-grade girl?"

Emma backed away, her hands spread. "Now wait a second, Mrs. Piggott. I didn't accuse Karl of tripping her. He as much as confessed to it when he blamed it on Eddie Vorpagel, saying it was Eddie's idea. Besides, I saw him laughing with Eddie before I approached them." Heat rose up from her neck. *God help me say the right words.*

"That is not what Karl told me, and I'm sure he wouldn't exaggerate at all. He told me it was an accident. That he didn't mean to trip Clara." Mrs. P. crossed her arms. "I'm sure he didn't mean to do it since that's what he said."

"I'm sorry, Mrs. Piggott, I disagree with you. I had to go by what he told me. And by the reaction of Eddie, I'd say it was planned. I had to deal with the boys the best way I could."

Mrs. Piggott waved her hand as if dismissing Emma. "Well, we'll see about that. I'm going to go talk to Mr. Dietz." She turned and stomped down the stairs.

Emma fled into her room, collapsed in her chair and, with elbows on her desk, propped her forehead on her hands. Heat coursed through her as if her veins flowed with fire. Taking a slow breath, she told herself to calm down. She couldn't lose her temper with Mrs. P.

It was only the end of the first month. Was she cut out to deal with this? *Lord, I don't know what to do. Please help me.* Why did that woman manage to irritate her in every possible way?

CHAPTER 9

Three minutes later Emma heard Mrs. Piggott talking as she climbed the stairs. She burst into the room followed by Mr. Dietz. And pointed at Emma. "—and that's what I told her. Now you tell her what to do about it."

Mr. Dietz calmly sat on a student desk and cross one leg over the other knee. "All right then. Now that we're all here, let's go over this again. I'm not going to discuss a problem with a student without everyone in the same room."

Mrs. P. jumped in before Emma could take a breath. "Like I said, she humiliated Karl by making him stand in front of the class for an hour this morning . . ."

Mr. Dietz held up his hand, palm out. "Now, hold on, Mrs. Piggott. I already heard your side of the story when we were outside. I need to hear what Miss Ehlke has to tell me."

Emma took a slow breath. "This morning when the first grade was walking toward my desk, I heard a clunk and turned quickly enough to see Eddie and Karl smiling at each other. Clara lay on the floor crying." She related the rest of the incident as it happened. "The two boys stood in front so I could keep my eye on them for about fifteen minutes while I finished teaching reading."

Mr. Dietz nodded toward Mrs. P. "You told me you don't agree with Miss Ehlke's conclusion about what happened. I tend to think Karl and Eddie were in cahoots for this incident after what she described. In fact, both of them had to be reined in during the tornado scare a couple weeks ago since they weren't behaving properly. Do you have anything to add now?"

Mrs. P. still had a scowl on her face, but her voice was subdued. "It may be reasonable that the boys planned to trip the girl, but I don't agree that humiliating them in front of everyone was the right way to discipline them. It seems to me since Clara wasn't really hurt so bad, the teacher could have forgotten about it entirely."

Trying to control her temper, Emma swallowed twice before speaking. "I did not make them stand in front to humiliate them. I was merely trying to keep my eye on them while I was teaching."

Mr. Dietz nodded. "I do that often with troublemakers. It's a good way to stop them from causing problems."

Mrs. P. raised her eyebrows. "Troublemaker? Are you insinuating my Karl is a troublemaker?"

"No, of course not. I wasn't speaking about him."

Emma toyed with her glasses lying on the desk. "Also, I couldn't just forget about them tripping Clara because it was the first major disruption in my class. If I hadn't come down hard on the two boys, someone else would try something worse next time."

Mr. Dietz nodded. "I agree with Miss Ehlke there. Children need strict discipline early in the school year to keep the classroom under control the rest of the year. That's important to parents, isn't it?" He looked directly at Mrs. P.

Mrs. Piggott nodded her head slowly, as if she were doing it grudgingly. She looked into Emma's eyes. "I'll concede the point this time. Just don't pick on Karl and single him out next time you're trying to make a point to the class. He always tells me what happens in school, so I know exactly what he's done each day."

Emma had to swallow a laugh. Karl told his ma *his* version of events at school. She returned Mrs. P's intense gaze. "Mrs. Piggott, I can't tell what I'll do or won't do to Karl, or any of the other students in my classroom, since it depends on their behavior, but I will promise I'll do the best I can to be fair to everyone in my room. I'll also promise that I will protect all of my students, especially the little girls, from others picking on them or trying to injure them."

Emma let out her breath. These children were under her care. She had a duty to God to protect them from others, especially the bullies in the class. No one, not even Mrs. P., would keep her from doing that.

Mrs. P. nodded. "I'll go home and discuss this with my Meyer and Karl. I don't want him injuring the girls either—accident or not. Have a good evening." She waved and left the room.

Emma slumped against the back of her chair. Exhaustion flowed over her. She wouldn't get any correcting done until after supper. This would be a long night.

Mr. Dietz cleared his throat. "I thought you handled her very well, Emma. You stood up for yourself in front of her. Mrs. Piggott likes to be important in our school, so she talks to me often during the school year. I listen to what she says, but she's not the teacher here. I think you did the right thing in class today. You needed to nip this problem with these two boys before it gets worse."

Emma sat up straighter, the burden gone from her shoulders. "Thanks so much. I didn't know how to react in the middle of the crisis today. God helped me get through this first test."

Would she be ready for the next one?

***

What a long day. Despite the evening gloom, she almost skipped down the sidewalk on her way home. She'd survived the talk with Mrs. Piggott and Mr. Dietz. At least, she didn't think she was in trouble with Mr. Dietz, and she really didn't care what Mrs. P. thought about her. Maybe she should, but right now she didn't.

When she passed Freddie's house, Jules's car was parked on the curb. Vivi. She hadn't talked to her much over the last couple weeks. Maybe she was here. She could tell her about the excitement at school. It was rather late, but Emma headed toward Freddie's porch.

As she raised her hand to knock on the door, it burst open, the squeaky hinges grating in her ears. Jules stumbled out, almost knocking her flat.

"Whoa!" Jules grabbed her arm. "Jeepers! Didn't know you were out here."

Freddie barged after Jules, starting the avalanche all over again. He bumped into both of them, reaching out to grab her other arm. Emma stepped back and straightened her hat.

"Hey, Teach, what are you doing here so late?" Freddie released her arm and brushed off her sleeve. "Haven't seen you around much this week."

The sky was rapidly changing from dusk to total darkness, but the light from the house illuminated their faces. She cleared her throat. "I was just coming to ask if Vivi was here." Maybe this wasn't such a good idea after all.

"No, she's not." Jules shook his head. "I was just leaving to go to her house. Do you want me to give her a message?" He fidgeted with his key ring.

"No, no. I wanted to tell her what happened at school today."

Freddie leaned against the porch railing with his hands in his pockets. "Tell us then. What happened?"

Emma crossed her arms. "My troublemaker acted up for the first time today. He tripped a first-grade girl and laughed with his buddy about it. They ended up standing in front of the class and then, during recess, writing sentences on the board. Anyway, his ma came in after school and gave me an earful for being so mean to her boy."

Freddie reached toward her arm. "You O.K.? That's a sticky situation there. What did you say to her?"

Stepping back, she shrugged. "I'm fine. She got the principal involved, but at least he agreed with me."

"Swell. Hope that's the end of it for you."

"I hope so too."

"I used to hate writing sentences on the board. So boring. But I learned a lesson doing it." Freddie smiled.

Jules glanced at her. "I sure couldn't do what you do with those kids."

Rubbing her hand up and down her arm, she smiled. "I couldn't either without God's help. Anyway, tell Vivi I wanted to talk to her."

"Will do, Emma." Jules nodded.

Since it was late, she'd best head home. She started down the steps. "Thanks, Jules." She turned to wave.

***

"Wait a second." Freddie hurried down the steps after her. "You don't have to run off so fast." Jules followed on his heels.

She stopped short and swung around, almost causing Freddie to plow into her. "After my long day, I can't stay. I'm so tired already." Sidestepping onto the grass, she switched her reticule from one arm to the other.

"Nah, don't be a wet blanket. Just a couple minutes, at least, so we can figure out what's up for this weekend." Freddie tucked his thumbs into his front pockets.

Jules studied the key in his hands before glancing up. "How about a movie?"

"Terrific idea." Emma's voice almost smiled. "That's one of the things on my to-do list."

"Now you're on the trolley, Jules." Freddie grinned. Perfect. He could sit close to her in a dark theater. Maybe put his arm around her.

Jules spoke up. "I hear there's a new one at the Kenosha Theatre."

"What's playing down there?"

"It's a Charlie Chaplin film, *The Gold Rush.*" Jules leaned against his car. "I hear it's a humdinger."

"Baloney, that's not a new movie." Freddie had seen an ad for it in the paper weeks ago.

Jules shrugged. "Well, it's new around here. Have you seen it?"

Emma crossed her arms and drew in her shoulders. "No, I've never seen it."

Was she cold in the night air? Her lilac perfume tickling his nose, Freddie stepped closer. "What do you think, Em? Sound like a plan to you?"

"Yeah." She rubbed her arms.

"Then it's decided." He put his arm around her to keep her warm. This was good practice for movie night.

She shivered. "I'll talk to Vivi then." She edged away from him.

"O.K., I'll go tell her. She's usually a pushover when it comes to flicks." Jules opened his car door. "See you Friday night about seven-thirty. Gotta run." Waving, he slipped into his car.

As Jules started the engine, Emma stepped away from Freddie and turned to go. "You don't have to scram so fast." What was her rush? Did his arm around her make her nervous? "Hey, fill me in on the rest of the week."

"Aw, it's so late." She clutched her purse to her chest and backed toward her driveway. "I have to teach tomorrow, so I'd better head home. I'll tell you when I tell Vivi."

"O.K. I'll surrender. I'll be in suspense until Friday." He flashed her a grin. "See you then." He watched her hips swing as she sauntered across his lawn and up the drive toward her house. His blood heated up just watching her. That movie night couldn't come fast enough for him.

But what was eatin' her? Skittish as a young colt tonight. Why did she run away so quickly? At least, it sure looked like it to him. He'd put his arm around her to try to keep her warm, but maybe she had misinterpreted his intentions. Such a shy girl, probably without much experience in dating. He'd have to help her out there, but he'd have to be smart about it.

***

Emma ran up the steps to her porch. Was it right to stand on the front lawn with Freddie's arm around her? Anyone in the neighborhood could have seen them. What would Pastor say? Living in a fishbowl, and all. She opened the front door and stepped inside.

As she got ready for bed, she scolded herself for rebuffing Freddie. Was he only trying to keep her warm in the cool air? She shook her head.

If only she hadn't made an issue of it by being rude to him and walking away. She needed to trust him more. She wasn't used to being with guys. That was the problem. Next time she wouldn't be so nervous.

***

Sitting in the school lunchroom, Emma opened her mouth to take a bite of her sandwich. A spine-chilling scream at the next table stopped her short. She whipped around and saw Lizzie Mueller staring into her lunchbox. Eyes bulging, Lizzie's face was as white as the tabletop. She typically didn't dramatize small events, so something must be drastically wrong.

Emma dropped her sandwich and hurried to the girl's side. "What's wrong, Lizzie?"

With tears streaming down her cheeks and her hand shaking, the girl pointed toward her lunch. "There's . . . a . . ."

Emma peered over the edge of the lunchbox and spotted a small green garter snake curled up next to a red apple. She gasped, but forced herself not to flinch. Her older students were testing her again. Probably trying to get her to panic in front of the others. She swallowed, willing her stomach to stay where it was.

Good thing it wasn't a mouse. She never could abide mice. However, growing up with four brothers, she'd had plenty experience dealing with garter snakes. She put her arm around Lizzie's shoulder. "I'll take care of it. Don't worry."

Emma took a big breath. *Lord, help me to stay calm in front of everyone while I deal with the snake.* She picked up the lunchbox, held it at arm's length, and hurried up the steps and out the front door. She dumped the entire contents behind the bushes, shaking it to make sure the critter wasn't still inside. Bringing the lunchbox closer, she turned it over to peer into it. Totally empty. No snake, but no lunch for Lizzie either.

Now to deal with the results of this trial by fire. She marched down the steps toward the table-lined room. As she turned the corner to enter the room, she spotted several third- and fourth-grade boys glancing toward the door and pointing at her. Yup, they were testing her again.

Emma raised her arm. "Can I have your attention, please?" Forty pairs of eyes stared at her. "We have a problem in our class. Lizzie's food has just been spoiled by a snake that mysteriously got into her lunchbox."

All the girls in the room gasped and stared at her. Emma had to press on. "Now, we all know that a snake couldn't get inside her lunch pail all by itself. I would like to know if anyone has any knowledge of this problem."

She glanced from one end of the room to the other, looking for anyone willing to confess. Silence reigned among all the children. "By the reaction of the girls, I'm going to guess that it wasn't a girl who put it in there." Eyes wide, the girls shook their heads.

First-grader Willie raised his hand. "I didn't do it. I don't know how to find thnakess," his lisp very pronounced.

Several more first- and second-grade boys chimed in. "Not me, not me."

The third- and fourth-grade boys remained very quiet. They slid glances from one to the other, but did not say a word. Did they know who did it? Would someone confess, or would one of them tattle on the culprit?

"It appears that one or more of the third- or fourth-grade boys ruined Lizzie's lunch. Now she doesn't have a thing to eat.

Since no one will tell me who did it, all of you will need to give one item from your lunch to Lizzie for her to eat. We don't want her hungry all afternoon."

She walked toward Lizzie with her now empty lunch pail. Putting her arm around the girl, she asked her to stand up. "You boys, let her choose whatever she wants from your pail."

When Lizzie was seated in her spot again, eating, Emma clapped her hands to quiet the room. "To make sure that no more snakes sneak into lunchboxes, those same boys will stand next to the school wall during recess this noon. Now let's hurry and finish eating so there's time to play yet." She walked back toward her place at the head of the first-grade table. Her appetite had vanished. No way would she be able to eat a bite.

Had she passed the test?

***

Emma had her answer later that afternoon when Mrs. Piggott once again barged into her classroom.

"What's this about you taking my son's lunch away from him and handing it over to the Mueller girl?"

Emma sighed. This was getting to be too much of a routine. "Karl is not telling you the whole story again, Mrs. Piggott. Did he tell you that Lizzie Mueller had a garter snake in her lunch pail?"

Mrs. P. gasped, her hand flying to her chest. "A snake? How did it get in there?"

Emma stood with hands on her hips. "How, indeed? That's what I had to figure out on the spur of the moment this noon. No one confessed, but comments made by other students led me to believe that it was one or more of the older boys. Therefore, they each donated one item from their lunches."

"But why take food away from them?"

"I don't think I'd be able to eat any food from a lunchbox formerly inhabited by a snake. Would you?"

"Uh, um . . . Well, no. I wouldn't *touch* anything that was near a snake."

"So why should Lizzie? I had to dump her entire meal out with the snake, so I couldn't let her go hungry. Thus the donations by the students."

"Oh, well," Mrs. P. hugged herself. "O.K. Karl didn't make that clear to me when he told me. I'll take him to task for this, that I promise you. Good day." She retreated from the room and walked down the stairs.

Staring out the window, Emma finally let out the breath that she'd been holding. At least she'd escaped Mrs. P's ire this time.

***

After school on Friday, Emma plopped into her chair. What a long week. But she still had to straighten up the classroom before leaving for the weekend. Papers were scattered on her desk, and the blackboard needed washing. She spotted specks of paper on the floor. Add sweeping to the list. Removing her glasses, she laid them on the corner of her desk.

Humming "I'm Always Chasing Rainbows," she worked on one task after another. After filling a bucket with water, she climbed the steps to her room. Time to clean the blackboard, or should she say milky-white board, since it was covered in chalk dust. She sighed. A knock on the door drew her eyes away from her task. "Hello, Pastor."

"Evening, Emma." Even though he was handsome enough in his usual black suit and tie, his coffee hair and deep brown eyes reminded her of the town undertaker at home. Good thing he couldn't read her mind.

Setting the bucket on the platform, she smiled. "I'm trying to finish up here, so I can leave for the day. Do you mind if I keep working?"

"Not at all. Don't let me stop you," he said with a wave of his hand. "So, how did you survive this week?" He sat on a student desk and removed his hat.

"You wouldn't believe what those kids tried on me." She bent to retrieve the sponge. Water poured over her hands as she squeezed it.

"Oh, what happened?" He ran his fingers along the rim of his hat.

"One of the days Karl Piggott tripped one of the first-grade girls. He was laughing about it with Eddie, so they had to stand up in front of the room for a time." Emma paused, looking toward Pastor. "They didn't sound very sorry, so they wrote sentences during recess."

"Your first altercation with him?"

She approached the filthy chalkboard. "Mmm-hmm, but that's not all. A couple days later, one or more of the boys put a garter snake in Lizzie's lunchbox. That was challenging to deal with. Good thing snakes don't scare me too much. On top of that Mrs. Piggott came in both days demanding an explanation of my actions—or at least, Karl's description of my actions."

He nodded. "Wow. I guess it was challenging for you. Sounds like you managed to live through it pretty well."

"I'm hoping the worst is behind me." She faced the chalkboard, her arm arcing back and forth, turning a streak of the milky-white surface to charcoal-black.

Pastor stood and stepped up onto the platform. "Let me help you with that." He took the sponge out of her hand and dunked it in the bucket.

"Thank you." Emma watched him reach his arm from top to bottom washing the board in straight even lines starting on the left edge. She'd never seen anything like it. Perfect strokes lined up side by side. She shook her head. "I think I'll sweep the floor if you're doing that."

"There's a plan. Then you can get out of here sooner."

After fetching the dust mop from the hallway closet, she chuckled. "I can't believe how chaotic the room is after school every day."

"Not at all surprising with so many little bodies in here. Now, about Karl—please let me know if there's anything I can do whenever a problem arises." He paused. "But that's not what I came to talk to you about." He squeezed out the sponge. "I was wondering if you were busy on Sunday noon."

Emma's mop froze in midstroke. She answered slowly, "N . . . no." Gazing at Pastor, she couldn't swallow past the lump in her throat. She clamped her hands on the mop to stop them from shaking. What was he going to ask her?

"I've been invited to the Hintzes' house for Sunday dinner. Would you like to join me for the visit? I thought it would be a good opportunity for you to get to know them better." He cleaned another stripe on the board. "Clayton is in your class, isn't he?" After rinsing, he squeezed the sponge dry.

"Yeah." Her blood started to circulate again. "He's in fourth grade."

"Perfect. Then I'll come and pick you up after church." Stepping back, he inspected the spotless chalkboard. "As usual, it will take me a while to finish greeting the people, but I'll come as soon as I can. Will you be here?" Dropping the sponge in the bucket, he picked up his hat and placed it on his head.

Emma glanced from the immaculate board to Pastor. Not a drop of water on the floor, or speck of chalk dust on his black suit. Amazing. Was he for real? No wonder his house was spotless when she'd been there weeks ago.

Back to the invitation. "Yes, but you said you were invited. Are you sure I'm invited, too?" She swept the dirt into a pile. "Maybe they want just you to come for dinner."

***

Neil glanced her way. She can't back out now. "I'm sure it would be fine if you come along. Mrs. Hintz told me she wanted to get to know the church workers better. That includes you." He peered into her eyes. "You'll come, won't you?"

"Sure." She nodded. "I need to get to know his parents. I haven't gotten to their house yet."

"Wonderful. Have a good weekend. I'll see you Sunday morning." Tipping his hat, he walked out the door.

He grinned as he trotted down the school steps. He had done the right thing. Mrs. Hintz didn't say she wanted him to come for dinner specifically to get to know their daughter Frieda, but he had a feeling that was the ultimate reason for the invitation.

The twenty-year-old young lady had been overly friendly with him after church services as of late. Frieda Hintz was a nice girl, but she was—as the saying goes—almost as wide as she was tall. Of course, that didn't matter to him. He shook his head. He just didn't like any mother trying to push a daughter at him with the idea of getting hitched. Nobody was going to play matchmaker for him. If only he could dispel any high hopes on Frieda's part by taking Emma along.

Now Emma was a different story. He would encourage a bit of pushing from her mother. He wouldn't mind it at all. They really weren't anything more than co-workers, but only God knew what would happen in the future.

Chapter 10

After Pastor left her classroom, Emma let out a pent-up breath. When he asked about her plans for Sunday afternoon, she'd assumed he wanted to take her on a date. Wild imagination. How wrong she'd been. Her mother used to tell her that assuming things got a person into trouble. She was right.

Emma would be going with Pastor only on a trip to visit Clayton's parents. What a relief. Or was there some disappointment way down deep?

She had told herself to be nicer to Pastor Hannemann, but that didn't include a date with him. He was her pastor, after all. She wasn't good enough for him. Or neat enough, for that matter. Shaking her head, she peered at the clean blackboard. There was the truth. He'd never consider asking her on a date.

The stack of papers on her desk stared at her. She sighed. Lots of work to do. Better get busy since she would now be occupied Sunday afternoon. And tonight was movie night with Freddie and his friends. She hurried to get as much done as possible in the short hour before heading home.

After supper Emma rushed upstairs to get dressed. She pulled on her print skirt and a cream-colored blouse. Combing her hair, the brush froze in midair. Fixing a hairdo took up so much time. Would a different style be easier? Her hand pulled her hair into its usual chignon. Maybe tomorrow she'd have time to think about that.

Trotting down the steps, Emma heard a knock on the front door. She swung the door open. Perfect timing.

"All dolled up and ready to go, I see." His hat in his hand, Freddie smiled at her. He stood on the porch dressed in a navy pinstriped suit with a red tie, a wave of his sandy hair drooping across his forehead. "Vivi and Jules just pulled up." He nodded toward the street.

"All set." Emma tugged on her gloves and straightened her hat, closing the door behind her. "Ready to paint the town." They headed toward Jules's car. "I need to forget this week."

"Count on me to help you with that assignment." Freddie winked as he helped her into the car.

Jules pulled away from the curb and headed toward Kenosha. After getting settled in the back seat, Emma leaned forward. "Thanks for suggesting a movie, Jules. I haven't been to one for ages."

"I have not been to the good film either." Vivi turned toward Emma, her arm draping over the seat back. "Charlie Chaplin is very funny, so I hope this is also. Some laughs will help me after the long week."

"It'll be terrific." Freddie patted Vivi's arm.

"How did the teaching go this week?" Vivi smiled. "You have not talked about the happenings."

"My first challenging week." Emma rubbed her forehead. "Two times my older boys acted up—once even involving a snake."

"A snake! You didn't tell me about that. What happened?" Freddie put his arm around her shoulder.

"Early in the week, my third-grade troublemaker tripped a first-grade girl causing a bit of a ruckus, but the next day a garter snake ended up in a fourth-grade girl's lunch pail."

Vivi gasped. "What did you do with the creature? I would have screamed for the help and run the different way."

"Nah, I just dumped the whole thing outside, but then I had to deal with the situation."

Freddie squeezed her arm. "Who did it? The same trouble-maker?"

They wound their way through the dark neighborhoods on the edge of town and into the lighted streets of the business district.

"That was the problem. No one confessed, so all the older boys had the same punishment. The worst part was having Karl's mother descend on me after both incidents. She managed to give me an earful. " Emma glanced at Freddie. "I only hope I did the right thing."

"I am sure you did the handling correctly. I know I could not get up in front of the whole room full of the children, and then face angry parents on top of it. My hat is off to you." Vivi swept off her hat dramatically, bowing her head to Emma.

"And how! Time to hang it up and forget about it." Smiling, Freddie put his hand over Emma's gloved one.

Emma nodded, gazing down. Should she let him do that? Did this constitute a fishbowl event?

"It is O.K." Vivi winked at Freddie before glancing at Emma. "We have the fun tonight."

"You betcha." Freddie patted Emma's hand. "The movie awaits us."

Emma leaned back in her seat. She had to stop worrying about fishbowls so much.

Jules found a place to park a couple blocks from the theater. Freddie clasped Emma's hand while they walked the short distance. Tingles raced up her arm. She refused to pull away this time. No one from church would be watching them here.

The four friends had to wait in line to purchase tickets for the movie. When they entered the lobby, Emma's eyes widened. An amazing kaleidoscope of colorful posters lit up the walls advertising upcoming films.

"Do you gals want to go pick out the seats?" Freddie glanced from one to the other.

"So now you're not including me in this party?" Jules crossed his arms and squinted at Freddie.

"You slay me, Jules." Freddie laughed and thumped him on the arm. "Ladies' choice tonight."

The four enjoyed a good chuckle. They headed toward the large doorway into the theater.

Emma's mouth fell open. This place was cavernous, larger than any church she'd ever been in. As they walked on the red plush carpet down the center aisle, the usher showed them to available seats. When they were about to sit down, she glanced up at the balcony looming over the back of the theater. Incredible. As large as the entire auditorium back home. A great crystal chandelier hung from the ceiling, spreading soft light to every corner, as if it were the heart of the building. So ritzy. She'd never imagined anything like it.

When the Wurlitzer organ started playing, she almost jumped into Freddie's lap. She cocked her head toward him. "Is it starting already?"

He whispered into her ear. "Two-minute warning."

"I hope he's a good organist. I've gone to movies where the music ruined the entire story. It made it hard to follow the plot." Emma lowered her voice when the theater was suddenly blanketed in darkness. Black and white pictures flickered across the screen with the dialog flashing between pictures.

Freddie reached for her hand. "Not the time to worry about it now."

***

After a brief moment of hesitation, Freddie slipped his arm around Emma's shoulder as they emerged from the theater into the crisp night air. "Did you like the movie?" They waited for Jules and Vivi.

She leaned toward him. "Ab-so-lute-ly. What fun!"

Vivi and Jules joined them.

"Terrific film, but I couldn't believe we had to pay twenty-five cents to get in." Jules put his arm around Vivi's waist. "Two weeks ago I went to one in Racine costing only fifteen."

"I have heard that they charge the more for the popular stars." Vivi poked Jules in the chest. "I bet Charlie Chaplin is more famous than the actors in the other movie."

As they headed down the block toward the car, Jules and Vivi led the way. The night air was filled with the distant sound of jazz emanating from the dance hall near the park.

Freddie forced himself not to tap out the contagious beat on Emma's shoulder. "I thought the movie was worth it."

Sitting in the dark next to Em with her lilac perfume had been worth more than two bits. He'd happily pay double that any day of the week.

"Yeah, I thought it was hilarious." Emma chuckled. "It was the exact thing I needed tonight."

Vivi glanced over her shoulder. "Me, also."

They laughed as they ambled past an ice cream parlor with an orange and yellow striped awning. Jack's Café, painted across the front window in three-foot cherry-red letters, beckoned to Freddie. His stomach growled in response to a three-scoop ice cream cone pictured next to the words.

Jules froze in midstride. "I hear an ice-cream soda calling me." He motioned with his head. "How 'bout it?"

"Hey, just what I was thinking." Freddie's noisy stomach agreed with him. "Perfect timing." The four of them laughed.

"Let's go then." Jules held the door open for the other three. "It's Friday night so no one has to get up early tomorrow."

"Says you." Vivi jabbed Jules's arm. "I have to be up early for the work by eight-thirty."

***

Emma licked her lips. "Oh, Vivi, ice cream sounds so good right now."

"So, I guess I am voted out." Vivi pointed toward the door and smiled. "Let us get a wiggle on then."

As they entered Jack's, Emma wasn't surprised by the patterned tin ceiling or the long soda fountain on one side of the large room. Those were typical of the ice cream parlors she had been to in Milwaukee during college. "I love the beautiful mural painted on the back wall. Is that a scene from the lakefront?"

"Yup. Several cafés around here have different scenes from the Lake Michigan area." Freddie placed his hand on the small of her back. "Let's see if we can find a seat."

The crowded room didn't offer much of a possibility. Her eyes searched every corner for a vacant spot. "What if we can't find a table?"

Could Freddie even hear her above the laughing and cackling?

Jules pointed with his finger. "There's an empty booth near the back. Let's hurry before someone else grabs it."

Jules clasped Vivi's hand and pulled her between the close tables.

Freddie followed suit with Emma in tow. They slipped between chairs occupied by other customers before finally sliding onto the benches of the booth.

"I worked up the appetite just getting to our table." Vivi smiled as she laid her clutch bag and gloves on the flat surface. "So many people."

"Everyone must have the same idea. It's Friday night, after all." Freddie slapped the table. "What goes better than ice cream on a Friday?"

The waitress came to take their orders. Sitting next to Vivi, Jules ordered black cows for both of them.

Freddie turned to Emma. "What would you like?"

She scanned the menu printed on a board behind the counter. "A chocolate ice-cream soda sounds good. I haven't had one of those in a long time."

Freddie raised two fingers. "Make that two. It will be easy to remember."

After the waitress left, Vivi leaned back in her seat. "I remember when first I came to this country, I could not understand what the 'black cow' was. It seemed a funny name for the drink made from root beer and ice cream."

"I've heard of 'brown cows' also." Jules winked. "Though I can't quite imagine combining cola and ice cream."

"And how." Freddie grimaced. "That doesn't sound good at all."

Emma watched as the soda jerk made the chocolate sodas. He put a squirt of chocolate syrup into the glass, followed by a couple pumps of soda water. Then he flung a scoop of vanilla ice cream into the air, catching it in the half-full glass. Blending this with a spoon, he added two more scoops of ice cream and filled the glass with carbonated water. Whipped cream and, of course, a cherry topped off the concoction.

"I've often thought of quitting my job at the factory and getting a job as a soda jerk." Jules watched the man behind the counter. "Looks like he's having fun."

"You? Baloney." Freddie shook his head.

"Why not? That would seem to be a great job. Sure thing. I could catch the ice cream in the glass just like he did. But I don't know how much they get paid."

Freddie raised his finger. "Bingo!"

"Besides," Vivi poked Jules in the chest, "they have to work in the evenings, especially the Friday and Saturday nights." She glanced from Jules to the soda jerk. "Would you want to work those hours?"

"Oh yeah, I didn't think about that." Jules wiped his hands back and forth as if to wash them of the idea. He winked at her. "Takes care of that plan. I couldn't miss those nights going out with you."

A smile tugged at the corner of Freddie's mouth. "Oh, come on. You should get a job here. Then when you're working, I can have Em all to myself." He flicked his eyebrows at Emma. "We could find all sorts of things to keep us occupied."

Heat rose up Emma's neck. "No, Jules had better keep the job he has now. Best for everyone. We don't want Vivi to be lonely on Friday nights." She pointed toward the restrooms. "If you'll excuse me for a moment, I need to check my hair."

Vivi pushed Jules aside. "I will also come."

The two hooked arms and headed toward the back of the café. They searched down a long dark hallway. Spotting the room marked "Ladies," Emma pushed open the door to find a small room with dark wainscoting on the lower part of the walls and beige paint above it. A bare light bulb hung from the ceiling, not quite reaching the dark corners with its glow. The musty scent permeating the room caused her to swallow.

Standing in front of the mirror, Emma glanced at Vivi. "After my crazy week, I was thinking that I might need a different hairstyle. This chignon takes so long to look right. What do you think?" She tucked brown strands back into her bun.

Vivi put her finger on her chin as she tilted her head side to side, studying Emma's hair. "You know, I think you would look swell in the bobbed hair. That *coiffure* would set off the face much. Almost frame the cheeks."

"*Coiffure*?"

Vivi shook her head. "Oh, I mean haircut. How you wear your hair. Like mine. Cut straight around—same length. About to bottom of your chin."

"Bobbed haircut? I can't picture myself with short hair." What had she started?

"But they are the rage everywhere. All young ladies are getting their hair cut like that. Have you seen the pictures in the magazines?"

"Sure, my mother gets *Good Housekeeping* all the time. Those haircuts look good in the magazines, but no one in my family has done that yet." If only Emma could remember if Ma had ever commented about those pictures.

Vivi laughed. "Well, then you would be the number one in your family. Or, how about the shingled look? That is shorter cropped hair with waves close to your head."

"No, I definitely wouldn't want to get it that short."

"Maybe right. Too short. But the bob cut is good length. Easier than long hair to take care of. Freddie would be, oh, enchanted."

Emma twisted her head, looking at her reflection. "You think so?"

Vivi nodded. "Ab-so-lute-ly. How about coming tomorrow morning to let me cut it for you?"

Nerves tap-dancing inside her, Emma shrugged. "I'm not sure . . ."

Vivi latched onto Emma's arm. "Think how much cooler it will be next summer."

They left the room and wandered back toward the café. "Cooler sounds great." Was she ready to do this?

"O.K. It is all set. We cut it in a bob tomorrow morning." Vivi slid a glance at Emma. "Then we will find you a cloche hat, and you will be all the spiffy."

"Wait. I'm still not convinced."

They approached the booth. "Let us ask Freddie what he thinks."

Freddie stood up to allow Emma to be seated. "Ask me what?"

Vivi spoke up. "Should our Emma get the bob haircut tomorrow morning? She would look terrific, no?"

Freddie turned toward Emma. "Yeah, sure. She would look keen with shorter hair. A real doll." He winked at her.

Heat rising up her cheeks, Emma finally nodded. "O.K. What time should I come?" Her insides quivered, not fully agreeing with the plan.

"I have an opening at the nine-thirty. We will have a good time making you all hotsy-totsy."

The four laughed as the waitress brought their order.

As Emma took a sip of her ice-cream soda, shivers crawled up her spine. What did hotsy-totsy look like?

CHAPTER 11

When Emma woke up on Saturday morning, she groaned. If only she could sleep two more hours. She'd gotten home at midnight after the four friends sat at Jack's Café talking and laughing for hours. Having such good friends in Racine was wonderful, but they should have cut their conversation shorter. She rolled over to peek at the clock on her dresser. No time to dawdle. She threw off the covers, not wanting to be late for her hair appointment.

After scurrying around to get dressed, Emma hurried down the steps and headed out the door as it slammed behind her. Only ten minutes to walk four blocks to Trudy's Salon. Vivi would understand if she didn't arrive on time though she did say her schedule was full this morning. Emma didn't want Vivi to fall behind on account of her.

Her heart racing, she tore down the street toward the salon. Was she doing the right thing? What if she didn't look good in bobbed hair? Would her hair frizz more on humid days than it did when it was long? The questions slammed through her head faster than her legs flew.

Trying to catch her breath, she rushed through the door two minutes overdue. "I made it. I woke up so late this morning." A distinct chemical odor saturated the air. Must be shampoo.

"I know what you mean." Combing out a woman's hair, Vivi glanced at Emma. "I had the hard time getting out of the bed, also. This will not take long." Vivi motioned to the chairs in the waiting area. "Be with you soon."

Emma had a chance to study the room. So this is what a beauty salon looked like. She'd never been in one before. The black and white checkered floor appeared uncluttered even though several hair cutting areas scattered the center. The three specialized chairs, each surrounded by two tables holding the hairdressing tools, took up the main section of the salon. Vivi stood by one of the chairs pinning up a French braid. She spun the chair around to be able to see every angle without having to move.

The side wall was lined with a row of sinks. Must be where women get their hair washed. She couldn't identify the odd-looking machines spread out across the back of the room. They had long hoses attached to a helmetlike center. She smiled. They resembled creatures from a scary movie. What were they?

Vivi motioned for Emma to come to her station. "Now, I am correct? You are wanting the bob cut today? *Oui*?"

Butterflies still floating around in her middle, Emma nodded. "Yeah, let's get this done before I get cold feet." She smiled. Would she be smiling later?

"I think you will look, what they say, spiffy." Vivi pointed to the sinks. "Come over here so we get started by washing the hair." As she seated Emma in the chair by the sink, Vivi asked, "Have you recovered from our night out?"

Emma leaned back. "It sure was fun, wasn't it?" She peered up at Vivi looming over her. "Now I just have to get busy this afternoon to get all my schoolwork done. I won't have time tomorrow to get anything accomplished."

Emma spluttered as water sprayed over her face.

"I am so sorry." Vivi dried her face with a towel. "What have you planned for tomorrow?"

Emma felt the cold shampoo seep over her scalp. "Oh, I agreed to go with Pastor Hannemann to visit one of my school families." She sighed as Vivi rinsed her hair. There were other things she'd rather do on a Sunday afternoon. "I'm not really too thrilled about it, but I guess meeting Clayton's parents is a good idea."

"Is this a social visit or about the school business?" Vivi draped a towel around Emma's wet curls.

"Pastor led me to believe it was about business when I said 'yes' to him." Emma sat up in the chair while rivulets of water ran past her ears. "I don't want to get involved with him on a social level."

Her eyes connected with Vivi's in the mirror's reflection.

"Why not?" Vivi's hands rubbed the towel over Emma's head.

"He's a pastor. How could I possibly get involved with someone who's my spiritual leader? He thinks of higher things. I'm not sure if he'd be interested in me."

"I was not hinting you were getting involved at all." Vivi led Emma back to her station. "Actually, when Freddie pointed him out at the ice-cream social, I thought he was the cat's meow. I did not think any pastor could be that young and good-looking."

Emma sat in Vivi's chair. "Well, yes, he is rather handsome." His brown hair, parted in the middle, and long face with a narrow chin came to mind. How could she forget his dark eyes? "He's been so kind to me lately. I'll have to see what happens tomorrow."

"Now, what about the hair?" Vivi spun Emma around to look into the mirror. "You have the beautiful long hair. I feel bad cutting it off."

Emma peered at her in the mirror. "Don't tell me that. I may change my mind yet."

"No, no, that is not what I meant." Vivi ran her fingers through Emma's hair. "I know the bob cut will be so much easier to take care of. Every time I cut someone's long hair, I feel bad." Vivi started combing it. "Have you told Freddie you will be with the pastor tomorrow afternoon?"

"No, I didn't think it was important." Emma sat very still in the chair while Vivi wielded her scissors. "It's more of a meeting to get to know the family than a social occasion."

"Are you sure Freddie will look at it that way?" Vivi snipped the hair. "I think Freddie thinks you are his girl and will not like the idea that you are with the pastor all day." Vivi's scissors stopped in midair. "*Oui*, he will be the jealous."

"Oh, come on." Emma shook her head. "Freddie doesn't have any reason to be jealous."

"Now, hold still." Vivi scowled in the mirror. "You better not to move, or your hair will be cut crooked." Vivi worked in silence for several minutes.

"I'll tell Freddie all about it later. He'll be fine with it." Emma turned her head. "How much longer will this take?"

"*Oui*, I am pretty well finished cutting the hair. Do you want to use the end curlers to make it wavy?" Vivi turned the chair.

Emma stared at herself in the mirror. "Let's just dry it and see what it looks like if I leave it straight." It would take a while to get used to seeing herself with short hair.

"O.K. You need to come over to the dryers." Vivi walked to the back wall by the strange machines.

"Is that what those are?" Emma laughed. "I couldn't figure out what they were when I walked in."

"*Oui*, air is heated on the inside and is blown out through the hose. It be faster than getting it air dried, but it be very noisy." As Vivi started up the electric dryer, she had to shout above the noise. "I have heard of the dryers small enough to hold, but I have not persuaded Trudy to buy one of those yet." When the dryer stopped after several minutes, the silence was deafening.

After sitting in Vivi's chair again, Emma drummed her fingers on the chair's arm as Vivi combed through her hair. What was taking so long? What would her new cut look like? As Vivi spun her around, Emma stared at the stranger in the mirror. "Wow!" She ran her hand down her now short hair. "It feels so much different with the extra weight gone." She turned her head this way and that.

"It looks terrific straight, but you could do the wave if you wanted." Vivi tilted her head as she gazed at Emma.

"No, I'll keep it like this for now." Emma pulse quickened. "I wonder what my students will think on Monday." She hadn't thought about that. Too late now.

"I am sure everyone will think it is keen." Vivi grinned. "They will love the new hair."

***

After hurrying home again, Emma opened the back door to the kitchen. She had to eat a quick sandwich and get over to school to get some work done. As the door slammed behind her, she spotted Hilda at the counter. The yeasty smell of bread dough spread throughout the room.

Turning to look at Emma, Hilda's hands paused over the large bowl. "Girl, what have you done to your hair?"

Emma patted her less-than-shoulder-length hair. "I got it cut at Vivi's salon this morning."

Didn't Vivi just say she looked great? Why the strong reaction?

"Yeah, I can see that." Hilda brushed the flour from her hands. "What will your mother think when she sees you with bobbed hair? Especially since you're living under my roof? You had such beautiful wavy tresses before."

"Hilda, don't worry. I'm sure she won't mind." At least she hoped she wouldn't mind. Her heart pounding, she brushed a strand off her face. Lots of women had bobs. It was getting more common every day. "Other girls at my home church have gotten their hair cut like this already."

"I know you're from a small town, so maybe your hair style isn't a big deal, but this is a city." She proceeded to pound the dough. "Around here that hairstyle is associated with flappers and floozies." She peered at Emma. "I wonder what Pastor Hannemann will think. Since you're a teacher, he might have something to say."

Emma swallowed, putting in check her rioting insides. Not the fishbowl thing again. In the middle of all the questions before her hair was cut, she'd never asked herself what Pastor would say. She hadn't done the wrong thing by getting a bob, had she? The deed was done, however, no going back now.

"I guess I'll find out tomorrow at church." She headed for the icebox to get out the milk. "I'm not going to worry since there's not much I can do about it now."

"I hope your mother doesn't blame me." Hilda put the dough in bread tins. "Are you eating early?"

"Yeah, I'm just grabbing a bite if that's O.K. with you. I need to get over to school as soon as I can to work on my lesson plans."

"There's bread in the breadbox and some meat in the icebox if you want a sandwich." She continued shaping the loaves. "Too bad this batch isn't ready for you. A fresh loaf always tastes better to me."

"I agree, but I can't wait that long. I'll taste it later. Thanks." Her appetite had disappeared anyway.

***

Shortly before dinner, Neil pushed the mower back and forth on the parsonage lawn, the sweet smell of cut grass invading his nostrils. The warm sun beat down on his head, but the crispness of fall kept the heat at bay. The rhythmic clacking of the mower sang as he walked. He was thankful to be near the end of this task for the season. Being outside was great, but mowing was so time-consuming.

He glanced up as he crossed the lawn once again. One of those young flappers walked toward him on the sidewalk. Her bobbed brown hair swung this way and that with each bounce of her step. Those women had such a bad reputation. He shook his head. Not much he could do about it.

He mowed to the edge of his lawn and turned to head back across the grass. Before he pushed hard to start the blades whirring again, out of the corner of his eye, he glimpsed the approaching woman. Emma. His hands froze. Impossible.

He shook his head and looked again. "Emma, what have you done to your hair?"

Her hands flew up to cover her head. "I, uh, got a haircut this morning."

"I can see that." Rubbing his temple, Neil took a deep breath, trying to control himself. He couldn't show the anger that seethed inside him. "Why did you get it cut so short?" He didn't even wait for her to reply. "When I saw you walking down the sidewalk, I thought you were one of those flappers."

This would cause more trouble for her than the dancing thing. Everyone in the entire congregation would see her with her bobbed hair. He ground his teeth and shook his head. Why, oh why, didn't she think things through before she did something so rash? And he would have to deal with the aftermath.

Her brown eyes widened on her ashen face. Emma ran her hands through her hair. "I got it cut like this so it would be easier to take care of."

"You'll probably accomplish that, but do you want to look like a flapper?" He forced himself to stay calm even though his blood pressure must have skyrocketed. It wouldn't help to lose his temper, but did she realize the trouble she was in?

The twittering birds filled the silence.

She'd been in Racine little more than a month. His first impression had been that she was a very levelheaded woman, kind to the children in her classroom. Did this change everything? Was her inexperience showing up again? She'd have to learn the hard way then.

Emma pulled herself upright. "No, of course not."

He shifted his feet and studied the ground. *God, help me know what to say to her.* Could he start over? "I know you don't, but for many people, that haircut represents a person with a bad reputation." He shook his head. "I'm not sure what the reaction will be when everyone sees you at church tomorrow."

"I certainly didn't change my hairstyle to make a statement about my life to anyone." Emma smoothed a hand over her throat. "I merely wanted to look more modern."

"It will grow out again." Neil crossed his arms. He didn't want her to feel too guilty. "People can easily get the wrong idea, so church workers need to be careful in their actions, even outside of the classroom. Same as dancing."

He smiled at her. Did she understand he was on her side in this matter?

"Yeah, I know. Fishbowl. I didn't think it would matter that much. It's just a haircut." Shrugging, Emma brushed her hair back from her face. "I'm going to work at school now."

"Better get the rest of my grass cut." He turned back to his mower. "I'll see you in the morning."

He waved before giving the mower a push. Most likely another fire for him to put out, then.

***

Emma walked past the parsonage and church before turning up the sidewalk leading to the school. If only Mr. Dietz weren't at school this morning. She didn't want to face the principal today, too. Getting admonished by Mrs. Mueller and Pastor was enough for one day. Oh, why had she decided to get her hair cut? Yesterday it had sounded like such a good idea.

She ambled in the door and climbed the stairs. Glancing right, she tried to see if Mr. Dietz was in his room. She didn't want to disturb him if he was. In silence, she opened her classroom door at the same moment he walked into the hallway.

"Can I help you, Miss?" He cleared his throat. "Emma, is that you?"

With her hand still on the knob, warmth rose up Emma's neck into her cheeks. She had a hard time getting the words out. "I'm here to work on my lesson plans."

She turned around. No choice but to face him now.

"What have you done to your hair?" His voice became louder with each word. "When . . .?" He pivoted and paced a few steps away before facing her again. "Why did you do it?"

Emma struggled to take a breath. Guess she couldn't escape the irate principal this morning either. "I thought it would be, uh, easier and faster to take care of my hair if it was cut shorter like this." She ran her hand through her hair. Shaking her head, she dropped her hand to her side. She had to stop touching her hair every time someone referred to it. That only brought more attention to its length. "My friend Vivi assured me it looked good."

"That is not the point." His arms flared toward her. "The problem is what lifestyle it represents. Don't you know people with those kinds of haircuts are usually young women with no morals? What are you planning to do next, get a flapper dress?"

Emma gasped, touching her fingers to her parted lips. How did he know about the dress? "Surely, you don't think I'm like that. I'm teaching children in a Lutheran school."

Why was Mr. Dietz attacking her for something so petty? It was only a hairstyle.

"I know you aren't." He paused. "But the people in our congregation who don't know you very well may jump to the wrong conclusion. You shouldn't have gotten your hair cut short precisely *because* you are a teacher in our school."

"It's just a haircut." Emma struggled to get the words out. How many times had she repeated the same words in the last hour? "What's so wrong with trying to look a little nicer?"

"In this case, the problem is your more modern look is associated with people who are morally questionable." Mr. Dietz stood with arms akimbo. "There is not much we can do about it now. You'll have to let it grow out again. I suggest you be very careful while it's growing so your actions are above reproach."

With that, he walked back into his room, leaving Emma devastated. She stumbled into her classroom and dropped into the chair behind her desk. How could he question her morals?

She put her head in her hands, a sob escaping her throat. Things were certainly complicated after a month of teaching. Why couldn't people judge her on her teaching ability instead of what she did in her free time, or how she cut her hair?

She'd dreamed of leaving home to have a more fun-filled life, but look what a mess she'd made of things. Was it wrong to want to be more modern?

Only the ticking clock answered her. Emma wished with all her heart that she were still with Ma and Pa. She put her head down on her desk and let the tears flow freely. All because of a haircut.

Chapter 12

Neil greeted his members with a handshake after the Sunday morning service. As she stood across the narthex, Emma's chestnut hair glimmered in the sunshine slanting through the doorway. He had to admit her new hairstyle framed her oval face perfectly, bringing out the color of her brown eyes.

Would she be able to handle the criticism that was bound to come her way? If only he could prevent the storm that approached. She stood to the side, nodding at the mothers of her students as they passed by. The women's smiles turned to scowls after glancing her way. Just what he thought would happen.

After the service, Neil went in search of Emma. Walking from the church to the school, he rehearsed what he wanted to say to her. He had come down hard yesterday after seeing her for the first time. As he finished mowing his lawn, he thought of numerous different ways to reword his thoughts without sounding so judgmental. He hadn't acted in a pastoral manner, by any means. He'd never been taught how to deal with situations like this at the seminary.

As Neil approached her classroom door, he closed his eyes. *Give me the right words to encourage the growth of Emma's faith.*

He knocked on her doorframe. "Hello, there."

She glanced in his direction and removed her glasses. "Good morning, Pastor."

"How are you today, Emma?" With papers stacked in unorganized piles on her desk, her usual sparkling eyes gazed up at him. He stifled the urge to rearrange the papers. She would be able to tackle her work more efficiently if she were organized, but that wasn't why he'd come today.

"O.K. Although I'm not so sure after all the looks I received in church. Everyone glared at me like I'd committed a sin." She fidgeted with her glasses before laying them on her desk. "I guess they agree with you about my short hair."

He removed his hat and nodded. "Well, Emma, you did surprise everyone."

"I hope what I did won't affect my relationship with my students and their parents." She started to comb her fingers through her tresses, but stopped midway and lowered her hand to her lap. "It was only a haircut. Now look at the trouble I've gotten into."

He hesitated, speaking as gently as he could. "Members in our congregation have seen too many young people with hair like yours who have bad reputations. They'll assume you're like them when they see your hair." He sat on one of the children's desks.

She sat up straight. "Mr. Dietz told me the same thing yesterday."

"Then I don't have to repeat what's been said." He rubbed his hands around the brim of his hat.

"But now it's too late. My hair's already cut off."

"You can demonstrate that you're different. Then they can see you're not like the rest of the world."

She peered into his eyes. "God will have to help me do that."

"I have no doubt He will." He took a deep breath. "But that's not what I came to say to you today. I wanted to apologize for my behavior yesterday. You certainly surprised me."

Her mouth formed a perfect *O*. "I'm the one who's sorry for this."

She reached toward her hair, but stopped midway, shaking her head.

Neil stood up. "Your hair will grow out before you know it."

She rose and stepped off the platform. "Not fast enough."

"Are you almost finished with your work so we can go?" Neil looked at his pocket watch. "I'll pick you up in thirty minutes for dinner. We don't want to be late."

"Oh, no." Her fingers touched her lips. "I forgot all about it. I'll hurry home and freshen up."

He waved before descending the school steps. As he walked back to his house, he thought about the afternoon ahead. He had to be careful how he treated Emma at the Hintzes' house. He wanted Frieda to get the hint they were more than just colleagues, but at the same time he didn't want to be too obvious to Emma. Frieda was a nice girl, but there was no way in the world he could conjure up a romantic feeling toward her just because that was her mother's wish.

On the other hand, he didn't want to offend Emma by being too forward since he was sure that in her mind, they were just co-workers. How was he going to manage this? It would be an interesting afternoon.

***

Emma dashed down the steps as Pastor's car pulled up to the curb. Good timing. She'd hurried home from school and combed through her hair. It didn't take long at all. She smiled. At least one good thing had come from her trip to Vivi's salon. Now time to face the music.

"All set?" Pastor opened the passenger-side door.

Walking across the lawn, Emma shook her head. "I'm not sure what we'll be doing over there, so I don't know what I should be ready for."

She climbed in and waited for him to close the door.

He hurried around the car and scooted behind the wheel. "I'm looking at this as a social visit while gathering a little family information."

Easing out the clutch, he pulled away from the curb.

The drive to the Hintzes' house didn't take more than five minutes. Pastor politely ran around the car again to open her door. "Have you met the Hintz family at church?"

"Sure, but I haven't talked to them much more than the usual greeting." She straightened her hat and brushed a black speck off her floral print skirt with her gloved hand.

They walked toward the front door. "You'll find them very pleasant. They have an older daughter, Frieda, about your age if I'm right."

He lifted the doorknocker and let it fall twice. The door opened to reveal a young woman with round, reddish cheeks.

Must be Frieda. Wearing a red dress, she resembled a combination of Mrs. Claus and a giant McIntosh apple. Emma averted her eyes and studied her shoes, hiding a smile.

"Oh, Pastor, and, uh, Miss Ehlke." The hue of Frieda's cheeks almost matched the color of her dress. "Mother is expecting you and, of course, you, too, Miss Ehlke."

By the sound of it, they were not expecting Emma at all. Why hadn't Pastor told them she was coming?

"Miss Ehlke, this is Miss Hintz." Pastor removed his hat and ran his hand around the brim, not making eye contact with either of them.

"Nice to meet you." Emma extended her hand and shook Frieda's. "Since Clayton is in my class, Pastor thought it would be a good idea for me to get to know your parents better."

"Of course." She opened the door wider. "Won't you come in, please?"

Pastor put his hand lightly on Emma's back as she preceded him into the house. Why was he touching her? She stepped away from him as she shook hands with Mr. and Mrs. Hintz. After glancing twice at Emma's hair, Mrs. Hintz greeted them warmly, as if she'd been expecting both of them from the start. At least more convincing than Frieda. She took their hats and gloves.

"Dinner isn't quite ready. Please make yourselves at home." Mrs. Hintz showed them into the living room.

Sitting near one end of the couch, Emma almost brushed her hair behind her ear again. She didn't need to call attention to her new hairstyle. Would their hostess comment on her bobbed hair?

With graying hair piled high on her head, Mrs. Hintz smiled. "Would you like some iced tea while we're waiting?"

Hostess's manners probably didn't allow for comments about inappropriate hairstyles. Emma smiled, relieved for the moment, until Pastor took a seat within inches of her. She gasped, clasping her hands tightly in front of her.

Why was he practically sitting on her lap? Guests' manners probably didn't allow for her to react to his inappropriate behavior either. Striving for a natural tone, she nodded. "Yes, tea sounds lovely."

Heat rose from Emma's neck onto her cheeks. She glanced Pastor's way, but he didn't move an inch. Having the entire rest of the couch empty, he didn't need to invade her space. Their elbows touched in the closeness.

Pastor slanted her a glance and cleared his throat. "I'd like some tea, also."

"Frieda, dear, could you please serve the tea for our guests?"

"I'll be happy to." She pushed off her chair and waddled toward the kitchen.

Emma couldn't sit still any longer. "I'll help you, Frieda."

"Perfect." Leading the way through the swinging kitchen door, Frieda looked over her shoulder. "I love your new haircut," she whispered. "You look terrific in it."

Emma's jaw dropped. After all the grief she'd had since yesterday morning, she never expected to hear this. Maybe it didn't look so horrible after all. She beamed in response. "Thanks. Some people have a different reaction."

"But it really looks good on you. Kind of brings out a sparkle in your chestnut hair. I've been trying to get the courage to get mine cut into a bob style, too." She pulled a silver tray out from a lower cupboard and placed it on the counter.

Wow! Emma was warming to Frieda more all the time. "I'm told it's the latest craze right now."

"Where did you get it cut? She really did a nice job." Reaching into the icebox, Frieda produced a pitcher full of tea.

"I went to Vivi at Trudy's Salon. I think she did a great job, too." Emma couldn't tell Frieda about the reaction she'd received yesterday from Pastor and Mr. Dietz. "Where are the glasses?"

Frieda pointed to the corner cupboard. "Everyone will get used to it."

When the tea was poured, they returned to the front room. After a brief glance Pastor's way, Emma sat on the opposite end of the couch.

At least she wasn't quite so depressed about her hair now. Maybe there was some hope it would all smooth over quickly. She'd have to wait and see what happened at school tomorrow. She shook her head.

She'd better rejoin the conversation. Mr. Hintz was telling Pastor about his job at the cheese factory.

Several minutes later, Mrs. Hintz announced dinner was ready. Pastor stood and waited for Emma to walk with him to the table. As Mrs. Hintz pointed out the table arrangement, Pastor's arm touched hers several times. Why was he standing so close to her? Was he doing this on purpose? He pulled out her chair at the table before taking his seat next to her. At least that was just good manners on his part. Maybe she was imagining things.

Pastor led the family with a prayer before bowls were passed around. Emma handed the potatoes to Clayton, sitting on her left.

Looking over his glasses placed low on his nose, Mr. Hintz reached for the meat platter. "Miss Ehlke, since you've been so busy with the start of the school year, have you had any chance to relax a bit?"

His jiggling jowls jumped as he talked. Wisps of graying hair struggled to cover the top of his head. He speared a slice of ham, placing it on his plate.

Setting her glass of tea on the table, Emma glanced at Pastor. She couldn't talk about attending the dance with Freddie.

He spoke up before she could get a word in. "We've had a picnic in the backyard at the Muellers' house. That's where she's living, as you know. We even managed to get in a game of croquet with Mr. and Mrs. Dietz."

His eyes roamed sideways in her direction as he grinned.

"That was a nice welcome to Racine." Mrs. Hintz smiled as she scooped some cucumber salad onto her plate and gave the bowl to Pastor.

"Then, of course, we were at the ice-cream social where she met many of the parents." Pastor dished out a small serving of cucumbers for himself before handing the bowl to her. "It's a terrific idea to have that event each year before school to reconnect the teachers and students."

"I agree completely." Mr. Hintz sliced his meat. "The best part is eating the ice cream, eh, Clay?"

"Yeah." Clayton's eyes widened. "The chocolate ice cream with strawberries on top is my favorite."

Emma listened as the conversation continued around her. Pastor answered every question addressed to her. Well, almost. What he said was true, but he referred to them as "we", as if they had done these things together, as if on a date.

Not the way it had happened at all, but what he said wasn't a fib either. What was going on here? Emma's pulse thrummed in her ears. Why was he doing this? She forced herself to swallow the food still on her plate even though the conversation had chased away her hunger.

"Save room for dessert. I made a chocolate cake, Clay's favorite." Mrs. Hintz sipped her coffee.

Frieda bounded out of her chair, keeping her eyes lowered. "Ma, I'll be happy to clear the table and serve the cake."

"Why, isn't that thoughtful." Mrs. Hintz patted Frieda's pudgy hand as she reached for a platter.

Emma started to rise. "Let me help you."

"Oh, no, no. You and Pastor are guests in our house today." Frieda held her hand palm out toward Emma. She scuttled in and out of the swinging door, ferrying out the dishes and silverware. Each time she returned, her face appeared to be a darker shade of red.

Emma shook her head. What was going on here? Frieda was clearly upset about the turn of events during their dinner, but why?

Finishing his dessert, Pastor made their excuses to leave. "I really must get back to church. I never finished cleaning up after this morning's service. I hope you'll excuse our abrupt departure." He glanced at Emma. "You had some things to finish at school for tomorrow, didn't you?"

"Yes, I have a couple hours of work to complete yet today, but thank you so much for the lovely dinner." Emma patted Clayton's head. "It was nice to see your home, Clayton. I'll see you at school tomorrow."

"O.K." He grinned up at her.

They waved as they walked out the door and headed down the sidewalk. Pastor rushed ahead and opened the car door for her. "Glad that's over."

Emma drew back before placing her foot on the running board. "Why did you say that? I thought they were a very nice family."

"That's not what I meant." He motioned for her to get in. After getting behind the wheel, he started the engine. "Before we came, I had a feeling Frieda was getting friendly with me for only one reason. I think she'll be over any thought of that now."

"What? You had me come with you so you could demonstrate to Frieda that you weren't available to her?"

Silence reigned in the car before he spoke again. "No, that's not quite how I'd put it."

Emma shook her head. "I'm sure that's how Frieda interpreted your actions. Didn't you see how depressed she looked by the time we left?"

"I just can't force myself to like a girl because her mother, or even the girl herself, thinks I'm a good catch. That's not how I'm made."

Her heart raced. How could he do that? "That's understandable, but using me to get the point across doesn't seem to be very honest."

"Um . . . I wasn't being dishonest with her." His face took on a reddish hue.

"Maybe not in so many words, but your actions weren't very honest. Sitting so close to me. Talking about things we've done together since I moved here." Emma clucked her tongue. She didn't want to say more and be disrespectful to her pastor, but she couldn't keep quiet about this.

"I didn't know quite how to handle the situation. I don't have any sisters, so how should I know what women think?"

Emma's eyes flew to his face. Was she the adult in this situation? "It seems that talking to her might have been a better approach."

The silence stretched between them.

"Maybe you're right." Gripping the steering wheel with both hands, he glanced her way. "Acting like that in front of her was a cowardly thing to do to her, and to you."

Emma tsked. "And it's not even true. We aren't a couple, or anything close to it. I . . . I don't know what to say. Not very professional, I'm thinking." After all the preaching he'd done to her about the fishbowl. Maybe no one else could see what he'd done, but she knew. And God.

After the drive back in complete silence, he stopped the car in front of her house and stared out the front window. Turning, he peered into her eyes. "Will you forgive me? I can see I have some praying to do about this."

She opened the car door herself and got out. "I guess we both have some soul-searching to do after this weekend."

CHAPTER 13

Soul-searching, indeed. Neil watched Emma walk up the driveway, her skirt swishing from side to side with the swing of her hips.

She veered toward the neighbor's house and quickened her pace when Freddie called to her from his porch. Twirling around, she smiled when Freddie pointed to her hair. His gestures spoke louder than words. As if Freddie's good opinion of her new hairdo could undo the negative reactions from members of the congregation. Emma surely found an empathizing ear in Freddie, as she no doubt explained the unfairness of her principal and pastor.

Neil clenched the steering wheel in his hands. What could he say? The different standards appeared to be inequitable to some people, but that's the way it was for workers in God's kingdom. He shook his head. He'd been over it time and time again with Emma. It wouldn't help if Freddie were on the other side whispering in her ear that things weren't evenhanded for her.

Neil sighed and pulled away from the curb, heading home. Anyway, what about the mess he was in? He should have been honest with himself, and Frieda, and admitted to her he could never be involved with her because of his attraction to the new teacher. Unfortunately, he couldn't even admit it to himself right now. At least it wouldn't do any good if he did. Emma's interests were concentrated on a certain blond-haired, blue-eyed callow young man instead.

***

Freddie turned to watch Pastor Hannemann drive away, his car belching out exhaust as he shifted gears. "Em, you've had a tough weekend." He faced her again. "I hope you aren't too upset about it all."

Emma shook her head. "Yesterday took me by surprise when Pastor and Mr. Dietz both judged my haircut in the same way. It sounded like they had taken notes from each other. Even Mrs. Mueller said the same thing. I guess I should have thought more before I did it."

He pointed to her hair. "The amazing thing is that it looks so great on you. You're a spiffy doll now. I wish you could get it cut like this all the time, but I bet that won't happen."

"Not on your life. I'll count the days until it grows out again." A sudden gust of wind blew in from the north, tossing strands of hair into her face. She brushed them behind her ear. "Won't make the same mistake twice." She glanced up into Freddie's eyes. "The interesting thing is that Frieda Hintz complimented me on my haircut this afternoon when we were at her house. She even asked me where I got it cut. At least it wasn't all bad."

"You and Pastor went over to the Hintzes' house?"

"Yes, he told me it was for a membership visit and for me to get to know Clayton's family better, but you should hear what was really going on."

"What?"

"On the way back here, Pastor hinted he had me accompany him for the sole purpose of discouraging Frieda from being interested in him."

"Interested in Pastor?"

"I think he thought Frieda's mother was trying to push her on him since he's a single man—you know, matchmaking. Some mothers do that to daughters. Well, anyway, he took me along to show Frieda that he was interested in me instead of her."

What was she getting at? Little hairs on the back of his neck stood on end. Frowning, Freddie crossed his arms in front of him. "How would she get that impression?"

"You should have seen how close he sat to me on the couch, and other things. I told him I didn't appreciate it one little bit."

"What did he do?" He forced his jaw to relax. Was Pastor trying to make a move on Emma himself?

"He pulled out my chair at the table. Touched my elbow when he was standing next to me. Sat too close to me on the sofa. Just little things, but altogether they seemed really strange."

Didn't sound like little things to him. Freddie took a deep breath. Was he allowed to get angry with a pastor? "Then what happened?"

"On the way home, he admitted it about Frieda and apologized. I guess this shows that pastors are human. They make mistakes like we do."

The tension left his shoulders. "Hmmm. I guess I never thought about it before. As long as he felt bad." He hoped that was all there was to the story.

"I'm sure he did. By the look on his face, he really was sorry." Emma edged toward the Muellers' house. "I'd better get home since I have work to do. I'll see you later."

"Yeah, sure." Freddie waved as she walked away. He rubbed his jaw. Would he have to compete for her against a rival?

***

What a weekend. Emma walked toward the school shrouded in an early morning fog, the trees blurred against the dark sky. Looked like the weather might soon match her mood. To lighten her spirits, she hummed "Beautiful Savior," a tune she'd heard in church the day before. Would she be going to war anymore about her hair?

It would be good to get back into the classroom after the tumultuous weekend. If only the children could cheer her up today.

Besides the morning thunderstorm, no excitement happened during the day until recess in the afternoon. Ringing her hand bell, Emma beckoned to the children when it was time to go back inside. Some of the boys didn't come running to get in line as usual. She rang her bell a second time for them. Two more boys ran toward the door, but three remained on the playground.

She marched toward them, her skirt wrapping around her legs in her haste. Why weren't they coming? As she got closer, she focused on one of the boys, Karl Piggott. Her hands clenched into fists. Was this another run-in with him? Was he testing her again?

"Phillip, Benjamin, Karl!" Emma's heart raced. "Did you hear the bell? Recess is over."

Benjamin and Phillip sped toward the line of children. Karl yelled after them, "Come back!"

"What do you mean, 'Come back'?" Emma strode toward Karl and grasped his arm. "I'll repeat. Recess. Is. Over."

"I don't have to listen to you anymore. Ma and Pa were talking about you. You can't be my teacher now. Ma said so. She said you had to be dealt with 'cuz you're a flapper. Flappers cause trouble."

She dropped his arm as if it were a hot kettle. Emma gasped, her legs wobbling under her. Oh, no! Karl's dad was the chairman of the school board. What could his wife have said to make Karl think such a thing? Why would Mr. and Mrs. Piggott have been discussing her in front of Karl? Not good news.

She pointed her finger at Karl. "Never use that word in school again." She took a breath before continuing. "I'm sure your mother wouldn't say such a thing. Come back into the room so we can finish our lessons."

She grabbed his shoulder, leading him across the lawn. She let out a silent prayer of thanks when Karl cooperated and scuttled toward the rest of the children, who stood like statues in complete silence.

The rest of the day flew by, her mind racing with Karl's announcement. As soon as school was ended, she'd have to go talk to Mr. Dietz. This was something she couldn't deal with herself.

When the children were gone, Emma hurried across the hall to find him. After knocking on the door, she barged into his room. He looked up from the stack of papers in front of him. "Mr. Dietz, I have something to tell you. You won't believe what Karl Piggott announced this afternoon. He told me his parents stated that I couldn't be a teacher anymore because I'm a flapper. Do you think they really said that? In front of him?"

Heat rising up her neck, her pulse thrummed in her chest. Why was it so warm in here?

"Slow down. You need to take a deep breath and start from the beginning." He motioned for her to take a seat. "I'm sure our school board chairman wouldn't have said such a thing. There must be a mix-up in the communication between Karl and his folks. What exactly happened?"

As Emma scooted into one of the student desks, she explained to him the scene on the playground, her muscles relaxing. Would he have a solution to the problem?

His head bobbed from side to side. "I'm really not surprised. You can't be too upset by what a young student says. I'm sure he misinterpreted something his folks mentioned yesterday. My guess would be that Mrs. Piggott was making a comment to Mr. Piggott about your new short hair."

"I can't believe people can be so biased about it." Emma's voice ground out the words. "I probably should never have gotten it cut."

"Maybe we should talk to Mr. Piggott after the school board meeting tonight. Get this cleared up." He glanced at papers he was shuffling on his desk.

"My grand idea of an easier hairstyle seems to be more trouble than it's worth." Mumbling, she stood. "I'll be here this evening doing work for tomorrow, so feel free to bring Mr. Piggott in after your meeting. Thank you."

She left his room and returned to her desk, piled high with work.

***

Emma gave Freddie a halfhearted smile as she spotted him sitting on his porch steps in the descending darkness. "I'm so glad to see you. What a day—and it's only Monday."

He rose and sauntered toward her. "What happened?"

He fell into step beside her, heading toward school, as she filled him in on the details of the Karl incident.

"Sorry to hear that. You'll just have to ignore all the critics. It sure looks swell on you, don't forget. Be patient for a couple weeks. Everyone'll get used to your new style and forget about it soon enough."

They plodded down the sidewalk. "Hope you're right. This is wearing me out. Tonight I have to meet with the school board chairman. What next?"

She rubbed her forehead. Was she getting a headache now, too?

"I don't get the prejudice against your hairdo."

"Me neither, but it's real. In this case, according to Karl." She sighed as they approached the school steps. "I'd better get going so I finish my work before the meeting's over. See you tomorrow."

She walked up the steps toward her room. What would she do if she couldn't vent to Freddie? The encouraging word from him made her feel better. For a short while, at least.

***

Sometime later, she looked up when there was a knock on her door. Mr. Dietz and Mr. Piggott walked into her room.

"The meeting's finished. Is this a good time to have a chat with you?" Mr. Dietz approached the platform.

"Definitely." Emma stood and stepped off the raised area to the floor. "Thank you for taking time to talk to me, Mr. Piggott. Something happened in school today that I think you should be aware of."

She proceeded to explain the circumstances of Karl's comments to his father.

Mr. Piggott's ears matched his red checked shirt as he fidgeted with the hat he held in his hands. "I'm so very sorry. Karl must have misunderstood what we said. Ethel may have mentioned something. If I remember correctly, she stated that some people would jump to the conclusion that you were a flapper—because of your short hair."

Mr. Dietz cleared his throat. "I've discussed all that with Miss Ehlke already."

"Of course, Ethel and I, that's not our opinion. It's not *my* opinion." Mr. Piggott shook his head. "We even have a couple girls at work with haircuts like that."

"I'm glad to hear it." Emma removed her glasses and turned to lay them on her desk.

If only she could have heard the conversation at the Piggott residence. How did Karl get the impression he didn't have to listen to her if his mother hadn't said so? But of course she couldn't ask his father.

Mr. Piggott glanced from Mr. Dietz back to her. "I'll talk to Karl and straighten him out in the morning before he comes to school. I don't want you to have any more trouble from him."

Great news. She hoped Karl would listen to him. "Thank you so much, Mr. Piggott." She brushed her hand down her hair. "If I'd known about all the trouble this haircut would cause, I would have left my hair long."

He put his hat back on his head. "Please accept my apology again for any trouble Karl instigated today. I'm very supportive of the work you're doing in our school."

"Thank you." She smiled. "Good night to both of you."

***

At the end of her long day, Emma rearranged her pillow for the umpteenth time, unable to sleep. She pounded it for good measure. Why was life so complicated? Oh, Ma, what would you say about all these troubles? They always had long talks about problems when she was growing up. If only she could transport herself magically across the miles and hear Ma's solution.

Some of her students had told her about having telephones in their homes. They were even able to talk to people in a different state. Pastor had one at the parsonage in case he was needed for an emergency. If Ma had a phone at home, Emma could pour her heart out to her. If only.

She let out a slow breath. She'd just have to get up the next day and face it head on. One day at a time. Would life ever get back to normal?

CHAPTER 14

On a sunny November afternoon, Emma sat at the desk in her classroom. The trees were almost bare, allowing her to see the clear blue sky. If only she could be outside enjoying the brisk fall air before winter set in. Too many spelling papers needed correcting. Rubbing her eyes, she found it hard to concentrate on anything.

The fall weeks had blurred together as she eased into the routine of teaching. The months rushed by faster than she thought possible. She was so busy keeping ahead of her large class she sometimes couldn't stop to take a breath. The weekends had produced a break in the hectic schedule, but often she didn't even have time to see Freddie and his friends. She missed her conversations with Vivi, but she'd make up for that very soon.

Now, on the Sunday before Thanksgiving, Emma could only think about the upcoming trip home to Juneau. Too bad her desk was covered with work for her to do. She couldn't escape all this for several hours yet.

Vivi planned on accompanying her to her hometown for the four-day break. She'd confessed to Emma she hadn't gotten away from Trudy's for more than one day, here and there, since she'd started working seven years before. It was about time she had a vacation from work. Emma couldn't stop smiling. They would be spending the long weekend together on the farm.

Her thoughts then turned toward Freddie. Even though she hadn't had much time to spend with him recently, it didn't mean she hadn't thought about him a great deal. He kept her life in balance when things at school got harried. His unruffled outlook helped to calm her down on her most chaotic days. If only she could figure out her feelings toward him.

In a way, he was someone to laugh with when she needed to unwind, but in other ways, Emma was becoming dependent on him. She could always count on Freddie to listen to her problems and give her ideas on how to solve them. He never lost patience with her, but there was something about him she couldn't put her finger on. Maybe she would have a chance to discuss all this with Vivi.

They would have all day Saturday for girl talk. Emma had promised Vivi they could take the train to Madison that day to buy an outfit for her. She hadn't had time to go shopping during the last month. The plan had been to purchase a new dress to match her new hairstyle, but after the dreadful reaction at church, she hadn't wanted to complicate things more by buying a dancing dress. Maybe now was the time.

Emma shook her head to clear it. No more woolgathering. Time to concentrate on the spelling papers in front of her.

***

Walking past the Charles Jonas statue in the park, Neil's footsteps crunched through the scattered gold and crimson leaves covering the sidewalk. He breathed in their musky scent with relish. His favorite time of the year, before cold winter winds blew in from the north.

And Sunday afternoon. His favorite part of the week. The morning church service under his belt and nothing to think about for the time being. Smiling, he strolled toward home. His walks helped him relax after his Sunday morning busyness.

As he rounded the corner of the school, he impulsively leaped up the stairs to try the door. To his surprise, it was unlocked. Who would be here on such a beautiful sunny day? He pulled the door open and headed up the stairs to investigate. Glancing to the left, he spied Emma bent over the papers on her desk.

"I wondered if someone was here working." Smiling, he leaned against the doorjamb. "And just why are you in this stuffy room instead of outside enjoying the beautiful fall weather?"

His eyes fell compulsively on her desk and opened wide as he surveyed it. Piles of papers rose like untidy ziggurats here, there—a dense colony of them. Some looked so old he wondered if coal, even diamonds might be found at their bases. My! He would never have been able to work amidst such chaos.

"I'm trying to get these spelling papers finished before I can go home. Hate to miss the nice weather, but I don't have a choice. Since I'll be leaving on Wednesday, I need to plan ahead."

Ignoring the paper pandemonium, Neil felt Emma's smile warm his heart more than the bright sunshine outside. Did her heart warm because of him? He looked down at the hat in his hands. "I'm glad you'll get to go home for Thanksgiving."

"Will you be heading up north to visit your family, also?" She removed her glasses and laid them on her desk. Neil noticed they disappeared from view.

"I wish. I'd love to go home. Haven't seen the folks since June." He sighed. He missed his family terribly, but it was impossible for him to be with them now. "Holidays are no time for pastors to be away from church. I have to prepare for the Thanksgiving service besides the usual worship on Sunday."

"I never thought about that." Emma's face changed as if a curtain had dropped over her sparkling eyes. "Sorry to hear you can't get away. I forget that while we're all on vacation, you are on duty."

He shrugged. "That's the life of a pastor. Will you be taking the train home?" He moved toward the raised platform, pulled by an invisible magnet.

"Mmm-hmm. Vivi's going with me."

"Vivi?"

"A friend of Freddie Neumann's. She's French, that is, she's actually from France and doesn't have family here, so I'm taking her along." The twinkle returned to her eyes.

"Good. Uh, *très bon.*" He smiled. "You've been working so hard the last couple months. You need a break." He sidled up to the edge of her desk: the hunter and the hunted. One of the paper ziggurats winked at him to form and square it into a proper, neat rectangle. "Hope you have good traveling weather."

Neil's eyes roamed to the window as if to study the weather, but his hands moved instinctively to deal with the unruly mob of papers before them. He heard Emma respond.

"I hope so, too. Maybe today's weather will hold out until then."

"Yes. There's no better time to travel than when the air is crisp in fall." He was looking at her but his hands were busily ordering the stack like a drill sergeant forming a platoon of recruits. He suddenly stopped, aware of Emma. She was looking at him questioningly.

"Pastor?"

"Well. Yes. I can see that you're busy." He released the papers and involuntarily squared them again. "Well, I'll, uh, just, um . . . let you get back to work, then." He headed determinedly toward the door, but pivoted at the last moment. "Have a very relaxing time with your parents over Thanksgiving."

Smiling, Emma replied, "Thanks so much. Happy Thanksgiving to you, also." She waved before he turned toward the steps.

***

Emma breathed a sigh of relief as she locked the school door. Finally finished with her work. She sauntered past the parsonage on her way home. She hadn't spent much time with Pastor during the last month. Even less than with Freddie, so why had her heart fluttered when she was talking to Pastor earlier?

He was so easy to chat with today, except for that quirky thing he did with her papers. When was the last time she'd had a nice conversation with him? They usually talked past each other. His perfectionism drove her crazy in some ways. But had she falsely placed him high on a pedestal when he was really much more approachable? No quick answer to that question.

As the sun fell toward the horizon, Emma strolled past Freddie's house. Spotting Jules's car in the drive, she sauntered up the sidewalk in time to see Jules and Vivi emerge from the house. "Hello, Vivi. You are still planning on coming with me to Juneau on Wednesday, aren't you?"

The four met up in the middle of the sidewalk before the guys headed toward the car. Jules and Freddie were involved in a discussion about the jalopy, as usual. Vivi dismissed them with a wave of her hand.

"But, of course. I am looking forward to it." Vivi nodded, her vibrant eyes adding more than words could say.

"Terrific." Emma gave her a quick hug.

"Let us sit and chat while they talk." Vivi pointed toward the porch steps. "I want it to be the Wednesday afternoon now. I am not happy about going to work for three days first."

"Exactly what I'm thinking. For the first time, I wish I didn't have to teach tomorrow."

"Are there any suggestions you can give me about what I should bring on the trip?" Vivi glanced at Emma. "I have never been to a farm in America before and do not know what to be wearing."

"The only thing I'd recommend right now is something warm. We may end up husking corn for all I know." Emma shrugged. "My mother wrote last week that they're a little behind on some of the fall work because of rain they've had lately."

"That is the good idea." Vivi glanced toward the street. "I will bring my winter coat along." By that time Jules was standing by his car beckoning to her. "How are we going to get to the train station on the Wednesday?"

"I haven't figured that out yet." Emma ambled toward the car with Vivi.

Vivi winked at Emma. "Let me handle the problem. I am sure I can persuade Jules to give us a ride over there. Have a good week." After she crawled into the car, she waved before he shut the door.

As they drove off, Freddie walked toward Emma. "It sounds like you two are planning a humdinger of a trip next weekend."

She smiled. "I don't know about that, but I'm sure looking forward to going home for a few days. Somehow I think Vivi may make it exciting just by being with me."

"We'll have to plan a night out on the town when you get back next week." Freddie accompanied Emma to her house. "We haven't had much time alone lately. Either you've been swamped, or Jules and Vivi tag along."

Emma slanted a glance his way. "Yeah, you're right. A night out would be great. When we get back, I hope things will settle down for a while."

"When they do, make sure to save time for us."

"I will." Emma reached the porch. "I'd better focus on school yet. Three days to go."

"That'll be gone sooner than you think." His eyes followed her up the steps.

"That's what I'm worried about. I have so much to do." She waved as she opened the door. "See you later."

As Emma trotted upstairs, her mind drifted back to Freddie. Was she making this too complicated? If she were falling in love with him, wouldn't her heart race? Wouldn't there be fireworks exploding when he was around? It didn't happen. What was wrong with her? Why couldn't life be black and white?

***

Emma practically skipped home on Wednesday afternoon when school was out. The children had been as excited as she was all week, but she kept them focused on their studies by promising they would learn the story of the Pilgrims and Indians if they finished their work early. That had motivated them to concentrate on Monday and Tuesday.

By this noon, they'd finished what she'd planned for the week, leaving the afternoon for telling the story of the first Thanksgiving and making decorations to take home. Overall, it was a very enjoyable day.

Glancing at her watch, Emma hurried to finish packing before Jules and Vivi arrived. He'd agreed to drive them to the station. What a relief. She didn't want to ask to Mr. Mueller for a ride. Would Freddie come along with them? She hoped. Since she wouldn't see him for four days, she wanted to say good-bye.

Minutes later, she stepped back to survey her packing job. Almost finished. Good thing since her suitcase was stuffed already. She froze when she heard a knock on the door. Racing down to answer it, she stepped aside as Vivi burst through.

"*Bonjour*, you ready to go?"

"Not quite. Come upstairs with me for a minute." She trotted up the stairs.

Vivi followed close on her heels and gasped when she entered the bedroom. "I love the blue counterpane and braided rug." Her eyes roamed the entire room. "*Oui*, it is my favorite color. I would not live in my own apartment if I could have the room like this." She plopped down on Emma's bed.

"There are some nice things about living with a family, but I sure wouldn't mind living on my own, like you." Emma crammed her comb and toothbrush into the corner of her case. "At least I could sit around the living room in my pajamas if I wanted. No way could I do that here."

"I never thought about the fact. Maybe I will appreciate my apartment more now." Vivi stood up. "Are you ready to go? Jules and Freddie are waiting for us in the car."

"Yeah, I'm all set." She leaned on her luggage, forcing it shut. "Let's go, so we don't miss the train."

"Goodness, I feel so outdated." Vivi pointed to the hard-sided case. "Even you have one of those new . . . umm, what is it called?"

"A suitcase."

"*Oui.* I still only have a carpetbag to pack in. But, of course, I haven't traveled for so many years I have not had to buy a new valise."

"My parents bought this for me when I graduated from college last spring. They figured I'd need one traveling to and from home." Emma grabbed the handle of the brown case. "We'd better hurry."

Vivi and Emma scurried down the stairs and out the door.

Freddie grabbed the bag from her and hauled it toward the waiting car. "Time to hit the road?"

"Absolutely, we don't want to be late." Emma watched as Freddie jammed the suitcase into the back seat, throwing Vivi's valise on top.

Freddie looked at her. "Not much room left back there because of all the luggage."

Emma clucked her tongue. "I'll crawl in back, and you sit next to Vivi."

"O.K. Slide over, Vivi. I guess I'm up front." Freddie ran around the car and opened the passenger door.

Jules closed the car door after Emma squeezed into the remaining space next to the luggage.

What adventures would the weekend bring?

Chapter 15

"What a long trip." Emma gazed at the ceiling, shadows from the candlelight chasing each other across the white surface. She was stretched out on her old bed in the farmhouse, her arms crossed behind her head. She was home.

"*Oui*, I am so tired. My head is spinning." Vivi propped her head up on her bent arm as she lay across from Emma. "I am glad we finally arrived."

"I know." Emma smiled, letting out a long breath. "After we bought our tickets, I was really worried about catching the train at all."

"That was my first experience of jumping onto one that was moving, but of course, I have not had too many train rides."

"It was rather exciting." Emma chuckled.

After clambering aboard the departing car, they'd searched for a place to sit together and finally crumpled into a seat near the back. Right when they were beginning to relax, it pulled to a stop in Milwaukee.

"And then finding the right train in the big city." Vivi shook her head. "I am glad I do not travel much. Not for so long anyway. It was so, uh, what they say? Confusing. Trains everywhere. How did you know which one to get on?"

Emma waved her fingers. "I've been to the Milwaukee station so many times over the years going to school. It wasn't hard to find the one to Beaver Dam." She grasped Vivi's hand and squeezed. "I'm glad you were with me this time."

"Me, too." Vivi's lips turned up in a half-smile. "I did not know your father would come to get us in a wagon. I forgot farmers do not have autos."

"I guess I never told you." Emma smiled in return. Waiting for them at the station, Pa had bounded out of the wagon to give her a bear hug. She sighed. It was so good to be back. "Life here is very different than in the city."

She looked at the candle on the dresser in her room. So different. No electricity on the farm.

"*Oui*, the outhouse." Vivi laughed. "Anyway, it was interesting climbing onto the high wagon seat. I am happy your father gave me a boost."

Emma nodded. "That's a necessity since these skirts are so constricting sometimes."

"And the ride in the wagon." Vivi smiled and rubbed her backside. "It has been so long since I sat on such a hard seat for the bumpy ride. It is good thing I brought along the warm coat."

"At least it was the end of the long day." Emma yawned and shook her head. "I can't believe I even taught school this morning."

"Now that we are here, we do not think about Racine. I plan on exploring this farm tomorrow." Vivi nodded and lay back on the bed.

"We can maybe do that after our Thanksgiving dinner." Emma sat up. "I'll feel like walking around then." Pushing herself off the bed, she opened her suitcase. "Time to unpack."

They were alone in the girls' bedroom, the room they would occupy with her sisters Maggie and Katie. At least she had a large enough bed to share with Vivi. No problem there.

Across the hallway, the boys' room was just as large. Since the entire upstairs was divided into the two rooms, many battles had taken place between them in her childhood.

"Sounds like the good idea." Opening her valise, Vivi shook out a navy dress that had been carefully folded.

Pointing to hooks in the tiny closet, Emma laid her nightgown in a drawer. "I was really happy to hear Pa say they were trying to buy a car if the corn crop was good. No more cold wagon rides then."

"That would be wonderful for the whole family. Your mother must be very happy about it. No?" Hanging her dress on a hook, Vivi glanced toward Emma. "She did not say too much to me when we arrived."

Emma finger-combed her short hair. "I'm sure she was too busy looking at my hair. Remember, she hasn't seen me since August. It's grown some since I got it cut, but it's still shorter than when she saw me last."

"I think you are right. I am certain she will get used to it soon. You look so chic like that." Vivi stacked the rest of her clothes on top of the dresser. "Did your pa say anything about helping out in the cornfield on Friday?"

"No, not yet. I bet we'll have to lend a hand, though, especially since he mentioned the car." Emma hung her church dress on the hook next to Vivi's. "They'll be in a hurry to get the corn to the co-op as soon as possible."

"Should be the swell weekend." Vivi placed her valise under the bed.

"Let's hurry back downstairs. At least it's warmer down there. Pa always reads the family devotions about this time." Emma led the way down the steps and headed toward the kitchen.

Memories poured over her as heat, radiating from the front room potbelly stove, overflowed into the warm kitchen. As a small girl she remembered grabbing her clothes on the way downstairs to get dressed next to the heater on winter mornings. It didn't take too much persuasion to dress quickly since the only heat in the upstairs bedrooms rose through the open floor grates from the front room below. She could remember some cold mornings when she found a thin layer of ice in the water pitcher on her nightstand. So long ago.

She linked her arm with Vivi's as they entered the kitchen. The entire family sat around the table. Danny had the newspaper open while Willie, Frank, and the two girls were bent over their schoolwork by lamplight. Little Johnny was reading a story to Ma from his school primer. Amazing that he was reading already.

Pa looked up from the almanac he was perusing. "Just in time. I was about to call you to join in the evening devotions."

"That's what I figured, Pa." Emma and Vivi took the last two chairs at the table.

"Let's fold our hands and listen while I read from the book of Galatians."

The rest of the children put aside their books and focused on him as his booming voice spoke words from the Bible. Peace settled on Emma's shoulders. Would the feeling last the entire weekend?

***

When Maggie and Katie were asleep in their bed, Emma and Vivi tiptoed up the steps. After blowing out the lamp, Emma crawled into bed. She hadn't had her long talk with Vivi about Freddie. "Vivi, are you asleep?" she whispered.

"I am not asleep now." Vivi turned to face Emma in the darkness. "What is on the mind?"

"I've been thinking a lot about Freddie lately." Emma flung her arm over her head.

"That is not surprising. You see him almost every day."

"I'm not sure what I'm feeling, though. I enjoy being with him since he brightens my day. I like to talk to him for advice when I'm confused about something." Emma turned over, but raced on. "Since I spend so much time with him, I should be falling in love already. Only I don't hear the bells and whistles going off in my head." She turned to face Vivi. "Do I love him? I don't know what love is."

"*Ma chérie*, slow down!" Vivi put her hand on Emma's arm. "Do not worry so much about it. Do you think love is magic?"

"Magic?"

"*Oui*. Magic. Something that suddenly happens. You are still getting to know him. If you are going to fall in love, it will happen on its own time."

"I don't know how to act with him anymore."

Vivi clucked her tongue. "You are worrying again. Be yourself. You cannot force love. Do you have any feelings for him?"

Emma smiled. "I sure like him. He's fun to be with."

"If the tender feelings for him are going to come later, they will. Trying to push yourself into love does not work." Vivi yawned loudly. "Love will hit you like the bolt of lightning when the real thing happens."

"Well, the bolt hasn't struck yet."

Vivi turned to Emma. "Just be patient. Go to sleep now, we have a busy day ahead of us."

Vivi was probably right. In the darkness, Emma shook her head. She was good at causing more problems for herself. Here she was worrying too much over something she couldn't control in any way. Ma always said, "Worrying never built any bridges." She'd been right about that. It didn't even answer the question about Freddie. Was love always so complicated?

***

Emma pried her eyes open. Someone was shaking her shoulder.

"Emma, I need you to help me." Ma whispered close to her ear before setting a candle on the dresser.

Oh, yeah. The cobwebs cleared from her head as she threw off the covers. She was back on the farm. Thanksgiving morning. So much to do to get ready. She mouthed, "I'll be down in a minute." She pulled on her skirt and blouse as quietly as possible. Let Vivi sleep longer since the sun was barely peeking over the horizon. At the last second before she slipped out the door, the creaking floor woke Vivi.

"What is going on?" Vivi rubbed her eyes. "You are dressed already?"

"Ma needs help in the kitchen. You can sleep longer."

"Not at all." Vivi threw off the blanket and jumped out of bed. "I will be ready soon."

"We'll go down together." Emma sat on the bed while Vivi pulled on her clothes. Minutes later they headed down the steps. "You make the necessary trip to the outhouse first and then hurry back."

"G'morning, Ma." Emma kissed her on the cheek while Vivi hurried outside.

Ma flicked a glance at Emma before concentrating on the bowl in front of her. In the lamplight, her arm whirred in circles as she continued to stir. "I wanted to let you sleep a little later this morning, but there's so much to do before dinner. We need to leave for church by nine, so our time is limited."

The scent of onions reaching her nose, Emma carried hot water from the stove reservoir to wash up at the sink. She pumped cold water into the basin until it was cool enough to use. "That's all right, Ma. We'd love to help you."

The door slammed behind Vivi. "Of course, Mrs. Ehlke, I will be also glad to help. I am just thrilled to be here." She joined Emma at the sink. "I have sat alone for so many Thanksgivings. I am thankful Emma asked me to come along with her."

"We're thankful you could come with our Em." Ma glanced at Vivi and smiled.

"What do you need help with?" Emma grabbed a towel and dried her hands.

"Yesterday your pa butchered the turkey. It's sitting out on the cold porch. I need to stuff it right away so it's ready for the oven." Ma continued stirring the dressing. "I baked the four pies before you got home, but all the last minute things need to be done yet." She walked out to the porch to get the turkey, wiping her hands on her white apron. "Maybe you girls can peel the potatoes," she said over her shoulder.

"Sure thing." With a candle in her hand, Emma headed for the cellar steps with a large kettle in her arm. "We keep our preserved food and other produce from the garden down here." She turned to Vivi who followed her. "Be careful as you come down these steps since they're very uneven."

"I will." Vivi shuffled from one step to the next. "It is so dark I can hardly see."

"I should have brought a lamp with us." Emma turned the corner into the dark cellar. "Duck your head. Don't want to bump it on the low ceiling beams."

She set the candle on the highest shelf. Wrapping her arms around herself, Emma tried to keep from shivering. Her long-sleeved cotton blouse didn't feel very warm at the moment.

"Jeepers! Look at all the jars down here." Vivi's mouth hung open.

The rows and rows of canned vegetables and fruits lined the shelves around the room like slats in a picket fence. In the middle stood a dozen or more baskets of food sitting in clusters. Some held bushels of potatoes while others were overflowing with different kinds of squash. A couple of the baskets were filled to the top with black dirt.

"While you're getting the potatoes, why don't you dig up a bunch of carrots, too." Ma's voice floated down from upstairs.

"O.K., Ma." Emma pointed to the baskets of dirt. "Vivi, maybe you can do some digging in those bushel baskets to find carrots for dinner."

"Why are they buried?" Vivi's hands burrowed into the dark soil.

Emma handed her a burlap bag from the stack in the corner. "So they don't spoil so easily after they're pulled out of the garden. They're often good until February or March that way."

The noise of the potatoes plopping into the kettle sounded like drumbeats in the echoing room.

***

After working side by side for a couple hours, the three women looked around the kitchen. Emma's mouth watered at the tantalizing aromas permeating the room.

The kettles of collected potatoes and carrots waited on the stove. The turkey was stuffed and roasting in the wood-burning Monarch range with a fire large enough to allow continuous cooking without burning the house down. They'd covered the freshly baked bread with towels, keeping them warm on the top of the stove.

The dish of cranberry sauce cooled on the porch along with all the pies. What a perfect place to keep things cool in the November weather as long as hungry boys didn't decide to taste the goodies first.

"Everything looks all set." Ma wiped her hands on a towel. "Thanks so much for all your help, girls."

"You're very welcome, Mrs. Ehlke. I am glad to lend a hand and look forward to eating all this good food, too." Vivi rubbed her stomach. They shared a good laugh.

Ma hung the towel on the oven door handle. "I couldn't have done all this myself. Maggie and Katie are big helpers most of the time, but since they're only thirteen and ten years old, they tire out easily."

"It feels good working in a kitchen again." Emma glanced at her watch. "It's getting late. There is no way I'm ready for church." The pain in her legs told her that she'd been working for hours already.

Ma gasped. "Only fifteen minutes left. Hurry, hurry! Pa hates to be kept waiting."

Emma and Vivi raced up the stairs to their room. Would they make it in time?

Chapter 16

Her heart pounding, Vivi flew down the steps slipping into her gray coat, matching hat, and gloves. She'd never moved so fast before, pulling on her stockings and dress in two minutes. Good thing Emma's room was large enough to accommodate the frenzied chaos of two women dressing in quick time.

"We barely made it. The wagon's parked outside already." Emma preceded her into the kitchen. "Pa doesn't like to be late for church."

The family, dressed in church clothes, filled the kitchen, leaving standing room only. Mrs. Ehlke inspected everyone as they entered the room. "Danny, I'm glad you and Willie helped Pa with the chores. He couldn't have finished the milking on time if you boys hadn't pitched in."

Danny's handsome face matched the red checked tablecloth as he slid a glance at Vivi. His square chin jutting forward, he scowled toward his mother with a wave of his hair dipping low across his forehead. "Ma, I'm twenty-four years old. I'm not a boy anymore."

Ma patted his cheek. "That's a matter of perspective."

Vivi swallowed her laugh before it escaped. He was cute when he blushed.

Entering the room, Maggie skidded to a halt before she bumped into her ma. "Sorry."

Maggie bounced across the room and stopped next to Vivi. "Good thing you're here with Emma. For once I didn't have to get up early to help Ma with all the food."

"I am so happy to be here, also." Vivi squeezed her hand.

"I needed a break." Maggie smiled. "I'm usually Ma's right-hand man." She pulled on her mittens.

"Well, you make sure you have some fun time while we are here, then." Vivi buttoned her coat.

Mr. Ehlke burst through the kitchen door. "Everyone ready? The buggy's not big enough for all of us, so we'll have to go in the wagon." He shook his head. "I can't wait to get us that car."

"Patience, Walter." Mrs. Ehlke laid her gloved hand on his arm.

"I know, Lena, but that's hard sometimes. I hope we can get it soon." He glanced at the family. "I packed the wagon bed with a good amount of straw to keep the cold away. The bales are covered with old blankets. They should protect your church clothes." He waved toward the door. "Let's go."

Maggie, Katie, Frank, and Johnny climbed into the wagon bed, huddling together to keep warm. Mrs. Ehlke, wrapped in a horsehide robe, sat up front with Mr. Ehlke. Danny's strong arms boosted Vivi and Emma into the back where they sat on top of the bales, using them as benches.

Vivi's head jolted back as the horses jerked the wagon into motion. They picked up speed rolling down the sloping driveway, the wind cutting through her coat like a knife. As the wagon started toward town, Emma shivered next to her.

"We should have brought blankets to wrap around us, I think." Emma scooted closer to Vivi. "Danny and Willie, come sit by us to help shield us from the wind."

"I'm all for that." Danny scrambled to sit beside Vivi, while sixteen-year-old Willie sat next to Emma. "Don't want you two to freeze to death." Danny turned his warm smile toward Vivi, causing her to well-nigh melt into a puddle on the blanket.

Why did his brown eyes do that to her? Jules would not want her having thoughts like that about another man. She forced herself to look away from his intense gaze. "This is real togetherness."

"You're right there." Danny's shoulder brushed against hers when they hit a bump.

To distract herself from his closeness, Vivi glanced up the lane toward the farm as they headed down the bumpy dirt road. The two-story brown house, trimmed in white, with the wide screened-in front porch perched on the edge of the hill. What a lovely place to grow up.

Were her eyes brimming with tears because of the wind, or because she had missed this family closeness for so long? She swallowed past the lump in her throat. "This is what being in a family is all about."

"You're not part of a large family?" Danny slanted her a glance.

Emma leaned forward, turning toward him. "No, she grew up in France and came over at the end of the Great War."

The conversation flowed between them as they swayed with each bump of the road. When they entered Juneau, Vivi rubbed her hands together. "I am so cold. Are we getting close to the church?"

Danny leaned toward her. "Mmm-hmm. It's only a couple blocks away."

After they turned the next corner, the tall white clapboard church with forest-green shutters loomed ahead of them. What a beautiful sight. Vivi smiled.

As their wagon approached, several families smiled and waved. Some of the younger children ran next to the slowing wagon, shouting hellos.

Such a strong bond between all these people—and they weren't even relatives. Vivi sucked in a quick breath. "I am surprised to see so many people on the cold day."

"They come every Sunday no matter what the weather is." Emma moved toward the back of the wagon as soon as it stopped. "They wouldn't miss Thanksgiving Day since it's the day to thank God for His blessings."

With Danny's help, Emma hopped off the wagon. "Come on, Vivi. It's time to go in." Vivi jumped next with Danny's strong hands at her waistline.

Before she knew what was happening, Vivi found herself seated between Emma and Danny in a pew, the potbelly stove taking the chill out of the room. A life-size statue of Jesus on the cross adorned the wall behind the altar. Visions from her childhood floated through her mind. She'd attended services in her French Catholic church so long ago. She could never understand the words spoken in church, but Mama had told her a little about Jesus' suffering. It never meant much to her then.

Light pouring through stained glass windows illuminated the entire church. Had she ever seen anything so beautiful? Jesus was the central figure of all the pictures. Scenes from stories she'd heard as a child flashed through her mind as she gazed from one picture to the next.

Vivi pulled her attention back to the pastor as he announced the first hymn. Her heart soared when the voices of the people joined with the organ music. Even though the words of the hymn were awe inspiring, their simplicity made them easy to understand. The pastor's message delineated the blessings God had poured out on His people. By the time church was over, she wanted to hear more about Emma's religion.

The trip home took forever as the organ music swirled through her head. She couldn't ask Emma about church now with everyone else so near. She'd have to wait until later.

Maggie and Katie chatted happily with Emma until she finally bumped her shoulder against Vivi. "What's wrong? You're so quiet."

The piercing wind blew down her neck, as the clouds grew darker with the threat of rain. Vivi shivered from head to toe. "I am too cold to even consider the talking." Her teeth chattered so loud Emma's parents could probably hear them in the front seat.

Danny moved closer. "I'll just have to do my part to keep you from freezing then." His smile warmed her on the inside. Too bad it didn't reach down to her toes.

"Thanks for trying. I'll need some tea to thaw me out when I get home." She shivered again. Was everyone else as cold as she?

Rain started to pelt the backs and heads of the huddled family. Vivi shook her head. She didn't think things could be more miserable than they already were.

"We'll be home soon." Danny pulled his collar around his ears.

They finally drove up the lane of the farm. Vivi waved her fingers in front of Emma's face. "They are oh so frozen. I cannot move them much."

"Hurry and jump down, so I can get the horses into the barn." Mr. Ehlke stopped close to the house. The children scrambled out, as Willie paused to help the women down. Danny stayed in the wagon to assist his pa while everyone else scurried indoors.

"I guess no more exploring the farm today." Shivering, Vivi unbuttoned her coat and shook off the water. She flexed her fingers, bringing them back to life. The heat from the wood-burning stove began to thaw her frozen limbs. Her stomach growled at the luscious smell of roast turkey coming from the kitchen.

Emma hung her coat on one of the hooks by the back door. "We'll find something else just as interesting to do. It's certainly too cold and wet to be wandering outside in this weather."

"Let's get this dinner finished as soon as possible." Mrs. Ehlke peeked into the hot oven. "The turkey is sizzling nicely. I think it'll be done soon. Vivi and Emma, can you help me with the rest of the food?"

"I'll get the potatoes and carrots cooking." Emma moved the kettles to the stove.

"Katie, go get Maggie, so she can help you set the table. We want to make sure everything is ready on time."

Everybody chipped in with the preparations. Vivi sliced the bread and put it into the breadbasket. The girls carried dishes and silverware to the table. Even Frank and Johnny helped by carrying in firewood from the woodpile on the porch, filling up the boxes in the front room and the kitchen. Impressive. It was fun to help out when everyone was working together.

When the food was ready and the family seated around the large table, Mr. Ehlke folded his hands. "We're going to start our Thanksgiving celebration with a special prayer. I'd like everyone to add what you thank God for this year. I will start. Lord, I thank you for the extra rain this summer to grow a bountiful crop of corn. I thank you for bringing Emma home for this holiday. I thank you—"

A prayer?

Finally Mr. Ehlke's voice stopped. In the silence that followed, Mr. Ehlke nodded to his wife.

Vivi sat stunned as each person took a turn.

Mrs. Ehlke started her prayer. "And I thank—"

What would happen when it was her turn to add to the prayer? She'd never done this before. The intoning voice got closer and closer to her. Her mind froze.

Now it was Emma's turn. "Thank you God for giving me so many new friends in my life in Racine. I especially thank you for my new best friend, Vivi." Such a short prayer.

Maybe Vivi could think of something, too. She was next. She panicked. "Um . . . thank you . . . for the chance to share this weekend with Emma's family." Whew! She did it. Now maybe she could listen to everyone else.

After the prayers were finished, silence reigned around the table except for an occasional clink of a fork tapping a plate. "All the food tastes so good, Mrs. Ehlke."

She hadn't eaten home-cooked food like this for a long time. It wasn't fun to cook a large meal when she was the only one eating.

"Thank you, Vivi." Mrs. Ehlke passed the potatoes to Danny.

"I am sure I am going to eat oh so much." Vivi forked a bite of carrots into her mouth.

"I think that's what Thanksgiving is for, isn't it?" Mr. Ehlke passed the turkey plate to Willie. "Every year I eat too much."

"Walter, you know that's not the most important part of the day." Mrs. Ehlke cut up the turkey on her plate. "Besides giving thanks to God, I think being together is the best part of this day. It's so nice to have everyone home again even if it's only for a weekend."

"I agree with you for sure, Mrs. Ehlke." Vivi lifted some warm bread to her mouth.

***

Emma crawled under the blankets later that night, her feet touching warm sheets at the foot of the bed. "I'm so glad Ma let us use their bed warmer before they needed it." She pulled the blanket up to her chin trying to stay cozy as she and Vivi faced each other. She whispered, "What a long day. I'm exhausted."

"Oh, no, no, I am not tired at all." Vivi's voice bounced with lightness. "I have never had the more wonderful day."

Emma's finger covered her lips. "Ssshhh. We don't want to wake the girls. What do you mean? It was just a typical Thanksgiving Day."

"No, I mean, it was the church this morning. I have never experienced what I did when all the people sang the hymns. I tingled from head to toe. Does that ever happen to you?" Vivi propped her head on her bent arm.

"Absolutely." Emma's sleepiness vanished. "Have you ever been to a church service before?" She wanted to share her faith without saying the wrong thing to confuse Vivi.

"*Oui*, we went to mass in France when I was very little. Back then church was the place to sit still in the quiet building while the priest kept talking in Latin up in front." Vivi squinted her eyes. "I am remembering *les vitraux*—um, the stained glass windows—also, but I did not understand the meaning at all." Vivi pulled the blanket higher.

"What was different about today?"

"Today I was able to listen to what the pastor was saying. Even the hymns and Bible readings, I could understand what the words meant." Vivi nodded.

"God is so good giving us so many blessings in our lives. That's what you heard today." If only she could explain it better. Emma's pulse raced.

"I have never heard it described like that before. Church was about what I had to do for God. I did not realize He affects me personally." Vivi's eyes twinkled in the dim candlelight.

"Oh, yes! If I didn't know God held me in his hand every day, I couldn't get up in the morning. He guides me throughout the day and watches over me at night. I trust Him to guide me home to heaven when I die, also."

"That must be the great comfort for you." Vivi sighed.

"The best thing God did for me was send his Son, Jesus."

Vivi rubbed her forehead. "I heard the pastor talk about Jesus, but I did not understand what it meant."

"Let me tell you about Him. Jesus came to this earth to die on the cross even though He had never done anything wrong."

Vivi gasped. "Oh, I remember seeing crosses in the French church we went to. My mama told me Jesus died on the cross, but she did not say why. What good does that do for us?"

Emma put her hand on Vivi's arm. "He had to die to pay for the sins of the whole world. Three days after He died, He rose from the grave showing His victory over death. Now, our sins are forgiven, and when we believe in Him, we'll go to heaven as soon as we die. As the Bible says, *'For God so loved the world that He gave His only begotten son, that whosoever believeth in Him shall not perish but have eternal life.'*" Emma finally took a breath.

Vivi shook her head. "That sounds more like a story. How can one man's death make it possible for everyone to go to heaven?"

"He wasn't just one man. He was God's Son. God accepted Jesus' death as the atonement for all our sins."

"Atonement? I do not know this word."

"It's sort of like friends that are angry with each other, but someone walks into the room and solves the problem for them. They are reconciled—not mad anymore, they're friends again. Jesus' death solved the problem of sin. We are at one with God."

"Why would He do this for us?"

Emma shrugged her shoulders. "The Bible tells us God did this out of love for us. We believe what He tells us."

"You mean, I do not have to do anything myself to get to heaven?" Vivi's voice faltered.

"That's why everyone today was singing their hearts out in church. We don't have to do anything to get to heaven. God has done everything for us. We just believe His promises, and then live a life of thanksgiving to Him." Emma smiled at Vivi.

"That explains many things around here today." Vivi lay back on her pillow. "The whole family was so happy to help out and work together. I have never been in a family that got along so well."

"You'll have a chance to come to church with us again on Sunday." Emma fluffed up her pillow. "If you have any more questions, maybe you can talk to our pastor."

"I would rather wait until we get back to Racine and talk to your pastor." Vivi put her hands behind her head. "I do not know Pastor Hannemann, but you must know him well. He is nice, no?"

Emma's insides fluttered as warmth spread up her spine. She hadn't thought about Pastor all day. Well, almost all day. There was the minute in church when she wondered what he was preaching today. And, of course, during the family prayer when she wondered if he were eating alone. But that was it.

"Oh, yes. I'm sure he'd love to answer your questions. I'd be happy to go with you to talk to him." After blowing out the candle, she turned toward the wall. "We'd better get some sleep."

The feeling deep inside her lingered long after silence covered the room. What was with her jittery stomach?

Chapter 17

"Wake up, girls! Hurry! The cows are out and wandering across the road."

Emma bolted upright in bed in time to see Ma set a lamp on the dresser and disappear out the door. Heart racing in her chest, she scrambled around the cold room. Shadows from the flickering light played across the others as they tumbled from their beds, even though it was still pitch dark outside. Maggie and Katie hopped from one leg to the other, pulling on old pants in record time.

Vivi yawned. "What is happening?"

"The cows escaped from the fence. We have to help out."

"Help out? How?"

Emma smiled. "I can tell you've never lived on a farm. We have to chase them back into the fenced area, probably the barnyard."

"What should I wear?" Vivi looked around as if she were lost.

Emma tossed a pair of blue jeans in Vivi's direction. "Here, put on these old trousers I usually wear out in the field." Emma pushed her legs into a matching pair of blue denim overalls. "Danny gave me a couple of pairs that were too small for him. I use them when something like this happens."

Emma stretched the straps of her pants over her shoulders and fastened the clasps onto the buttons on the bib. Did Vivi have a clue what was ahead? "We should be in for a fun time."

"Nah, you know it's not." Maggie shoved her arms into her sweater. "It's so cold and wet out there. I hate doing this."

That didn't help much. Emma tugged on her warmest socks.

"You're wrong. It's fun." Ten-year-old Katie's grin covered most of her face. "I love chasing cows. They are so hilarious when they run the wrong way."

Emma turned to Vivi. "The cows get out of the fence from time to time when one of the bolder ones pushes his way through the barbed wires to get to the grass on the other side." Emma sighed. "Since it rained so much yesterday, it's going to be a muddy mess."

"Do you mean we have to actually be close enough to the cows to make them go into the fence again?" Vivi slipped into her sweater. "They are so big."

Emma headed out the door. "Don't worry. If they come straight at you, just shout and wave your arms. They're really scared of people."

"That is not much comfort." Vivi followed her into the hallway.

The four ran down the steps into the kitchen, finding Johnny and Frank pulling on their rubbers at the door. "Put on these old galoshes and coat of my mother's." Emma shoved her feet into her work boots. "Make sure you have a hat and mittens. It's probably very cold out there so early in the morning."

Bundled up from head to toe, they headed outside. Pa, Willie, and Danny stood next to the wagon waiting for them. "When we called the cows in for milking, they didn't come. We saw several heading west for Schmidt's place. The rest were going south across the road." Pa pointed toward the waiting wagon. "Danny, you take Ma, Emma, and Vivi in the wagon toward the Schmidt farm and see if you can head them off. You need to get in front of them."

"O.K., Pa."

"I'll go with the rest across the road. I don't think they're far away. Let's go, kids." Pa, Maggie, Willie, Katie, Frank, and Johnny started toward the road on a run.

Danny helped the women clamber into the wagon, and then jumped onto the high seat. When they reached the road, Emma pointed toward the pink eastern horizon. "Maybe it'll be light enough to see them." She hadn't done this for a long time. Her pulse drumming with excitement, she took a deep breath and turned to Vivi. "Chasing cows in the dark is always harder than in the daylight. They can disappear on you into the black night. Not a good thing."

***

With the wind whipping in her ears, Vivi squinted toward the harvested cornfield. "Is that where the cows are supposed to be?"

"They should be somewhere over there." Emma pointed westward.

Bouncing with each jolt of the wagon as it careened down the road, Vivi hung on to the sideboards. "At least the corn is cut. They cannot hide in a bare field."

Emma nodded. "You're right there."

"We'll cut across our field by the line fence. I don't think they've gotten this far yet." Danny turned the wagon into the field. The horse slowed to a crawl as the wagon wheels sank into the muck.

When the wagon came to a stop, the women jumped to the ground, Vivi's boots landed with a splat. Yesterday's rain had turned the soil into sludge. How would they chase the cows in this greasy mess?

"Try to walk on the brittle corn stalks." Leaving the wagon, Danny headed across the field. "It won't be so slippery then."

Looking up, Vivi saw silhouettes advancing toward them in the predawn. She glanced at Emma. "What happens now?"

"We need to spread out and walk toward the cows that are coming." Emma stretched out her arms and moved them up and down.

"Toward them? Why not wait until they get here?"

"Our job is to turn them around so they go back to the barn. We don't want them to come this far." Emma pointed toward the right. "Let's head that way. Ma and Danny will spread out toward our left."

Vivi stepped carefully from one row of corn stubble to the next trying to stay on drier ground. The pink sky allowed her to see the approaching herd as the cows lumbered in their direction. The lead cow veered right, straight at her. "Here comes one." Her heart pounded with the same tempo as the approaching cow's hooves.

As if on cue, the rest of the herd followed suit, aiming straight toward them. Emma scooted closer to Vivi, waving her arms. "We have to close the gap so the cows can't sneak between us."

Fear pouring through her veins, Vivi froze to the spot like the statue of Charles Jonas in the park back home. "The cows are so fast. They are so *gros*, big." The shrill cry from her mouth surprised even her.

Emma's gestures were not enough to stop the first cow. It shot between Vivi and Emma and continued on its course for the neighbor's front yard. "Come on, Vivi, we need to stop the rest from escaping. They're scared of you if you make noise. Shout with me."

Pulling herself together, Vivi clapped her hands and shouted. "Do not come near me, you stupid cows. I do not like you."

"That's telling them. I've never heard anyone tell them off like that." Smiling, Emma draped her arm around Vivi's shoulder.

The herd loped toward the left, heading for Mrs. Ehlke and Danny. They did their part to turn the cows back in the direction of the barn. The crisis was over.

Vivi started to breathe again. "Are we finished with this unpleasant job?" She watched Danny walk toward her.

"Not quite. You, ladies, follow them back to the barn to make sure they don't turn around again." Danny veered in the direction of the Schmidt's house. "I'll go after the one that got away," he said over his shoulder.

As he turned toward the neighbors, his foot slipped on the soggy soil. A screech pierced the early morning sky as Danny's legs flew up in the air before he fell on his back.

"Are you all right?" Mrs. Ehlke hurried in the direction of her supine son. "Did you hurt yourself?"

He lifted his head to look at the women. "I'm fine." He tried to pick himself up from the ground, but fell back again a second time.

Vivi coughed to cover a threatening giggle. She lost the battle and started to snicker. The tension she'd felt a few seconds before poured out of her, turning her snicker into a chuckle. Before too long, she was doubled over laughing with tears running down her cheeks. Emma soon joined in the merriment.

"Whoops!" Vivi's foot slid out from under her. Panic followed as she tumbled into the oozing mud. She plopped on the gooey ground, looking sheepishly at Danny sitting three feet away. That's what she deserved for laughing at him.

A smile spread across Danny's face as he scrambled to his feet, covered in mud from head to toe. Striding toward her, he reached out his hand to help her up, her finger tingling on his contact. Shaking with laughter, he waved his arm toward the barn. "Just get the rest of the herd home." He turned his back on the women and continued after the lone cow.

Vivi dragged her eyes away from the retreating mud-splattered man. What was the tingling about when he grabbed her hand? She turned toward her friend.

Emma's eyes chuckled at her, even though she managed to keep a straight face, as she put her hand on Vivi's arm. "Are you O.K.? What would Jules say if he could see you now?" The suppressed smile finally broke into the open.

"You are not in much better shape than I am with the mud splotches on your nose. Freddie probably would think it was the cat's pajamas though." Vivi looked over her shoulder, glimpsing the damage to the back of her pants. "I guess I should not have laughed at Danny's fall."

"Don't worry about it." Emma jumped over a pile of manure in the field. "We needed a good laugh."

In the growing morning light, Mrs. Ehlke, Emma, and Vivi trudged after the cows as they wandered back toward the barn. Vivi's legs ached with every step she took. "All I can think about is falling into bed again to sleep for a couple hours. Are you so tired, too, Em?"

"I think I'm more cold than tired." Emma pulled off her mittens and flexed her fingers. "My fingers feel like they're frozen through."

"When we get the herd situated in the barn, we can all go warm up in bed." Mrs. Ehlke nodded toward the building. "I suppose Pa, Willie, and Danny will have to finish the milking before breakfast, though."

When the last cow entered the barnyard, Vivi helped Emma close the gate. The rest of the family had already returned with their renegade herd. The children were as mud covered as she and Emma. "Looks like you had fun, too."

Maggie's shoulders drooped as she walked toward Mrs. Ehlke. "I'm exhausted and the sun's not up yet."

"I just told Em and Vivi that we could go warm up in bed a bit before breakfast." She put her arm around Maggie's shoulder. "Let's head into the house right now. Come on, Katie." They started toward the house, looking like worn-out immigrants finally getting off the ship.

Following behind, all Vivi could think about was the warm bed Mrs. Ehlke promised. "It seems like it has been half a day since your ma came into our room."

"I know what you mean." Emma trudged by her side.

"I think I agree with Maggie, chasing cows is no fun."

***

"Breakfast is ready." Pulling herself from the brink of sleep, Emma yawned when Ma's voice echoed up the stair steps.

She and Vivi had been in bed half an hour. Enough time to warm up, but not to get any sleep. "That's the end of rest for today, I bet."

Beside her Vivi stretched. "At least I am warm again in my toes."

"Let's go down and see what Ma cooked up to eat." They hopped out of bed and slipped on their day dresses, hurrying down the steps. The smell of bacon met them when they entered the warm kitchen. "We're famished, Ma."

"It's about time you got up. Sit down to your breakfast then." Ma pulled the platter of bacon out of the oven. "I made oatmeal to keep you warm today."

"Warm? You mean after the cow chasing?" Emma retrieved the milk from the icebox and set it on the table in front of Pa.

"No, I could really use your and Vivi's help out in the cornfield for several hours today." Pa heaped his bowl with oatmeal and brown sugar. "We're trying to get in the rest of the crop so we can take it to market tomorrow."

"O.K., Pa." Emma passed the meat to Vivi. "We've been wondering if you wanted us to work this weekend. If we help out in the field today, Vivi and I would like to take the train to Madison tomorrow for shopping."

"That sounds good to me if your Ma doesn't need your help." Pa poured himself a second cup of coffee.

"You girls deserve a day off after all the assistance you gave me yesterday and your dad today." Ma went to get the last of the bacon from the frying pan. "Does anyone want more bacon?"

"I'm fine, Lena." Pa pulled out Ma's chair. "Come eat your breakfast before it's cold."

Danny reached for the plate of bacon. "You girls better eat up because it's going to be a long cold morning out there."

After breakfast, Emma stacked her dishes in the sink. "We need to find Vivi some dry warm clothes since she sat down on the job in the cornfield this morning." She nudged Vivi with her elbow.

"Very funny." Vivi's face blushed a deep shade of pink.

"We'll have to search in Willie's drawer since you got my extra pair muddy." Emma started up the stairs. After spending time searching, they found some pants in Danny's drawer. "They're pretty huge on you, so you'll just have to put on a couple extra layers of clothes to make them fit."

"I guess they be big." Vivi held the waistband six inches away from her waist.

"You'll probably be glad for the extra layers once we're out in the field. I don't think it's warmed up much since our cow-chasing adventure this morning." Emma pulled her own overalls up by the straps.

Once they were bundled in hats, mittens, and scarves, they went outside to meet Danny and Pa. Willie and Frank were also enlisted for the task, but they didn't look happy about it. They all scrambled into the wagon, which contained several empty bushel baskets.

Ma came running out of the house with a bundle of towels. "Here's a jug filled with hot chocolate, wrapped in extra towels to keep the heat in. I hope this helps you to warm up when you take a break."

"Thanks, Ma. That will taste mighty good by midmorning." Danny grabbed the bundle from her.

They bounced their way out to the field in the wagon bed, rocking side to side over each trench in the cornrows. Finally Pa pulled the wagon to a stop. He turned around on the seat and pointed back toward the barn. "Danny, you take the girls in that direction and start husking. I'll go with the boys toward Schmidt's place and husk that way. The wagon will be in the middle so it's convenient for all of us to empty the baskets. How does that sound?"

Danny jumped off the seat and came around to the back of the wagon. "Let's go, girls." He emphasized the last word. Grinning, he assisted first Emma and then Vivi off the wagon bed.

Emma slapped him on the sleeve as he let go of her waist. "Girls, indeed. You can stop that right now. Pa can get away with it, but not you."

"Now, now. We can't be having a dispute when we have to work together all morning." He grabbed three bushel baskets out of the wagon. "I'll show you what to do so everyone gets the hang of this."

Vivi shrugged her shoulders. "Whatever you say."

Pointing to the rows of corn shocks stacked in the fields, Danny pulled his gloves on. "It's not hard. Here's how this works. The corn was cut down several weeks ago and tied into these bundles—shocks. Now that it's completely dried, we need to cut apart the shocks, husk the cobs, and throw them in the baskets. We'll use this thing called a husking pin." Slipping the metal device over his gloved right hand, he cut the binder twine holding up the corn and pushed it to the ground.

Emma showed Vivi how the husking pin worked by grabbing a cob of corn, stripping the husks off the cob, breaking it from the stalk, and tossing it into the basket. "It's easy to do. It just hurts your hands and knees after a while." She continued to find the cobs, husk, and toss them in the basket as she talked.

After slipping the husking pin over her glove, Vivi watched them for a few minutes. "That doesn't look too hard."

"Join us whenever you get the idea." Danny tossed her a cob.

The three worked side by side to the rhythmic motion: strip, strip, snap, toss, strip, strip, snap, toss. After a time, their hands moved faster in the same routine, filling up the basket. Danny lifted the heavy bushel of corn, dumping it into the wagon. When the first shock was finished, they moved onto the next one.

"Now that you've practiced, let's see how fast you two can go." Danny smiled at them as he cut a new shock and tipped it onto the ground. "I bet I can work faster by myself than you can together."

Vivi's head snapped up. "A race?"

CHAPTER 18

Vivi rubbed her hands together. She loved challenges like this.

Danny stood with his hands on his hips. His half-smile tipped up the corner of his mouth. "Yeah, a race to see who's fastest. I'll beat you two, hands down."

Imitating Danny's pose, Vivi felt her spine tingle as she watched the smile tug at his face. "No, you will not." How could she resist him when he was so appealing?

"No way. Four hands are better than two." Emma stood shoulder to shoulder with Vivi. "We can win this competition any day. Right, Vivi?"

"Ab-so-lute-ly." Vivi nodded once.

"O.K. I'll even cut open your shocks for you." He walked down their row, tipping the shocks onto the ground. "Now you have an advantage."

"*Merci*, but we do not need the help." If only she was as confident as she sounded. She and Emma bent to the challenge, pulling at the husks. Their rhythm increased as cob after cob flew toward the waiting basket. "We can keep ahead of him. Will we, Emma?"

"Or we'll die trying." Emma smiled at her friend. "See, we're finished with our shock at the same time as Danny." They moved to the next one.

When the basket was filled, they hurried across the space to the wagon, dumping it over the sideboard. Heading back toward the next shock, Vivi leaned toward Emma. "Why did you not tell me your brother was so handsome?"

Emma drew back with her mouth open. "Danny?"

"Mmm-hmm." Vivi couldn't hide her smile.

"How would Jules react to that question?" Emma placed the bushel basket next to the shock lying on the ground.

"I am not saying I like him, just that he is the real sheik." Vivi snapped off another ear.

"Guess I never thought about it before."

Thunk. Emma's corncob landed in the bottom of the empty basket. Vivi followed suit. She looked up to see Danny pull away from them and move down the row ahead of where they were. "We need to move faster, or he will win." Their hands flew from the shock to the basket and back again.

Emma pulled with the husking pin. "You must think about Danny as I do about Pastor. He's good-looking, but it doesn't really matter. You have Jules who adores you. And of course, Pastor is out of my reach since he's a pastor."

Vivi remained silent. She certainly had Jules, but the thought of Danny tugged at her mind.

"Come on, girls! I knew I'd do this faster than you." Danny laughed while he dumped another basket in the wagon.

"Oh! My hands are getting so sore." Vivi shook her hand before grabbing another cob. "We are going to have to dump this full basket again, Emma."

They trudged across the field with the weight of the basket between them. The wagon bed was completely covered with rigid wrinkly dry cobs, piled high, a volcano ready to erupt. Were they almost finished? Vivi's shoulders ached as she lifted the basket over the side.

Danny called to them from down the row as they knelt beside the new shock. "I think all the talking is slowing you down over there."

Vivi smiled at Emma across the shock lying between them. "We have lots of important things to discuss." She whispered to her friend in a low voice. "We need to work faster."

They bent over their task with concentrated effort. A few minutes later, Vivi's hands froze in midair as she listened. She looked up from her cob toward Danny. "Do you hear that? He is humming something."

He suddenly belted out the words:

Yes, we have no bananas
We have no bananas today!
We have string beans and onions, cabBAGes and scallions
And all kinds of fruit and say
We have an old fashioned toMAHto
A Long Island poTAHto, but
Yes, we have no bananas
We have no bananas today!

"I know that song." Vivi stood up to stretch her legs. "How come you were humming the first part?"

"I heard the song on the radio at my friend's house in town a week ago. I don't remember all the words, just the refrain." Danny lifted his full basket into the wagon.

"I love this song. Jules's friends sing it down in Racine." Vivi grabbed a cob ready to work again. She proceeded to sing all the words for Danny and Emma.

"'Yes! We have no bananas," Danny joined in the chorus. "We have no bananas today!"

The fieldwork zipped by the louder they sang. Soon they had Emma joining in on the song. They switched to other songs as the morning flew by. Vivi beamed as she sang and tossed corn into the basket. What would Jules think of this?

***

On Saturday morning, Emma had to drag herself out of bed. "Vivi, time to get up." Emma stroked her aching arms. "I feel as if a train ran over me. How are you?"

Vivi rubbed her knees in response. "I have never hurt so much."

"Yeah, too bad we didn't win the race with Danny. At least there would have been some reward for all this agony." Emma massaged her hands, ignoring the pain shooting to her fingertips.

They had worked all day, stopping only at noon for lunch and warming up at home. When the bright sunshine of the day had melted into a cold gray blanket at dusk, they dumped the last basket of cobs into the wagon and headed home.

Pa had declared the day a huge success since there were only two patches of corn to finish on Saturday morning. They would be able to go to the feed mill by noon to get the crop weighed.

Vivi and Emma had taken long hot baths in the portable tub to warm up, but Emma's tired muscles had still screamed at her when she fell into bed later in the evening.

As the sun peeked into the window, Vivi sighed. "I think my knees will not be the same. I do not know how I will be able to do the shopping this morning."

"Oh, come on. I can't believe anything will stop you from shopping in Madison." Emma finger-combed her hair after she pulled a sweater over her head. "Let's not waste time. We need to get a ride into town to catch the train."

When they entered the kitchen, Emma's stomach growled as the smell of Ma's warm cinnamon coffeecake invaded her nose. "Thanks, Ma, for making my favorite while I'm here." Kissing her on the cheek, she gave her mother a hug.

"You're welcome." Ma squeezed her arm. "I'm just glad you could be home for a couple days."

Pa pulled out his chair and sat down at the table. After the table prayer, he announced, "Good news to tell you. Thanks to all your hard work yesterday, Willie and Danny finished up husking the corn this morning while I did the chores. That means we'll be ready to head into town shortly after nine o'clock."

Emma sat down next to Vivi at the table. "That's great. The train leaves for Madison at ten, so we can ride along with you to town." Emma scooped some eggs onto her plate and passed the dish to Vivi.

Danny shoveled a forkful of eggs into his mouth and washed it down with milk. "What's so special that you have to go shopping all the way to Madison?"

"She has been wanting to buy the perfect dancing dress since September." Vivi took a bite of her coffeecake.

Emma wiped crumbs off her face. "I haven't had time to go shopping with all my schoolwork."

"Dancing? You can do that even if you are a parochial school teacher?" Ma scraped the last of the eggs onto her plate.

"We haven't gone often, but Pastor Hannemann said we have to go to Milwaukee or farther away so no one from our church will be there." Emma folded up her napkin. "I'd just like a more modern dress. Maybe I won't even wear it dancing."

"Well, dear, just remember you are God's representative in your church, so be careful of the choices you make. You don't want the same kind of trouble you had after your haircut, even though I think it looks very nice." She ran her hand down Emma's hair.

"Believe me, Ma, I don't want to go through that again." Emma brushed her hair behind her ear.

"Well, anyway, I hope you two have fun today." Ma stood up. "You can finish getting ready for your trip. I'll get Maggie and Katie to clean up the kitchen this morning."

The response from both girls was unanimous. "Awww, Ma!"

***

Pulling up the collar of her coat, Emma stepped off the train in Madison. The northeast wind whipped around the corner of the station, sending a chill to her bones. Even the sun didn't do much to warm the air.

Vivi turned her head as if searching for someone. "Where are all the shops?"

"We're only at the station, Viv. We need to find out how to get downtown." Emma pointed toward the depot. "Let's ask an agent for directions."

Emma opened the door, allowing Vivi to enter the building first. The wood-burning stove in the corner spread warmth around the room as they approached the ticket agent's window. Vivi waved her fingers at him. "*Oui*, could you please help to direct us to the stores for the shopping?"

"Sure, ladies. Just walk a couple of blocks straight toward Lake Mendota and then turn left and head up the hill to the Capitol building." He pointed across the street. "Lots of stores up that way."

"Thanks so much." Emma's nose tickled from the smoke in the room. She sneezed as they left the depot.

"I guess we have a walk ahead of us." Vivi turned up her collar and pulled her hat lower over her ears.

Emma and Vivi hooked arms and headed across the street. "Let's get this adventure underway, then." After walking half an hour, their steps slowed heading up Mifflin Street near the Capitol.

"Let's hope this is all worth it." Emma panted as she put one foot in front of the other.

"I am sure it will be fine."

"Leastwise, we made it to the shopping district, but what have we found—a grocery store, a barber shop, and a hardware store. Not what we're looking for." Emma shook her head.

"I have not seen the clothing store at all." Vivi sighed.

"Oh, we can't give up so easily. With a city this big, I'm sure we'll find something." Emma didn't feel the confidence she tried to portray.

Gasping, Vivi pointed down the street. Tucked between the mercantile and the shoe store, a small shop with a bright red and gold striped awning caught Emma's eye.

Vivi clutched Emma's arm. "Look there! 'French Shop.' With a name like that it has to be wonderful." Grinning, she grabbed Emma's hand and almost flew across the street.

They jumped the last foot to avoid getting run over by an approaching car. "Jeepers. Are you trying to get us killed? If this is the place we're looking for, it will wait for a couple more minutes." Emma straightened the sleeve of her coat while her heartbeat resumed its normal pulse.

As they opened the door, two bells jingled, announcing their entrance. Emma's pulse quickened. It was indeed a dress shop, even though it was rather dark and narrow. A few colorful dresses hung on display along both walls, catching her interest at once.

A silver-haired woman, dressed in an elegant blue ensemble, approached them. Her hair, piled high on top of her head, tilted off center as she nodded toward the door. "Hello, *mesdemoiselles.* Can I help you find something?"

Vivi's eyes glowed as she chattered to the woman in a foreign tongue. Emma smiled. Obviously, French. They conversed for a couple minutes before turning to Emma again.

"Oh, I am so sorry." Vivi tugged her toward the back of the store. "We did not mean to leave you out of our discussion. Madame Angele says she has the couple dresses for you to look at back here."

"Yes, my dear Emma. I did not mean to ignore you like that. I have not had the chance to talk to anyone in French for the long time." Madame Angele squeezed Emma's hand and smiled. "I am so happy to help you out."

They walked between rows of yard goods of every imaginable color. Sparkling evening gowns were hung high up on the walls for display. "You have to understand that most of the gowns purchased in this store are prepared by the orders *specials* only, but I do have the few you can look at right back here. Since the summer wedding season is over, this is the slower time of the year. I have been able to stock up a few more dresses that are for the sale today."

Vivi gasped as she pointed to a lovely dress in a silky tan crochet, having tiny tangerine-colored flower appliqués with pale green stems accenting the skirt that ended midcalf. The low, scooped neckline was outlined with hand-stitched clear beads. "You simply have to try this on, Emma."

Stepping into the dressing area, Emma slipped the gown over her head and caught her breath. The dress clung to the contours of her body like a peeling to an orange. The dropped waistline and flutter sleeves added to its risqué aura. There was no way she could wear this in public. "Umm. I'm not sure I could wear this anywhere, especially in Racine. I can't imagine what Pastor would say if he saw me in this."

"Why are you thinking about Pastor Hannemann now?" Vivi circled Emma, eyeing the dress. "I can imagine Freddie would say *Ooh-la-la* if he saw you in that."

"I think I'd better try on something else." Emma walked back toward where Madame was glancing at a rack of garments.

She held up a black sleeveless gown elegantly ornamented with interwoven silver threads. Accented with flowers shaped from tiny silver beading, the sheer black material looked like a silky river flowing through Madame's fingers. "How about this one?"

Emma's hand flew to her throat. No need to look further. "I'd like to try on that one now." That was an understatement.

When she came out of the dressing area this time, Vivi's and Madame's eyes widened. "*Magnifique!* You are really lovely in the gown." Madame motioned Emma to turn around. "It fits you *très bon*!"

"Oh, Emma. You are right. This dress is much more stunning than the other one. I can picture you dancing around the ballroom in Freddie's arms." Vivi grabbed Emma's hands as if she were going to whisk her away in a dance step.

Emma squeezed Vivi's fingers. "Do you think it looks good on me?" The gown flowed around her slender body, hinting at the curves beneath without emphasizing them. "Would Pastor approve?"

"What is it with Pastor again? But I think it would pass his test." Vivi stepped back and clasped her hands in front of her. "This is the dress for you."

Emma walked over to the mirror. "I don't think I need to look any further. That means our shopping trip won't take so long." She went back to change into her skirt and sweater. "Maybe we can leave it here for a while and look around for some shoes to match."

"By all means. I will pack up the dress for traveling while you finish the shopping." Madame reached for the gown and waved her fingers, dismissing them. "The perfect dress needs the perfect shoes, also."

"And we can't forget the cloche hat." Vivi spun Emma around in a circle.

During the next half-hour, the two visited several stores purchasing the finishing touches for her new outfit. Emma gathered all the bags ready to head back to the French Shop. Did she really need all these new items just to go dancing? After all, Pastor had warned her about doing that. And apparently, her mother agreed. She needed some new clothes anyway. She could wear the dress and shoes to other events.

But was she kidding herself?

***

Stepping off the train late Sunday afternoon, Emma searched the crowd looking for Freddie and Jules. She sighed as her shoulders sagged. The trip was finished, but the ache from saying good-bye to her family still weighed heavy in her heart.

Vivi poked her ribs. "There they are." She waved, jumping down onto the platform.

She ran toward Jules who grabbed her, whirling her in a circle before kissing her soundly on the lips. "Man, Viv, it sure is swell to have you home again. It was tough having you gone so long."

"I missed you, too, but I had a terrific time." Vivi planted her feet on the ground. "We did so many great things. Oh, Freddie, you should see the chic dress Emma bought in Madison, with matching shoes and even black silk stockings."

"Hold on there! You need to slow down." Jules picked up Vivi's carpetbag.

"Yeah, I didn't even get a chance to say hi to Em." Freddie approached Emma with open arms. "And I see your new hat. Looks real swell." He touched the curls peeking out from under her cloche hat.

She stepped into his hug, only to find his lips pressed firmly against hers. As her eyes widened, she drew back. She wasn't expecting this. He hadn't tried to kiss her since the first time they went dancing months ago. Maybe this was what was missing between them. She tilted her head to smile up at him. "It was good to see my family, but I'm glad I'm back."

"And how. I missed you, baby." Freddie whispered in her ear. "We have lots of those to catch up on."

What did he mean by that?

Chapter 19

With her coat buttoned up to her neck, Emma sat on the porch swing waiting for Freddie. At least it was Friday. She could sit for a minute after her hectic school week. From the time she'd returned from Juneau, she'd been running all week trying to keep ahead of her students.

The children had a hard time concentrating after the Thanksgiving vacation. She had to discipline Karl Piggott on Tuesday because he would not keep quiet. Karl ended up standing in the corner for half an hour. She was sure she'd hear from his mother, but so far, nothing had happened. That was a good sign.

The snow floated toward the ground as Emma watched Freddie saunter up the drive. Snowflakes rested on every tree branch in the Muellers' front yard. She smiled and waved. "Such a gorgeous evening tonight. Just like being inside a shaken snow globe."

"Sure thing. I say we go for a walk." Freddie headed up the steps. "We haven't had much time together lately."

"Sounds good." Emma stood as the swing swayed backward. "I love walking through snow like this."

"Get your warm hat and gloves." Freddie nodded toward the door. "You don't want to get cold ears or fingers."

Emma smiled as she ran up the steps to her room to look for her hat, scarf, and gloves. She located her things in the bottom drawer of her dresser. Throwing the scarf around her neck, she headed out the bedroom door. The idea of a walk with him in the falling snow put a bounce in her step.

Would the snow make Freddie more romantic, like the welcome-home kiss last Sunday? He had surprised her that night. A nervous sensation shot through her. Was he going to be more amorous tonight as well?

Pulling on her gloves, Emma stepped onto the porch. "All set. It doesn't feel too cold out here." Emma slipped her knit hat on her head. "So, where do you want to go?"

Freddie stepped closer to Emma and gently pulled the scarf snugly around her neck. He didn't step away from her, but took hold of her gloved hand. "Let's walk toward the North Beach Park by the lake and see how long we can stand the cold." He matched his steps to fit Emma's stride as they headed down the sidewalk. "You haven't told me what you did on your trip to the farm yet."

Emma glanced at Freddie and smiled. Somehow, everything fell into place, so perfect. The gently falling snow sparkled in the streetlights as they strolled from one pool of light to the next, walking block after block. Her hectic week melted into a soft peace. She must be falling in love. The cold didn't even penetrate to her toes as she walked through the deepening snow, telling Freddie the details of her trip home.

Freddie threw back his head and guffawed. "Ha! That must have been hilarious! I wish I could have seen Danny lying in the mud. And you, dressed in overalls? That must have been a sight."

Emma nudged Freddie with her shoulder. "Hey, that's not nice." Even though a smile tugged at the corner of her mouth, she stuck her lower lip out. "In winter I always work outside on the farm dressed in my brother's clothes."

"I'm sure you're cute in them." The snow-covered trees of the park beckoned them. "The only way you'd look spiffier would be in a snow bank." With that, Freddie pushed her into the deep soft snow.

"Ohhh!" Emma landed with a thump, her arms outstretched. She was giggling as she struggled to stand again. "Why'd you do that?"

"Just wanted to make you into a snow angel." Freddie grabbed her hand, tugging her upright. "I'm not in hot water, am I?" He helped brush off the snow from her arms and continued to the front of her coat even though no snow was on it.

Emma gasped. What was he doing? Was it her imagination, or did Freddie's hand drift too close to forbidden territory? His hand slipped around her waist as he gently cupped the back of her neck and pulled her toward him. Her mind was a whirr as the cold air melted away. Surrounded by the dark sky filled with swirling whiteness, his lips touched hers—warm, soft, and lingering. She stepped back. If only she could think straight.

"Turn around." He put his hands on her shoulders and gave her an about-face, then brushed off the back of her coat and hat.

She must have been imagining things. Freddie wouldn't let his hands stray. It would be too fresh. When he turned her again, he offered her a peck on the cheek.

"Sorry for getting you wet. Couldn't stop myself. You're too cute." His fingers brushed the side of her face.

Emma blinked. Back to reality. She shivered. "Brrrrr. Some snow must have gone down my neck." She took off her glove, reaching into her collar to brush away the cold.

***

"Here, let me help." Freddie whipped off his glove and put his warm hand inside the collar on her neck. "I didn't mean to get you cold." He couldn't let her get too frozen in this weather.

"I'll survive." Emma said, her teeth chattering as he removed his hand. "At least the snow is gone."

Freddie grasped her hand. "We better get you home, pronto." They headed back the way they had come.

Since they were going at a much faster pace, Freddie clutched Emma's hand firmly as they walked in silence. The snow had stopped, but a breeze blew in from the northwest. "This wind isn't helping at all. How're you doing?"

"I'm O.K. I'm warming up since we're walking faster." Emma darted a glance his way, smiling.

What he'd done while brushing Emma's coat didn't seem to put her off too much. So what if his hands strayed where they shouldn't have. Anyway, he didn't regret it. He'd been patient with her for the past several months, acting like a gentleman every night when he walked her home from school. It was about time for her to start paying him back for his patience.

He'd tried to make it clear the Sunday before by kissing her at the train station. He reckoned since he bought her ice cream, movie tickets, and other things last fall, she should expect to return some favors. He couldn't push too fast since she was a farm girl, and a teacher, but, hey, maybe she would get the hint after tonight.

Emma rubbed her hand back and forth on her sleeve. "I didn't realize how cold I was until we started back. I can hardly feel my feet anymore. Time to get inside and warm up."

"How about coming over to my place for some hot chocolate?" Freddie squeezed her hand. "I owe you. I kept you out in the cold too long."

Emma nodded. "I'd love hot chocolate on a night like this." Her teeth clicked as she spoke.

"Ma'll make some to warm you up." He linked arms with her and tucked her close to his side. "C'mon, we'll be there soon."

"Brrr. The ache from my feet is spreading up my legs." She snuggled close to him. "I can't feel my fingers and toes anymore."

"That's not good. Only one more block to go. We'll get you as warm as toast in no time." Raising his eyebrows, he smiled at her. She could count on him for that.

***

"Thanks, Mrs. Neumann, for the terrific hot chocolate." Emma pushed her arms into her coat sleeves.

"I'm glad we were able to thaw you out. Least we could do seeing Freddie froze you." Mrs. Neumann waggled her finger at her son. "Next time don't keep her in the cold so long, young man."

"Jeepers, Ma." Freddie shook his head. "I'm gonna walk Emma back to her house. Be back in a jiff."

"Well, of course, you're going to walk her home." Mrs. Neumann blew Emma a kiss. "Take care, you two."

They walked out the door heading toward the Muellers' porch. At the bottom of their porch steps, Freddie grasped her hand, bringing her to a halt. He turned her toward him, enclosing her in his arms. Before she knew what was happening, he drew her close, his kiss deepening. A fluttering within her rose up, spreading faster than butter in a hot skillet.

Yet, at the same time, the muscles in her neck tensed as her heart raced. Thoughts flew through her mind. She'd never been kissed by anyone like this before. When she was growing up, she imagined she would swoon when she was kissed passionately, but she didn't feel lightheaded at all. Her feet were firmly planted on the cold ground. She stepped away from Freddie, feeling a void. Something was missing. She had no idea what.

"Bye, Em." Freddie abruptly turned and walked away. "Catch ya later."

What did all this mean? She still had a nagging feeling about his actions when he was brushing off her coat. It had been quite a surprise. Maybe she should expect things like that to happen now since she was in love. She was in love, wasn't she?

***

Neil stood in the pulpit looking over his Sunday sermon for the last time. During the hour before church each week, his nerves always threatened to take over his brain. When would he get over these last-minute jitters? Six months of preaching should make a difference, but it hadn't happened yet.

He was finally on the last paragraph of his manuscript when he heard the church door close. He looked up to see Emma strolling down the aisle with a young woman dressed in a knee-length black dress and cloche hat. Hmmm. What were they doing here so early?

He'd tried to stay away from Emma since early fall when he realized she was more interested in Freddie Neumann. If only he could change her mind, but he didn't know how. It didn't mean he didn't think of her often, however. Was it even his place? He wanted to be more than her "spiritual guardian."

It was simply easier to stay away unless he could open her eyes to the fact that Freddie was a skunk. Of course, he had no proof. But every time he saw that blond-haired, blue-eyed lad with the quick and ready smile, he always got the feeling Freddie was the type of person who was used to getting what he wanted when he wanted it. *Forgive me, Lord, for being so judgmental.* That was not something that a pastor should be thinking. When it came to Emma, he couldn't stop himself.

"Good morning." Neil stepped out of the pulpit and walked toward the two women. "Miss Ehlke, what can I do for you this morning?"

"Pastor Hannemann, this is my friend Vivienne Cohen." Emma nudged the stranger toward him. "She went to church in Juneau with me and has some questions to talk to you about."

"I do not know if I can think of the questions. Not . . . not now." Miss Cohen's cheeks turned red. Understandable. Emma had put her on the spot.

He extended his hand to her. "I'm glad to meet any friend of Miss Ehlke's." How could he calm her nerves? "How can I help? I only have a few minutes before the service starts, but I'd be happy to answer any questions you might have later."

Miss Cohen gingerly grasped his hand. "Emma took me to the church with the family. *Oui.* Then told me why Jesus died on the cross. It was amazing to hear, but I am certain I do not understand."

"Oh, well, there are so many concepts about the gospel to understand. It's not surprising you have many questions." After slipping his pocket watch back into its place, Neil tugged on his vest to make sure it was straight. "Maybe we can get together this afternoon and talk further. You'll have to excuse me. I need to greet people coming to church now."

"That would be *très bon.*" She looked at Emma. "You will come along this afternoon with me?"

"Of course, I'll be happy to come." Emma's lips tilted in a half-smile. As if she really didn't mean the words she spoke.

All the more reason to avoid her, but how could he if she'd be at the meeting? "That sounds like a good idea." Neil nodded. No way to get around the situation. He didn't want to have any appearance of something inappropriate with either of these young ladies. "Do you think we could meet in my study at the parsonage? How about two o'clock?"

"That would be terrific." Miss Cohen glanced at Emma. "I will look forward to talking to you."

Emma smiled. "We can go see my classroom before church, then. I've wanted to show it to you anyway. Pastor, we'll see you at church." They headed back down the aisle, their shoes clicking on the wood floor.

Interesting. What would this afternoon bring?

***

Emma and Vivi walked up the steps toward her classroom. "What did you think of Pastor? I mean, just meeting him and all."

"*Oui*, he seemed very nice to me."

"Did you tell Jules you were going to be talking to Pastor about religion?" Emma unlocked and opened her door.

"I have not had much of a chance to talk to him about God. Whenever I try to tell him how much it meant to hear about Jesus, he changes the subject. I do not think he wants me to ask these questions of the pastor." Vivi tossed her reticule onto one of the student desks. "But I really do not care what he thinks. I am going to find out all about the Bible whether he wants me to or not."

Emma smiled. "Good for you. God is more important than the opinion of any man. Jules will just have to deal with it."

***

Hours later, Emma gazed at the bookshelves in Pastor's study. Every book stood straight at attention, lined up on the edge of the shelf from tallest to shortest like children at a Christmas pageant. Did that resemble his life? Perfect?

Vivi sat beside her, fidgeting with her gloves. Two minutes ago they'd knocked on his door on the stroke of two. Was Vivi ready for this meeting with Pastor?

Walking into the room, Pastor carried a tray with glasses arranged in straight rows and set it on the corner of his desk. "Here is some water for you."

Flawless as always. Emma smiled, even though her heart fluttered with nervousness. "Thank you so much."

A chill running up her spine, Emma squeezed Vivi's hand. Vivi wanted to learn about faith in God, but that didn't necessarily mean Emma wanted to spend more time with Pastor. Her stomach was tied in knots. If only she didn't feel so confused about him.

Pastor sat behind his desk and looked at Vivi. "All the teachings that we believe come from the Bible, the Word of God. Of course, learning about these takes a bit of effort. I mean, it can't be done in one afternoon."

Vivi nodded. "Oh, I am willing to study, as long as it takes." She opened the Bible lying in front of her. "It seems so large. How can anyone find what they need with so many pages?"

"It is divided into sixty-six books." Pastor stood and walked around the desk. "They are arranged into chapters and verses." He leaned over Vivi to demonstrate.

Why was he leaning so close to Vivi? He almost touched her shoulder. Emma herself could have shown Vivi about the chapters and verses. She'd been using the Bible and looking up passages since her childhood.

"The first part of the Bible is called the Old Testament, which covers the years before Jesus' birth." Pastor flipped toward the back of the book. "The last part covers Jesus' life and the writings of the Apostles, His close followers. This is called the New Testament."

He moved back to his chair before turning toward Emma. "Did you tell her the story of Jesus?" His eyes locked on hers.

"Yeah, I explained the basics to her on Thanksgiving." Emma stared into his warm brown eyes.

Time stopped, ever so briefly. The seconds stretched their limits. She couldn't look away. Unable to control it, her heart hammered in her chest.

As reality emerged again, she broke the spell and fidgeted with her pencil. "Of course, I'm not sure how good a job I did."

Vivi looked from Emma to Pastor and back again. "I maybe did not understand everything she told me on the day, but I knew what she told me was important."

"We'll talk much more about Jesus' life and death next week." Pastor's smile radiated toward Vivi. "But for now, let's start at the beginning." Pastor continued for the next hour to explain more about the origins of the Bible.

"So, we'll meet every Tuesday evening at seven-thirty to continue our studies." Pastor smiled and handed Vivi and Emma their coats.

Vivi slipped her arm into her sleeve. "That is what we decided. Emma, you will come also? I need you to help me understand what I am learning."

"Of course." She wrapped her scarf around her neck.

Pastor held her coat for her. "I know that you've learned all these Bible teachings already, but it will help Vivi grasp the ideas if we all talk about them."

"Makes sense to me." Smiling, Emma buttoned her jacket. Vivi would be learning about God, but that would also mean she'd see Pastor every Tuesday. Was that a good thing?

Pastor's smile was turned toward Vivi again. "If we have a class every week, you should be ready to join the church in a couple months."

Why did he smile at Vivi so much? And she grinned back at him. Maybe he was just being friendly. Or did he find Vivi attractive? She had a boyfriend already. What about Jules? Emma's mind raced too far ahead of the situation. Enough of that.

She waved as they headed down the sidewalk. "Let's hurry, it's cold out here."

"*Oui.* My ears feel the wind already." Vivi pulled her hat down farther. "Pastor is oh so nice. I think I will learn *beaucoup*, I mean, so much from these classes. I am excited about them."

Emma pulled her coat closer to her neck. "Good thing he can teach you. I can't explain the Bible as easily as he does."

Vivi turned toward Emma. "Thank you for coming along with me. It will be good to have you there. Say, what happened between you and Pastor? At the one moment, sparks were flying between you two."

The cold seeped into Emma's bones as they quickened their pace. "What moment?" She knew exactly what Vivi meant, but she couldn't admit it.

Smiling, Vivi grabbed Emma's arm. "The moment when you two were staring into each other's eyes, and we all sat and listened to the clock."

So Vivi did notice. Swallowing Emma shook her head. "Don't be silly. I have no idea what you mean. Not a thing was going on between us."

If only that were true.

CHAPTER 20

Only two hours until the Christmas Eve program would begin. Sitting at her desk, Emma breathed out slowly to calm her jitters. Were her students as nervous as she was? She brushed fuzz from her black A-line skirt and straightened the ruffles of her bright red blouse.

Maybe she would have time to go over the last minute details of the program before the first student arrived. She'd spent a major part of December working with the children on the recitations and hymns they'd be presenting to their parents this evening.

She smiled when she thought of William trying to memorize the songs with his lisp. He'd managed to do very well by the rehearsal yesterday morning.

Tonight was the culmination of their work. She didn't want to lose sight of the reason behind it, sharing the Christmas story with the congregation.

Studying the printed program lying on her desk, she reviewed the logistics of the service to keep the details straight. It would be dreadful if she told one grade to stand up when it was actually time for another grade to speak. They would most likely be even more nervous than she was. The older ones had done this before, but this would be the first time for the littlest children. Clara and William were especially shy. They would need extra encouragement to open their mouths when it was their turn to speak or sing.

And what about Karl Piggott? Could he sit still that long?

The chairs in the front of church had been arranged so the children would sit facing the adults in the pews. During the rehearsals, it looked like a giant anthill, little bodies squirming every which way.

During the week Emma sat in amazement watching Mr. Dietz. The principal knew exactly how to plan everything to get the children to learn their parts and, most importantly, when it was the right time to stand up and sit down. For four days, they had gone over to church to practice the recitations and routines. Mr. Dietz was like an army general during those rehearsals, but they learned quickly that way. Tonight all the hard work would pay off.

Emma looked up when fourth-grader Lizzie Mueller walked into the classroom. "Hi, Miss Ehlke. Am I the first one here?"

"So far. You're a little early." Emma straightened the papers in front of her.

"I wanted to walk to school with you, but you left before I was ready." Lizzie sauntered toward Emma's desk. "Do you like my dress?" She spun in a circle showing off her light blue Christmas dress with a large bow in the back.

"Very pretty. It matches your blue eyes." Emma tipped her head and gazed at Lizzie. "Um, do you feel alright? Your cheeks are so red tonight."

"My tummy doesn't feel too good." Lizzie sat quietly in her desk. "But Ma told me not to worry. She thought it was just my nerves."

"I'm sure that's it." Emma walked toward the window to see if other families were arriving. Snow was falling gently outside—perfect for Christmas Eve. "The other children should be here soon."

She turned at the sound of a knock from the doorway. Pastor Hannemann stepped into the room, his mouth tipped up in a grin. "Blessed Christmas!"

"Thank you." Heat rose up Emma's neck.

"Are you ready for tonight?" He removed his hat and brushed off the snow. "Since this is a first for you, I thought you could use a word of encouragement before the service started."

"Thanks." Emma's mouth felt as if it were full of sawdust as she smiled. "I guess I am a bit nervous." She folded her hands to stop them from fidgeting.

"I'm sure you are. You've worked so hard for this." He studied his hat.

Emma glanced out the window. Did he really understand what this meant to her? "I'll be glad when it's over." At least the hot spell was passing.

"The important thing for the children to remember is that the Christmas story proclaims God's Word." Pastor placed his hat back on his head. "In a sense, they are the pastors tonight."

"I'll remind them when we're ready to go." She ambled toward her desk.

"I'd better get over to the church to greet parents. When do you want to leave for the train station?"

"Oh." She covered her mouth with her hand. She'd forgotten in the nervous excitement. Immediately after the service she'd be on her way home for almost a week. "I should be ready as soon as the children leave with their parents. I'll have to stop at the Muellers' to get my suitcase, but I'm already packed. I really appreciate that you're taking time on Christmas Eve to drive me to the station."

"It's my pleasure. After all, what would I do with myself after the service? I don't have any family in town either. And of course, I can't go home." He edged toward the door. "I'll talk to you later."

As Pastor walked out, second-grader Sarah and her brother Phillip sauntered into the room, followed by Karl Piggott and his mother. Wearing a bright red hat with a huge feather in the band, Mrs. Piggott approached Emma. "I want to make sure Karl has a visible place to sit tonight. Last year he sat right behind the baptismal font, so I couldn't see him when he was sitting down." She wagged her finger in front of Emma's nose. "I hope I don't have the same problem this year."

Why did Emma always have trouble getting a word in edgewise when Karl's mother was around? "Good evening, Mrs. Piggott," she said with a smile. "I don't think you will have the same problem this year. When we set up the chairs, we tried to make sure the children could be seen by us, and we could see them."

"Well, you better be right, or you'll hear from me after church." Mrs. P. turned and stomped out of the room.

Merry Christmas to you, too. Emma had the sensation she had just been run over by a freight train. Not one of her favorite ladies in the world. She shook her head, clearing it of those thoughts. At least she wasn't feeling nervous about the service anymore.

Over the next half-hour the children arrived in the classroom, spiffed up in their new church clothes. Their flushed faces declared to Emma that they shared Lizzie's nervous attack. When they were seated in their desks, Emma tried to calm them down. "I know you will do your best to sit still and speak your words loudly and clearly. It's our turn now to be the ones to tell our parents the story of our Lord's birth. Remember we are praying and singing to Jesus tonight during the service."

Emma arranged the children in the correct order before they left the classroom. When they were standing in line at the back of the church, Clara burst into tears. William raised his hand. "Mith Ehlke, Karl thpoiled Clarathz hair."

Emma hurried to Clara's side to fix the first-grade-size calamity. "Karl, keep your hands at your side from now on." Biting her lip to control her anger, Emma finished retying the ribbon, trying to match the look of its twin on the other pigtail. Someday Karl Piggott would have his comeuppance.

Waiting for the processional music, she took one last look around to make sure everything was perfect. Time to start down the aisle and sing:

> Oh come little children, oh come one and all.
> To Bethlehem haste to the manger so small . . .

***

Two hours later Emma sat in her classroom with her head in her hands. What a disaster. It had to be the worst Christmas program ever. Lizzie, who had been the Virgin Mary, threw up on the Baby Jesus in the cradle. She was thankful Baby Jesus was only a doll, so no damage was done there, but that had caused a wave of illness among the children.

Out of the eighty children in the program, Emma was sure twenty of them had gotten sick. The sour smell lingered with her still. By the end of the evening, buckets of sawdust were standing everywhere waiting for another explosion. Swallowing to keep herself from gagging, she had taken out one sick child after another during the span of the service, hardly waiting for the next child to erupt.

Tears spilled onto Emma's cheeks. That wasn't how she thought the service would turn out. She swallowed her tears when she heard footsteps hurry up the stairs. Who could that be?

***

Freddie charged up the steps toward Emma's classroom. He'd never witnessed such chaos during a program. What a circus. What was going through Emma's head right now? She was probably devastated, but it sure was funny. He burst into her room, smiling. "Are you all right? That was pretty entertaining." The dour look on her face told him she didn't agree.

She sprang from her chair and leaned forward. "Entertaining?" She raised her voice, and her cold eyes bore into him as she clenched her fists. "How can you say such a thing?"

Freddie sidled toward her desk. "It wasn't your fault, but it sure was a memorable service."

Emma's face took on a reddish hue before she exploded. "It's not supposed to be memorable because so many children were sick." She walked toward the window, keeping her back toward him. "It was awful. How many people were thinking about the Christmas story during that hour?"

"You got me there. At least the program didn't break down in the middle." Freddie perched on the edge of a desk. She sure was upset.

"I don't find much comfort in that." She glared at him before facing the window again.

"Don't get balled up about it. It turned out fine in the end." He sauntered toward her.

She started speaking before he reached her side. The room grew cold, matching her icy words. "I'll be leaving for the train station soon. Pastor is taking me. Make sure you wish your parents a Merry Christmas for me." She turned toward him and tried to smile. "I hope you have a Merry Christmas, also, and I will see you when I get back."

Was she dismissing him?

A knock at the door interrupted them. Emma faced the door as Mr. Dietz walked in. "Oh, excuse me. I didn't know anyone else was in here."

"No problem." Emma headed back to her desk. "Freddie was leaving anyway." She didn't even look his way.

"Have a Merry Christmas, Emma." Freddie exited her room and loped down the steps muttering to himself. What had just happened? Why did he open his big mouth? Now she was upset with him. If only he'd handled things differently. He would have to repair the damage at the dance on New Year's Eve. Shrugging, he walked toward home. He'd worry about the problem when Emma was back in town.

***

Emma stared at Freddie's retreating figure. She shouldn't have lost her temper, but the tension behind her eyes kept building, like a pressure cooker needing the relief valve opened. His comment triggered her valve. He had no clue how she felt about the service. No empathy at all. She took a deep breath and turned her attention back to the principal.

"Emma, I don't want you to feel bad about this evening." Mr. Dietz sat on a small desk. "There is no way we could have known that would happen, or done anything to prevent it."

Emma shook her head. "Lizzie told me before the service she wasn't feeling well. I told her it was probably nerves."

"Mrs. Mueller should have kept her home then. Not your fault. I should have guessed it was coming. I had a couple children home earlier this week with the stomach flu. The siblings came down with it tonight." Mr. Dietz stood, running his hands around the band of his hat.

"You're probably right. I didn't have anyone sick earlier."

"Actually, the program itself wasn't ruined. The Christmas story was still spoken and the songs were sung. I thought they did a nice job."

"Guess Freddie agrees with you there." Maybe she shouldn't be so upset about it.

Mr. Dietz placed his hat on his head. "Don't let this ruin your Christmas holiday with your family."

"I'll try not to let that happen. Thanks for stopping in tonight." Emma stood up. "You should get home to celebrate with your wife."

"Have a safe trip and a Merry Christmas." Mr. Dietz waved as he walked out the door.

Emma slipped her arms into her coat sleeves. "Merry Christmas to you and Caroline, also."

***

Neil locked his door and headed toward school. Would Emma be ready? She'd looked stunning this evening. Her rosy cheeks and her red blouse made her look like a Christmas elf.

He wished again there could be more between them than there was now. But at other times he tried to persuade himself to stay away from her. *God, please show me what to do, soon.*

As he took the steps two at a time toward her classroom, the lights in her room went dark and Emma emerged.

"Oh, I thought I heard someone coming up the steps." She pulled the collar of her coat tight and fastened the buttons.

"Are you ready to go?"

"Yes, I want to completely forget about tonight." Her shoulders drooped as she headed down the steps. She shuffled from step to step, as if she had lost her best friend. "I'll have to go to the Muellers' to get my things."

Neil had never seen her so despondent. He didn't know what to say to her. Silence reigned between them until they were on their way to the station. If only he could figure out how to make her smile again.

Finally he summoned the courage to broach the subject hanging between them. "I felt so bad for you since this was your first Christmas program as a teacher."

"Wasn't it terrible?" Emma shook her head. "Lizzie told me before church her tummy felt funny, but I thought it was nerves. Then I saw her looking ghastly pale right before she erupted. I knew the domino effect it would have on other children." Her voice broke. "Henry was next, even before I could reach Lizzie and get her out of there. I've never seen anything like it."

He glanced in her direction as she swiped unwanted tears off her cheeks. "Don't let it haunt you next year when you're working on the service." He reached out and placed his hand over hers. "The Christmas story was still proclaimed." He withdrew his hand when a hot surge ran up his arm as if he had touched a heated stove.

Emma's head flew up as she faced him with widened eyes. "Thanks. I . . . I'll try to remember that." She rubbed her other hand over the one he'd touched.

Despite the cold weather, heat rose under his collar. Was he making things worse for her? He didn't know how to handle women, especially ones with tears on their cheeks. Should he apologize for touching her? Should he simply ignore the last two minutes and pretend he hadn't touched her at all? What was the proper thing to do?

They rode in silence for a time. As they approached the station, Neil slanted a glance in Emma's direction. "We're almost there." A smile lit up Emma's face. Good thing the tears had disappeared. "A penny for your thoughts."

"Earlier tonight Karl Piggott pulled Clara's ribbon out of her hair right before we were ready to walk into church. I thought to myself Karl would get his comeuppance sometime." Her grin was contagious. "During the service Phillip Schneider threw up all over Karl. It was an awful thing, but that little boy can be naughty on occasion."

Neil's mouth tipped up into a half-smile. "God manages to even things out in the end. Sometimes I think He has a sense of humor." He pulled the car into the station parking area. "Will you need to be picked up next week when you get back?"

"No, Vivi and Jules, her boyfriend, will pick me up." Emma was much prettier with a smile on her face.

Neil sprinted around the front of the car and opened Emma's door as she tied her scarf around her neck. She stepped out of the car and stretched out her hand. "Thanks so much for taking time on Christmas Eve to bring me down here. And, uh, thank you for being so understanding."

Neil grasped her gloved hand in both of his. Don't make another mistake tonight. He dropped her hand. "The pleasure was mine." That was an understatement.

The train whistle in the distance brought him back to reality.

"We'd better get your things so you're not late." He headed toward the trunk to get her bag.

Following him toward the station, she turned up the collar of her coat. "No, I don't want to spoil the rest of the night by missing the train."

Carrying her bag toward the waiting train, he handed it to the porter. "Have a blessed Christmas, Emma. Say hi to your family."

As the train pulled away from the station, Neil sauntered to his car. In his opinion, the night would have ended better if she had missed her train. He wouldn't have had to sit alone tonight, or on Christmas Day if she were still here.

If only.

CHAPTER 21

As swirling whiteness filled the dark sky, Freddie searched the crowded platform for Emma. Her train had been over an hour late. At long last, she stepped down from the car looking as if she carried the world on her shoulders. He hurried to her side. "You're a sight for sore eyes." He gathered her into his arms and kissed her. "Did you have a bad trip?"

She sighed. "Yeah. I was afraid I wouldn't make it back in time." A smile pulled at her lips, but there was no sparkle in her eyes. "It was snowing so hard in Milwaukee I barely found the Racine connection."

"At least you made it, but there's not much time to get spiffed up for the New Year's Eve dance." Freddie grabbed her suitcase and put his hand on her back. "Jules and Vivi are waiting in the car."

When they were settled in the back seat, Vivi glanced at Emma. "Welcome home. How was the trip?"

Trying to keep her warm, Freddie snuggled Emma close to his side. "Did you have a swell Christmas?"

"It was nice, but very quiet. After sitting around there for a week, I'm happy to be back." Emma leaned forward, putting her hand on Vivi's shoulder. "We had more fun at Thanksgiving than I did by myself."

"You're right there. We had the great time with your family." Vivi put her hand on top of Emma's. "Sorry to hear the holiday was not very enjoyable."

Emma leaned back again. "Oh, don't get me wrong. It was good to spend time with them, but it wasn't too exciting." She smiled at Freddie. "Put it this way, just being back makes me feel better. I'm ready to party tonight."

He returned the grin. "Then I'm your man." Had Emma forgiven him for his untimely comments on Christmas Eve? It appeared so, or at least she must have forgotten the incident. Let sleeping dogs lie. He squeezed her shoulder. "We'll paint the town tonight."

"Sounds like a plan to me." Emma settled against his arm.

Vivi turned around, leaning on the back of the seat. "Say, Em, I have the swell idea. Maybe you should stay at my apartment tonight instead of disturbing the Muellers since we will be out so very late."

"Perfect. That way I won't have to worry about waking them. I'll let them know as soon as I get to their house."

"We'll drop you both off at the Muellers' house." Jules connected with Freddie's eyes in the rearview mirror. Freddie agreed with a nod. "Will you gals be ready in an hour?"

Emma looked at Vivi. "We'll make it happen somehow."

***

Sixty minutes later, Freddie found himself sitting on a couch glancing at his watch. Twirling his hat in his hands, he glanced at Jules. Where were those two gals? About the last thing in the world he wanted to do was make small talk with Mrs. Mueller, but that's exactly what he was doing. After all, she wasn't even Emma's mother. "Yeah, the snow finally stopped out there."

"I am thankful she got here safely. I hope it doesn't spoil your fun tonight." Mrs. Mueller twisted a kitchen towel in her hands.

"We'll be fine." As long as they aren't late, but he couldn't say so out loud.

Freddie rose as he heard footsteps on the steep stairs. Wow! He clamped his mouth shut after the first gaping reaction. Emma was ravishing in her black dress. The silver beads threaded through the dress put a sparkle in her eyes and made them glow. Soft curls surrounded her face, highlighting her wide smile. He couldn't wait to get her alone in the back seat. "You're gorgeous tonight, Em. You'd rival any Sheba."

"Thank you." Emma continued down the steps. "This is a result of the shopping trip to Madison." She grinned. "Vivi was my fashion adviser."

"It was well worth the trip." Vivi smiled and walked up to Jules, giving him a hug.

"These shoes aren't what I'm used to. Hope I can make it to midnight." Twirling in front of them, her knee-length skirt flared out, showing off her shapely legs in black silk stockings.

Freddie swallowed hard. "Nice gams." He needed to get out in the cool air.

Emma stopped in midtwirl. "They're not gams. They're legs."

"And they look nice in black. *N'est-ce pas,* Freddie?" Vivi slipped her arms into her coat as Jules held it for her.

"Ab-so-lute-ly. Your hair looks terrific, as well." Freddie ran his hand down a curl.

Vivi nodded. "I totally agree. I love your *coiffure,* all curly peeking out of the cloche hat."

Emma nodded once and picked up her handbag. "Are we ready to go?"

Freddie held Emma's coat for her. "Yup. Let's get a wiggle on."

"The jalopy is waiting." Jules bowed to Vivi, as they joined in laughter.

***

"We've been driving forever. Good thing it didn't snow so much here." Emma turned toward Freddie. "Where are we going?"

"Well, Pastor Hannemann said we shouldn't dance in Racine. Twin Lakes is thirty miles southwest, so that should be far enough. He shouldn't complain now." Freddie clasped her hand in his.

Finally Emma saw neon lights sparkle in the black countryside. "Twin Lakes Ball Room" blinked at her in pink and green letters as Jules's car pulled into the crammed parking lot. She sat up straighter. "Jeepers, everyone else must have the same idea we do."

"Man, I didn't expect such a crowd." Jules cranked the wheel, finding a spot to park.

"Yeah, guess New Year's Eve is for celebrating." Freddie exited the car and hurried to open her door.

Emma heard the music blaring when she emerged from the car. Her feet were tempted to tap out the rhythm already, but they weren't even near the building. "It's been such a long time since I've danced. I probably forgot all those steps you taught me." She clasped Freddie's arm as they sauntered toward the lighted doorway.

Freddie looked down at her, patting her hand, and smiled. "Just stick with me, baby. I'll help you out." He leaned in closer. "You'll be the bee's knees in there, all dolled up in that dress."

"Thanks." Heat rose in Emma's cheeks. Excitement coursed through her veins.

Would this night be a dream come true?

***

As the clock approached the hour of midnight, Emma floated around the ballroom. Since the first beat of the music, this night had turned out to be as wonderful as she'd hoped. She had remembered all of the fancy steps previously learned, dancing either with Freddie or Jules. Now with Freddie's arms around her, Emma waltzed across the floor. Or was she floating in the clouds? If only the evening could go on forever.

As the music stopped, the crowd gathered around the stage anticipating the stroke of midnight. Draping his arm around her shoulder, Freddie winked. "You're sure a terrific hoofer." He gave her shoulder a squeeze. "I could dance with you all night." He leaned over, giving her a peck on the cheek.

Her cheeks burning, Emma stepped away from Freddie. She wasn't used to a show of intimacy in front of people. "I'm having a great time, too." She nodded to Vivi. "Let's go to the powder room, Viv."

"Swell idea." Vivi looked at Jules. "Be right back. We still have some time."

A few minutes later as Emma and Vivi approached the guys, Jules slid an object in Freddie's direction. Freddie pocketed it as fast as possible, but not before the tips of his ears turned red. He looked like a kid caught with his hand in the cookie jar as his eyes met Emma's. What was that about? Jules and Freddie laughed as Emma and Vivi rejoined them.

Freddie leaned close to Emma's ear. "Are you ready for the celebration? It's time for my New Year's kiss."

A shiver running up her spine, she turned to him and smiled. "I've never had a New Year's kiss before." This would be the icing on the cake, a kiss to usher in the New Year from this man, whom she surely loved.

"Five, four, three, two, one! Happy New Year!" The room erupted in a symphony of shouting with the song "Auld Lang Syne" playing in the background. Freddie wrapped his arms around Emma and tilted her backwards. She clasped her arms around his neck and hung on. She had expected a warm romantic kiss but was instead surprised by a loud, wet smack.

"Happy New Year, doll." Pulling her upright again, Freddie grinned and winked.

An acrid smell overwhelming her, Emma pushed away from him. What was the odor on Freddie's breath? Did it smell like her Uncle Max, when he'd been drinking the night her cousin got married? Was that mysterious object in Freddie's pocket a flask of whiskey?

The bubble burst on her nice romantic New Year's celebration. "What were you and Jules doing while we were gone?"

"We didn't do anything." Freddie stood with his shoulders back. "You were only gone for a couple minutes. What do you mean?" He crossed his arms.

"Oh, come on, Freddie. I can smell something on your breath." Emma put her hands on her hips. "Did I see you stick a flask in your pocket?"

"You betcha. Did you want a swig?" Freddie put his hand on his suit coat.

Emma gasped. "Are you serious? I've never even tasted any . . . any . . . stuff like that."

"Don't be a Dumb Dora." Freddie glared at her, his nostrils flaring. "What's a sip now and then? It's a New Year's Eve party. It's what everybody—" He froze. Scrubbing a hand through his hair, he stared at his feet. "I'm sorry. Um, I didn't mean to snap at you."

Biting her lip, Emma shook her head. Unbelievable.

Jules sidled over and put his arm around her shoulder, giving her a brief hug. "Hey, come on, doll. Where's the crime? Nobody's going to get plastered."

Emma narrowed her eyes and peered at him. "What do you mean? What about Prohibition? Last time I checked, it was a crime."

With a shallow smile on his face, Jules shrugged. "It's only a crime to sell the stuff, not take a drink."

Emma scowled. Was that true? Oh yeah, what about Ella's wedding last year? The scowl faded. "Maybe you're right. Our neighbor brewed homemade beer for a wedding since it wasn't illegal. Our pastor even drank some that night."

Vivi smiled at Emma as she leaned against Jules. "Let's not ruin the night with this." Vivi took Jules hand. "I hear the Charleston starting up. Let's go dance, big daddy."

Not sure what to say, Emma stared at her feet. "I'm sorry I jumped down your throat." She couldn't make herself look at him.

Freddie put a finger under her chin, tipping her head until she gazed into his blue eyes. "No, you don't have to apologize. I'm the one who needs to apologize for getting angry at you." He drew her in and pressed his warm lips against hers.

Melting against him, this kiss meant so much more than the one at midnight. She'd been angry the first time, but this one made up for it.

He used his thumb to brush a tear off her cheek. "I don't want to spoil your special night." Smiling, he took her hand. "The music is calling."

Confusion filling her mind, she followed him onto the dance floor. If only her thoughts didn't act like a kaleidoscope—change the angle a little and a completely different view emerged.

***

Brushing her hand in front of her nose to stop the tickling, Emma refused to open her eyes. She wasn't ready to face the morning. Prying one eye open, she found a feather an inch away from her face. Her eyes flew wide open to discover Vivi on the other end of the irritating intruder. "You can stop now. I'm too tired to feel ticklish this morning."

Vivi propped her head on her arm. "Wake up, sleepyhead! I have been watching you for some time now, and you just keep sleeping."

Emma rubbed her eyes and yawned. "Well, you weren't lying awake for hours staring at the ceiling."

"Why could you not go to sleep right away? I was exhausted from the dancing." Vivi snuggled lower into the blankets.

Emma turned to face Vivi. "I'm so confused about Freddie. Sometimes I think I'm in love with him, and other times I don't like him at all."

"I know what you mean." Vivi jumped right in. "All men are like that. Sometimes I feel like strangling Jules, but when he is acting like the cuddly bear, I could hug him."

"At least, I'm glad it happens to you, too. I thought Freddie was so callous on Christmas Eve after that disaster in church. He didn't seem to care that I was so upset. At other times, like our walk in the snow, he's so sweet to me." Emma wiped a tear off her cheek. "Last night when I was hoping for a romantic New Year's kiss, he gave me a silly one instead. Then he offered me whiskey!" She drew in her breath before rushing on. "I was so angry. Later he apologized, giving me a sweet kiss."

"*Oui,* I know." Vivi hugged Emma. "Men can be so . . . What do you say? Uh, exasperating? As the saying goes: you cannot live with them, but you cannot live without them." Vivi patted Emma's shoulder. "Maybe you should let it rest for the while and see what happens."

"I don't know what to do." Emma lay back on her pillow. "Maybe I just need time to sort this all out."

"Perhaps you should talk to Pastor about this." Vivi squeezed Emma's hand. "He could possibly help you."

"No!" Emma's insides slammed shut as she turned to face Vivi. "Pastor won't understand anything about this. All he knows is religion."

Her eyes widening, Vivi's head jerked back. "What do you mean? I do not get this impression of him at all, but I have not known him long."

"Well, he *is* a pastor, so of course he knows the Bible."

Vivi clucked her tongue. "That is obvious. But he knows so much more, also."

"I don't want to talk to him about Freddie. Period." Emma let her pent-up breath out bit by bit. She was no doubt being ridiculous about it, but she couldn't imagine talking to Pastor about Freddie.

After Pastor had taken her to the train station on Christmas Eve, Emma couldn't get him off her mind. It was as if he had known her thoughts that night and had the exact words to comfort her. Several days later, she was still comparing his reaction to Freddie's thoughtless comments.

What would it feel like to have Pastor's arms around her? But he would never think about her romantically. No way should she be thinking about him like that either. She shook her head. And she positively couldn't talk to him about Freddie.

"It is about time we get out of the bed." Vivi pulled back the covers and touched the floor with her foot. "Brr. We will have to hurry." She looked over her shoulder at Emma. "I am surprised by your reaction to my suggestion. Why would you not talk to Pastor Hannemann? He seems like the kind man and is very easy to talk to."

Emma swung her feet out of bed. "He is a very nice person, but I don't think he has much experience with dating and such. He's above all that, studying the Bible all day long. That's what I mean." If only she could quiet her pounding heart.

Emma wrapped her arms around herself trying to keep warm. Why did Vivi keep talking about Pastor? They'd had several instruction classes so far, but nothing had happened there. Maybe Vivi was starting to like him more than she should. Emma found the thought troubling. Vivi shouldn't think about him as a man—he was a pastor, concerned about the spiritual lives of his entire congregation. Pastors wouldn't be interested in mundane things in life, like dating and relationships, would they? Emma glanced over her shoulder as Vivi pulled on a stocking.

"Well, if you can't talk to him, have you tried praying about Freddie?" Vivi reached for a dress in her closet. "From everything Pastor has said in class, Christians should turn to God in prayer when they are confused."

Emma froze with her arm pushed halfway into her sleeve. "Uh . . ." She tried to swallow through the thickness in her throat. Vivi, who was a new believer, understood what she herself needed.

"No, I haven't." Heat crept up her neck and face. How could she have failed to do something that should have been second nature to her? After all, she was a lifelong Christian and now a Lutheran school teacher. "Good advice."

She reached out and gathered Vivi in a long hug. "Thanks for being such a wonderful friend. I needed those words of wisdom."

That night when she had time to be alone with her thoughts, Emma fell on her knees in her room. *Dear Father in heaven, I have forgotten to turn to you in my time of trouble. Forgive me. I am so confused about what you have planned for my life. I am here to teach your children, but I find myself wanting to do other things. I want Your will to be done, but right now I don't know what Your will is concerning my future. I don't know if Freddie will be part of my life or not. Sometimes I feel as though I love him, and other times it's not so clear. Please show me what Your will is. Amen.*

She crawled in bed and pulled the blankets up to her neck. How would she know God had answered her prayer? She sighed.

If only Freddie could be more like Pastor.

CHAPTER 22

Tuesday evening came so fast this week. Neil bustled about his parlor to make sure it was shipshape and ready to receive his visitors. When all was to his satisfaction he moved to his study to prepare it for the class with Vivi and Emma. With great care, he dusted the top of his desk and then, like a general marshaling his troops, set out his books and notes while humming the hymn tune, "Onward, Christian Soldiers." His Bible lay open strategically in the center flanked by the *Small Catechism* on its right and *Nave's Topical Bible* on its left. Papers were spread out like flankers. He was just squaring the last of these unruly troops when he heard a knock at the door. He moved his desk calendar an inch to the right—Perfect!—and headed to the door. "Good evening, ladies. Come in. Come in out of the cold."

Vivi and Emma entered, stomping their feet to rid their shoes of unwanted snow. Emma patted her cheeks. Neil noticed they were bright red. "Good thing I live only two blocks away. My cheeks feel frozen as it is."

He wished he could tell her how pretty they made her look. "Glad you made it O.K. The cold wind only makes it worse."

Vivi slipped off her coat and hung it on the wooden peg on the wall. "I am tired of the winter already, and it is not even February."

Vivi's coat hung crooked on the hook, but Neil resisted the urge to straighten it.

"We might as well get settled in the office since it's warmer in there." Neil ushered them toward the left and they entered his study. "We'll be talking about baptism tonight," he announced as he sat behind his desk with the women facing him.

"Oh, I was baptized when I was the baby. My mother spoke of it often when I was little." Vivi opened her Bible and laid it on the desk. "Of course it was in the Catholic Church in France. Is that all right?"

Neil nodded. "That's an interesting question." He leaned back in his chair. "First of all, no church owns baptism. God's promises attached to baptism don't rely on those who do the act, or the church they belong to. As long as we baptize as Jesus commands with water and in the name of the Father, Son, and Holy Ghost, the baptism is valid."

"So then, my baptism counts." Vivi beamed, but then her forehead wrinkled. "What do you mean by promises?"

"The promise of salvation, Vivi. God tells us in 1 Peter 'baptism doth also now save us . . . by the resurrection of Jesus Christ.'" Neil sat back and steepled his fingers. "So you see, our baptism links us in faith to Jesus. Then, following Him, we'll go home to heaven when we die."

"That is *très* importance." Vivi smiled.

"Yes, it is."

Brushing her hair behind her ear, Emma tilted her head. "It makes me wonder about our neighbor back home. He told us he was baptized two times."

"Two times?" Vivi glanced at Emma.

"Yes, once when he was born. And then when he joined our church. Our pastor baptized him again, 'just to be sure,' our neighbor used to say." Emma's eyes connected with Neil's.

"That must have been . . ." Neil lost his train of thought staring into those deep cocoa eyes. He blinked and cleared his throat. "Um, a unique situation." How could he ever finish a complete thought with Emma in the same room?

***

Freddie glanced up from the mahjong tiles lined up in front of him. The tiny table in Vivi's kitchen hardly had room enough to hold all the pieces in one row, much less leave room for the extra tiles.

"Emma, you've really got the hang of this game." He smiled. "Of course, we've been playing mahjong for the last six Friday nights."

Vivi squeezed Emma's hand. "She has done the terrific job. This is hard to learn since it came from China." She rearranged her thirteen tiles on the table.

Freddie winked at Jules. "Maybe we should play for money tonight."

"You betcha. Swell idea." Jules chose the last tile from the pile in the center of the square.

"Now hold on. That would be gambling in my book." Emma's cheeks took on a pinkish hue. "My mother wouldn't cotton to that at all."

"Oh come on. Don't be a flat tire. It's only for pennies. You can't call that gambling in the least." Heat rose under Freddie's collar. He took a breath to calm down. "How 'bout if we throw the pennies back in the pot when we're finished and start again from scratch next time."

"Well, maybe it would be O.K. then." Emma shrugged.

"Then let's get crackin'." Jules made the first bet of the game.

They played for an hour before taking a break. "You know what's been spinning around in my head?" Freddie pushed back his chair before standing. "We've been stuck at Vivi's place playing mahjong every Friday night way too long. February is almost over. It's time we did something a little more exciting for the weekend."

"What do you have in mind?" Jules rubbed his chin.

Freddie spread his arms for the announcement. "My Aunt Esther, who is . . . let's just say she has lots of dough. Anyway, she asked us to come visit her. She lives in this swanky house up in Milwaukee."

"Your Aunt Esther?" Emma's brows knit together.

"Yeah. I'm her favorite nephew, so she insists I visit her a couple times each year. I haven't been up there recently." Taking his seat again, Freddie turned to Jules and Vivi. "We could plan to go next weekend. Let's drive up on Saturday. We can find a dance to go hoofing that night and come back on Sunday afternoon."

"Hey man, that sounds like a humdinger of an idea." Jules slapped his hand on his knee. "I'd be happy to drive us there."

"If we're going to see your aunt, how can we plan to go dancing?" Emma glanced between Freddie and Jules.

Freddie fidgeted with his tiles. "Oh, we'll have plenty of time to visit with her before we leave for the dance."

Narrowing her eyes, Emma tilted her head. "Where would we sleep?"

"We could easily sleep at the aunt's house." Vivi's grin filled her face. "I have seen the house before." Her arms spread wide. "It has the many bedrooms. We could each have one with more left over."

"Are you sure it's O.K. with your aunt?" Emma sat up straight. "I wouldn't want to put her out."

Freddie rubbed his forehead. "You don't have to be such a wet blanket, Em. Aunt Esther loves to have company. She entertains people all the time."

Glancing around the table, Emma sighed. "I guess that sounds like fun, then." She finally smiled. "It'll be terrific to get out of Racine for a couple days."

"Then we're all set." Freddie clapped his hands. "Next weekend it is."

***

Hearing the tick of the clock, Emma turned over to face the wall in her bedroom. No sleep in sight. She must have been lying awake for hours already. What should she pack for Milwaukee? Even after a week of thinking about it, she still hadn't decided.

It would be wonderful to get away though. She needed a change in scenery. Cabin fever, and all that. But was this really a smart thing to be doing? At least Vivi and Jules would be with them. Plus, of course, Freddie's aunt would be there to chaperone.

She rested her arm above her head. She had followed Vivi's advice to stay clear of Freddie for the last couple months. The cold weather helped her accomplish that. Since she had stayed at the Muellers' every night to study, she'd seen him infrequently. Their Friday night mahjong sessions had been almost the only contact she had with him during a week.

Maybe that's why Freddie suggested the trip away. Would he want to make this more than a fun-and-games weekend? What would the next two days bring?

She'd been pouring her heart out to God trying to decipher His will for her life. So far she hadn't heard any answers from Him—at least none loud and clear enough for her to hear. Why couldn't life be more black and white? She liked being with Freddie, but no bells and whistles went off around him. Why couldn't God give her a clear sign from heaven to settle her dilemma?

***

As Emma stared out the window with her mouth open, Jules pulled to a stop in front of a red brick mansion in Milwaukee. "Oh my. This is your aunt's house?" Steps leading from the front door down to the sidewalk ended at the street with a gated stone archway. What had she gotten herself into? She swallowed. Too ritzy for her. Could she even get out of the car?

Freddie smiled at her. "Once you get used to the idea, you'll see it's just a normal house. My uncle struck it rich doing business with oil companies."

"Oil? In Milwaukee?" Jules looked over his shoulder.

"He had some connection with an oil company in Texas." Freddie shrugged. "They built the house last year. It's nifty coming here once in a while."

"I agree." Vivi stared out the window. "I have been here before, but I am um, *impressionnée.* How you say it? Impressed."

The red brick house with the matching tile roof rose beyond the welcoming archway. Palladian windows, framed in white trim, fanned out evenly across the front. The corners of the house extended out further, resembling turrets. This would probably be the closest she'd ever get to being inside a fairy tale castle. "I haven't even been inside it yet, and I'm already impressed."

"Let me show you around." Freddie exited the car first and opened Emma's door. They all proceeded through the archway and up the flagstone sidewalk and steps. Freddie knocked on the door, repeating the process after no response. "I wonder where Aunt Esther is." He reached under a rock close to the front door. "Good thing I know where the extra key is hidden."

When Emma entered the house, she admired the tile fireplace in the living room. The sky-blue walls contrasted beautifully with the white, arched ceiling. The intricate chandelier hung suspended above the tapestry-covered furniture. "It's beautiful." Emma glanced over her shoulder at Freddie.

"I'll go see if I can find Aunt Esther in back somewhere." Freddie started down the hallway. After a minute he returned with a small paper in his hand. "She left us a note. Apparently, Uncle Frank's sister is ill. She had to go to their house this morning but hopes to be back later." Staring at the note, Freddie fidgeted with the paper.

"Oh, no." Emma searched Freddie's face. "Maybe we should leave, then."

His eyes widening, Freddie shook his head. "She specifically says in the note to stay and make ourselves at home until she comes back."

"That is fine with me since we are here already." Vivi picked up a glass figurine shaped like a Japanese geisha. "I love your aunt's things."

"Aunt Esther has very good taste in decorating." Freddie clasped Emma's hand and led her into the hallway. "Just wait till you see the sunroom."

He pulled her into a bright room with floor-to-ceiling windows in a bay that included a cozy window seat. To the left was a wall fountain with water splashing into a basin, almost as large as a bathtub. A fountain in a house? Incredible. It was magnificent, but who would have money to waste on something like that? "I can see why you like this room so much. It's so warm and welcoming with all this light."

Freddie tugged Emma down the hall toward the kitchen. "Uncle Frank made sure Aunt Esther has all the modern conveniences in here." The white cabinets arranged along the walls were interspersed with a gas stove and large electric refrigerator. Emma wanted to dig in and start cooking on the spot.

"Vivi, why don't you take Emma upstairs and show her around?" Freddie pointed to the stairs. "We'll give you gals an hour or so to get ready. Aunt Esther should be here by then." He smiled at Emma. "How does that sound? Make yourselves at home."

"Sounds good to me." Vivi hooked arms with Emma. "Let us go explore."

***

As Emma and Vivi headed down the hallway toward the steps, Freddie opened the door to the basement. "Actually, I think the best part of the house is downstairs." He led Jules down to the lower level.

The spacious basement room was dominated by a large bar area. The wallpaper and tin ceiling reminded Freddie of many speakeasies he had been in. Behind the bar were shelves filled with every kind of liquor bottle imaginable. They'd hit a jackpot.

"How can your uncle's shelves be stocked full with all this great scotch during Prohibition?" Jules picked up one bottle after another, inspecting the labels.

"Oh, you can obtain anything for a price." Freddie grinned. As long as he could enjoy it, too.

"Do you think we can try some of these?"

Freddie pulled a partially emptied bottle off the shelf. "I'm sure we can taste a couple." He took two glasses out of the built-in wall cabinet. In the beams radiating from recessed ceiling lights, the crystal glasses sparkled with rainbow hues. "How about this one?"

"Looks great to me." Jules took the glass from Freddie. "Do you think that your aunt's sister-in-law is seriously ill?" He took a swig of the strong drink. "Ah, great stuff."

"Man, I gotta level with you." Taking a sip, Freddie let the silky scotch spread warmth down his throat as he sat on one of the bar stools. "I know she's not sick 'cuz I made all that up. My aunt is gone on vacation for a couple months."

"What?" Choking on his scotch, Jules propped himself on the bar stool next to Freddie. "Are you pulling my leg?" A grin spread over Jules's disbelieving face.

"I knew Emma wouldn't come up here without a fire extinguisher." Freddie shrugged his shoulders.

"Huh? Fire extinguisher?"

"You know, chaperone. I can just hear her objection to having no chaperone with us, so I told her Aunt Esther would be here today." Freddie took a sip. "Now that we're here, I'm making it up as we go along."

"But that's lying to her, old chap." Jules peered at Freddie. "This is getting to be tricky. How's it going with her anyway?"

"I'm getting frustrated with her. She can be a pickle sometimes." Freddie took a mouthful of the golden liquid. "Things were going well after Christmas, but I'm not sure anymore."

"What do you mean?" Jules turned his glass in the light. "I thought you two got along well."

"Oh, we get along well all right. We just never have any time alone to progress with things." He took another sip. "No one can say she's a pushover. The bank's closed for me—no cash—no spooning."

"Ahhh. No kissing. Now I understand your dilemma." Jules started smiling. "I'll make sure you have lots of time alone with Emma during this weekend to . . . shall we say . . . make up for it."

Freddie returned Jules's grin. "That's my plan. I'm just hoping she'll never find out that I told her a fib."

"That's a sticky situation." Jules set his glass on the bar. "Where did you get the note from?"

"I, uh, wrote it at home before we left." Freddie looked down at his drink. "I have to tell Emma and Vivi that Aunt Esther called while they were getting ready to say she has to stay overnight at her ill sister-in-law's house." Freddie glanced at Jules. "Level with me. Does that sound believable?"

"Leave me out of this one." Jules held up his hands palms out. "Emma's no sap. She'll probably get suspicious."

"I know what you mean, but I just need to get her alone for a while." Freddie finished off his glass. "The way I see it is this . . . if we guys pay the way for the gals for movies, dances, and such, we should get paid back from them. Emma won't put out for me."

He opened a different bottle of whiskey. "Do you want to try this one?" He poured a splash into his glass. "Let's just say, I have some tricks up my sleeve if things don't go quite as planned."

Chapter 23

The two women climbed the steps to the second floor. "I can't believe how huge this house is." Emma peered down the lengthy hallway.

"You are right there." Vivi pointed down the passage lined with doors. "Let us look in all the bedrooms before we decide the room we like."

"Terrific idea. We can see how they're decorated." Emma opened the first door, a faint hint of rose scent greeting her. "Look in here." The rose-patterned wallpaper complemented the tiny flowers dancing among green vines on the counterpane. "I love it."

After inspecting the accommodations, they stood in the hall. "They are all *fantastique.* Freddie said we could have our own rooms tonight, but it would be nifty to share one." Vivi nodded toward the first door. "Should we pick the rose room? The bed looks so comfortable."

"Perfect. I was feeling terrible about getting so many sheets dirty for only one night. It won't be so much work for Aunt Esther's cleaning lady if we share." Emma placed her bag on a chair in the room. "Besides, my sister and I used to sleep together every night. I miss the quiet whispered talks after lights out. It'd be great to do that tonight."

Vivi laid her valise on the four-poster bed. "Are you still so confused about Freddie?" She glanced at Emma. "Have you been praying?"

A breath catching in her throat, Emma swiveled toward Vivi. "We better discuss this later." She opened her bag and took out her brush. "The guys probably won't like it if we're late." She pulled it through her hair. She'd been praying but was just as confused as she had been months ago. "Do they have a bathroom upstairs?"

"If I remember correctly. We will find out." Vivi led the way down the corridor. "*Oui.* Here it is."

Emma entered the last room on the left. The bathroom had tan walls and a white-tiled floor with a blue-painted ceiling. "Oh, my. The ceiling makes me feel as if I were outside." She pointed above her.

Looking up, Vivi frowned at her. "I never thought of it like that."

Emma noticed a small square area, surrounded in tile, next to the tub. It had a drain in the center of the square and a faucet coming out of the wall above the level of her head. "What's this?" The square area had a clear door separating it from the main area.

"You have never seen the shower before?" Vivi put her hand on the shower door. "Not too many people have them in the homes yet."

"Shower?" Emma brushed her hair behind her ear. "How does it work?"

Vivi opened the glass door and turned a knob three feet below the faucet. "This is the hot water, and the other is the cold. A shower is like taking the bath standing up. It is actually much quicker than using the tub." As she turned the knob, water sprayed out, getting her arm wet. "The trick is to get the water to the right temperature." Vivi quickly turned the knob in the other direction. "Do you want to try it while we are here?"

Emma nodded. "Do I have time?" She couldn't stop grinning. "Won't it take too long?"

"Not at all." Vivi handed her a towel. "You can wash up and wash the hair at the same time. That is the beauty of showers." Vivi turned to head out the door. "We will save our discussion for later."

***

The downstairs barroom swam in front of Freddie's eyes. The golden liquid in his glass splashed over the edge as he shook his head. "Whoops!"

"What do you mean, tricks up your sleeve?" Swirling his drink in his glass, Jules glanced sideways at Freddie. "I hope you aren't planning something stupid. Em's a nice gal."

Freddie shot a glance back at Jules. "Don't get out of joint. I won't get in hot water. You know me better than that." He swayed on his stool, laughing as he righted himself. "I'm tired of her silly prudish act. She can be a real Mrs. Grundy once in a while."

Jules put his hand on Freddie's shoulder. "Of course she's a Mrs. Grundy. She has to be tight laced since she's a parochial school teacher. Besides, she grew up on a farm. Not much chance of her being anything else but a bluenose. If she's special to you, she's worth waiting for."

"I'm tired of waiting." Freddie brushed off Jules's gesture, knocking over his glass.

Jules grabbed Freddie's arm. "Hey man, you're about tanked there. You tasted a bit too much scotch." Helping him to a standing position, Jules led Freddie across the room.

"What's eating you?" Freddie jerked his arm away. "Are you trying to tell me I'm plastered?"

Jules latched on again and continued toward the couch. "Let's just say I think you need to rest before we go dancing."

"All right." Freddie plopped on the sofa and lay down. "I'll just close my eyes for a while."

***

Emma worked a towel through her hair as she walked back into the bedroom. "That was fantastic. Wish I could use a shower all the time."

"I knew you would love it." Vivi pinned curls into her hair. "Now we can have time to talk."

"Hmmm. I can't even remember what we were discussing." Emma ran the brush through her hair.

"How are things going with Freddie?" Vivi reached for her dress.

"Oh. Yeah." Emma's hand froze. "You asked if I was still praying about Freddie. I am. Every day. I don't think God's answered me yet." She resumed brushing. "I enjoy Freddie's company when I'm with him, but it doesn't seem to go any further. I wonder if my feelings will turn into something more. Maybe things will change this weekend."

Vivi paused with her arm halfway into her sleeve. "Could that be your answer? No passionate feelings may mean Freddie is not the one for you."

"But I have so much fun when I'm with him."

"Time will tell." Vivi pulled her dress over her head. "We had better hurry before the guys give up on us."

***

Freddie's arms flailed as a soft fluffy object slammed into his head. He shot upright and spotted a pillow sitting on his lap. "Did you just toss this at me?"

Speaking with a fake British accent, Jules sat on a stool across the room. "Yeah, old chap! You'd better pull yourself together before the gals come down."

"Thanks, man. I must have dozed off."

"I'll say. You've been sleeping the better part of an hour."

Freddie stood up, balancing himself. "Everything's spinning. Guess I sampled too much hooch."

"No kidding. That's what I said before."

Freddie rubbed his forehead. "Um, what did I say before about Emma?"

"Well, it wasn't too complimentary. I'll put it that way."

Freddie sat on a stool. "You'll keep it to yourself, won't you? I wasn't, uh, thinking clearly."

"Don't worry. I'll never mention it." Jules patted him on the back. "It was the combination of a dame and too much juice."

Freddie pulled himself together, straightening his shirt. "I want you to know Emma is a great gal and worth waiting for, no matter what I said."

"Now you're on the trolley." Jules nodded, putting a hand on his shoulder.

Freddie headed for the stairs. "It's time to tell them about the phone call from my aunt."

Jules followed him. "There must be a better way to do this than telling stories."

Glancing back at his friend, Freddie's foot stopped in midair. "I can't think of another plan, so here goes—"

As they walked toward the front of the house, Vivi and Emma ambled down the staircase. As he looked at Emma in her black silky dress again, heat rose in Freddie's midsection.

"We are ready to paint the town," Vivi announced.

"Bad news first." Freddie studied his feet. "Um, my aunt called. She's not coming home tonight. Her sister-in-law is so sick she needs to stay with her."

"How awful. Hope it's not really serious." Emma rubbed a hand over her arm. "We should leave, then, since she won't be here tonight."

Vivi nodded. "Absolutely. We do not want to cause the mess in her house when she is taking care of her relative."

Freddie shook his head. "Can't do that." He'd anticipated their response. Would he sound convincing? "I suggested it, but she insisted we do as we planned and stay here. She was adamant that we shouldn't change anything because of her." He stepped closer to Emma. "Since there are four of us here, no one should think this is inappropriate."

Vivi put up her hands, palms out. "I am not so concerned about that, but we will be dancing when your aunt is worried about her sister-in-law. How can we have the fun? I think we should head south. What do you think, Jules?"

"Uh . . . I don't know." Jules nodded toward Freddie. "Freddie should decide since it's his aunt."

"Right you are, Jules." Freddie's shoulders sagged. Maybe this would work out. "Since my aunt was so insistent, I assured her we'd go and have a good time. We'll see her tomorrow when she gets home. Let's get a wiggle on before we run out of time to eat. The dance is waiting for us."

As Freddie held Emma's coat, she slipped her arms into the sleeves. She glanced over her shoulder at him. "If you're sure. It still doesn't seem right, but I trust you to make the right decision."

Freddie breathed a sigh of relief as Emma buttoned her coat. Now he was in a fine mess. Could he extract himself from the web he had woven?

***

Three hours later Emma settled in the car's back seat on their way to the dance. "What a lovely dinner." She put her hand on Freddie's arm. "I'll have to dance all night to work it off."

"Sounds like a plan to me." Freddie put his arm around her. "We'll dance till dawn if need be." He kissed her cheek. "After that we'll snuggle in the back seat to keep warm."

"I can think of other things to do in the back seat." Jules winked at Vivi.

"Just what are you insinuating, big daddy?" Vivi punched his arm. "This back seat is not the usual struggle buggy some people make it out to be."

Jules managed to drive one handed while rubbing his arm. "I was just kidding."

"That just reminded me of something I heard yesterday." Turning around, Vivi peered over the seat. "Did you hear Charlotte and Mel are having a shotgun wedding?"

"No surprise there." Poking Jules in the back, Freddie laughed. "Mel likes to use the struggle buggy."

"Yeah, guess he used it one too many times." Jules slanted a glance at Vivi. "Remember Mel and Charlotte necking in the back seat last summer at every dance?"

Sighing, Emma shook her head. "Oh, I could never do anything like that before I get married."

"What do you mean?" Freddie glanced her way. "Do you mean doing *it* together, or just necking in the back seat?"

Emma's arms had goosebumps on them. "All of it."

"How can you be so behind the times?" Freddie took his arm from around her. "Everybody does that kind of stuff. It's life today."

"Freddie, you're wrong." Emma gazed into his blue eyes. "I don't act according to what's popular today. I act according to what God tells us in the Bible."

"Never thought of that before." Freddie took Emma's hand. "You're right, of course." He squeezed her hand so hard her fingers cried for help.

"God wants people to wait until they're married." Emma watched Freddie as he stared out the window. No reaction to her words. Even if she could read his thoughts, she refused to change her mind on that subject.

Jules pulled the car to a stop in front of the Riverview Ballroom. "You wanted to dance off your dinner, so here we are." They could hear the muffled music inviting them in.

Freddie smiled as he helped Emma out of the car. "Let's go get busy." At least his smile had returned.

Freddie and Emma followed Jules and Vivi into the ballroom. It was much larger than any dance floor Emma had seen before. The floor was crowded with couples dancing the Charleston. Women danced past Emma with feathers tucked into headbands and strings of beads swaying to the music.

This crowd was much younger than the dancers in Kenosha. They would fit right in. "The music sounds great."

Freddie held out his hand to Emma. "Let's hoof it."

***

"I've never danced so much in my life." Emma and Freddie stopped to take a breath. "They sure don't play many waltzes up here." She fanned her warm cheeks. The stale air in the ballroom didn't allow her any relief from the heat. At least she'd worn off most of her dinner.

Freddie put his hand on her back and guided her toward the punch table. "Are you thirsty?"

"And how." Nodding, she accepted the glass from Freddie.

"When we're done, let's go find Jules and Vivi."

Hand in hand they walked around the large room searching for their friends. With rhythmic jazz filling the room, Emma leaned close to Freddie's ear. "There they are." She pointed across the dance floor. "Looks like they're looking for us, too."

Jules's face lit up when he spotted them. He motioned toward the door.

"He's trying to tell us something." Avoiding the gyrating bodies in front of them, Freddie led the way across the room. "Let's find out what's up."

The four emerged into the hallway. Emma rubbed her ears. "It's not so noisy out here."

"Can you believe he is hungry again?" Vivi shook her head. "We just finished the eating."

"Are you kidding? I already worked off all that food dancing the Black Bottom." Jules's stomach rumbled emphasizing his words.

Emma laughed. "Guess you weren't kidding."

"Do you have something in mind?" Freddie put his arm around Emma. "I could use a bite, too."

Jules looked at Vivi. "I haven't been up to Milwaukee for so long I can't think of a place to go right now."

"How about Harry's Hideaway?" Freddie led Emma toward the coatroom. "I haven't been there in forever. I'd like to check the place out again."

"Yeah! Swell idea." Jules helped Vivi put on her coat. "They have great food."

Vivi glanced over her shoulder at Jules. "If the food is good, let us go. We do not want you two to starve to death."

Emma shared a laugh with Vivi. Such fun she had with her friends.

Winking at Jules, Freddie opened the car door for Emma. "I'm sure we'll enjoy ourselves there. Eh, Jules?"

***

Minutes later, Jules pulled to the curb in front of a row of shops lining the entire block. Freddie spotted Harry's Hideaway, the name screaming to him from large orange block letters on a dark green canopy. The entire storefront was covered with translucent glass blocks. They glowed from the interior lights, illuminating the life within. He pointed toward the restaurant. "Here we are."

"Why would Harry call it a 'Hideaway' if he's not trying to hide anything with those orange letters?" Emma laughed as she glanced at Vivi. "This should be interesting."

"Let us go see what they have to eat." Vivi led the way toward the door. "I hope we are not too late."

As they entered the cozy restaurant, Freddie helped Emma with her coat. The aroma of a juicy hamburger taunted his stomach. "Smells like they're still serving food."

Flanking the left side of the long narrow room was a curved wooden bar surrounded by high stools. The shelves behind the bar held large and small glasses lined up like soldiers ready in the line of duty, waiting for ice-cream floats or sundaes.

Several round tables filled the remainder of the space, creating an inviting atmosphere. Freddie pointed toward an empty table near the back. "How 'bout that one?" After they were seated, he perused the menu in an instant. "Hamburger and French fried potatoes sound good to me."

Vivi squinted at him. "How can you eat that much when it is so late? I could not possibly eat all the food and then go to bed on the full stomach."

"Who says anything about going to bed?" Freddie snapped the menu shut as several people exited a door in the middle of the back wall. Boisterous laughter and raucous music poured out the opening, like a wave. "The night's still young." Smiling at Jules, he raised his eyebrows twice.

Closing the menu, Emma glanced toward the door. "I'd only like a chocolate sundae."

"Hmm, ice cream sounds perfect." Vivi laid her menu on the table. "Maybe I will change the idea a bit and have the banana split."

Emma slanted a glance toward the door as it closed again. "What's going on back there?"

Freddie choked. If only she knew.

"I'll join Freddie in his order. Ice cream wouldn't do it for me tonight." Jules looked over his shoulder. "Somebody's painting the town."

The waitress approached their table to take the orders. When she turned to leave, Emma pointed toward the now closed door. "We were wondering what's going on back there? It sounds like a party."

The waitress winked at Freddie. "Oh, sugar. There's always a party here on Saturday night."

Chapter 24

His face burning, Freddie's heart pounded in his chest. His eyes followed the waitress as she walked away. Why would she wink at him? He'd only been here once. Sure, he knew what was behind the door, but now wasn't the time for Emma to find out.

Grabbing her hand, he had to get Emma's mind off the door. "That was quite a shindig tonight, wasn't it? The band was a humdinger."

Jules drummed his fingers on the table. "You betcha. The music was tremendous."

"It sure was." Emma's eyes sparkled. "I love dancing. Wish I didn't have to be so careful about where we go." She turned to Vivi. "Pastor told me last fall not to dance where church members would see me. I almost feel like I'm lying to them."

"Pastor talked about sinning against your conscience in our class." Vivi laid her hand on Emma's arm. "If you feel like you are deceiving them, I think you should not go anymore no matter how much you like to dance."

Her shoulders dropping, Emma sighed. "I never thought of that before." She studied her hands. "Maybe you're right, Viv. It may be time to stop. I know the importance of being truthful since trust is a hard thing to earn."

Swallowing, Freddie fidgeted with the saltshaker. Whoa, now what should he do? In too deep with the lies, how would he dig himself out? "Now wait a minute. You can't stop dancing just because someone else thinks it's wrong for a teacher to do that."

"Might be what I have to do." Shrugging, Emma gazed directly into his eyes. "Maybe putting other concerns ahead of my own desires is part of growing up."

"Then who wants to grow up?" Laughing, Freddie sat up straighter. He'd buried himself in a huge hole. Would he ever be able to crawl out? "Besides, here comes our chow." Nice diversion.

The table was quiet as everyone dug into their food. "This really hits the spot." Jules took another big bite of his burger.

"Absolutely. This is really tasty." Vivi scooped a spoonful of her ice cream.

The door near them opened and closed as a man, dressed in a caramel-colored flannel suit with a brown fedora, slipped out of the back room. Laughter and shouting followed him through the door. He walked past their table, eyes staring straight ahead.

"It sounds like they are having the fun back there." Vivi motioned toward the brown door.

Emma scraped the last of her ice cream from the sides of the bowl. "Yeah, too bad we can't join them." She turned to Freddie. "We weren't invited."

"I've been here before." Freddie winked at Jules. "You don't need an invitation—only a password."

"Who would know the password?" Vivi pushed her empty bowl aside. "Do you have a clue how to get in?"

"I think I can remember." Freddie shoved his chair back. "It was a long time ago."

Minutes later the foursome stood outside the door as he knocked three times. "I hope I remember this."

Vivi grasped Jules's hand and whispered, "This is one of those places, no?"

"Ssshhh! Don't let Emma hear you." Jules flicked a glance at Emma, who was gathering her coat and gloves from their table. "This is Freddie's joke, but I don't think she'll find it funny."

"But I have to tell . . ." Vivi got no further.

Freddie slanted a glance toward Emma. "Walt sent me," was all he said as the door opened a crack. At those magic words, it flew wide open, admitting the four friends.

***

Emma peered through the haze as acrid smoke filled her nostrils. The area, much larger than the restaurant, held a wooden bar, mirroring the bar out front. Instead of ice cream bowls lining the shelves, liquor bottles filled the space. The textured crimson wallpaper, accented by golden leaves, winked mockingly at the dark wooden wainscoting encircling the entire room. In the corner, a piano played tinny music while on stage several half-dressed young ladies strutted their stuff.

The crowded room exploded in cacophony, loud enough to drown out the music. Women were dressed mostly in knee-length fringed flapper dresses with feathered headbands and long strands of beads. In most cases, cigarettes dangled from one hand while the other hand clutched a glass of liquid, some golden and others coffee colored. Glancing around her, Emma recognized other full glasses of amber liquid topped with snowy white foam—beer. She coughed, gasping to get her breath. Was this a speakeasy?

Emma had heard stories about these places, but had never in her life imagined she would set foot in one. She whipped around and glared at Freddie. "How dare you bring me into a place like this! What were you thinking?" She shouted to be heard above the din.

Or was it because of her intense rage? Before anyone could answer her, she pushed her way out of the secret door and flew toward the front of the restaurant. She slammed her arms into her coat sleeves as she reached the door and pushed her way out into the cold night.

Inhaling a deep breath of the clean air, Emma regained her composure. She hurried away from the wretched place not knowing where she was, or where she was going. In a matter of seconds, she had calmed down enough to hear Vivi calling to her.

"Em, wait for me." Vivi trotted to Emma's side while pushing her arms into her coat. "Slow down. I am with you, but we have to think here for the minute."

"I've never been so angry and embarrassed at the same time. How could he take me into a place like that?" Emma gasped, the cold air filling her lungs. "Did you see how the girls on stage were dressed? Those people were all drinking liquor. That was a speakeasy, wasn't it?" Her heart racing, Emma's hands shook.

Nodding, Vivi glanced back toward Harry's. "We cannot stand out here in the freezing cold too long. And I do not know if we are dressed warm enough to walk far. Let us head toward Aunt Esther's house. Jules will find us." Linking her arm with Emma, she proceeded down the sidewalk. "Take some deep breaths, Em. You need to stop the shaking."

***

Looking out the window in the door of the ice cream parlor, Freddie felt a hand on his shoulder and glanced at his friend.

"Hey, bud, what have you gotten us into now?" Jules rubbed his hand through his hair. "Did you see the look on Emma's face when she walked in there?"

"I saw." A sudden coldness penetrated to Freddie's core. "I knew Emma wouldn't like the idea of going into a speakeasy, but then she spotted the dancers in there. Now I'm really in for it. I wouldn't have gone in there if I had known about them. Harry didn't have a cabaret when I was in here last time." His head pounding, he dropped into the nearest chair. "How will I be able to explain myself out of this one?"

"That's your problem." Jules sat in the chair across from him. "What are we going to do now?"

"Let's wait for a bit." Freddie rested his forehead on his hands. If only he could turn back the clock. "I'm sure the girls will be back in a minute after they calm down."

"I can't imagine how you're going to explain this to Emma, but at this point, I don't even know what Viv thinks." Jules's forehead wrinkled as he rubbed the back of his neck. "This weekend has been totally ruined."

"It's not that bad."

Or was it?

After waiting two minutes, Freddie looked at the front door for the umpteenth time. No sign of them.

"Where do you think they are?" Jules threw a glance in Freddie's direction. "Maybe we should go look for them. It's too cold out there to last long."

Freddie stood up and headed for the door. "Right again, Jules. We better get going." He buttoned his coat. "I hope they didn't start walking back to the house."

***

Emma and Vivi scurried as fast as they could. "I don't know what to think about Freddie anymore." Emma's hands were buried deep inside her pockets. Was she shivering from the cold, or from anger? She wasn't sure of anything right now.

Vivi kept her arm linked with Emma's as small icy pellets began to rain down. "Let us wait to hear what both of them say." Vivi glanced over her shoulder. "Where are they? Maybe we should have gone back inside Harry's instead of walking away."

Emma couldn't feel her feet in her dancing shoes anymore. "I was way too upset to set foot inside that place again." She concentrated on taking one step at a time. If only she could head back to Racine tonight rather than stay another minute in Milwaukee.

Why had she come in the first place? Next time she'd stay home. The driving snow pelted their faces as they walked into the wind. She pulled her scarf tighter around her neck. "It's really miserable out here."

***

Freddie piled into the front seat with Jules. "I'd better sit up here to help you look for them."

Jules drove down the street toward Aunt Esther's house. "Hope they headed in the right direction."

As Freddie peered into the inky night looking for any sign of the girls, he noticed the snow crystals flying toward the windshield. "Terrific, it's starting to snow. Where are they?" After two blocks, Freddie spotted two figures in the distance trudging down the street. "There they are."

The two women stopped as the car approached them, and with arms linked, turned to face the bright lights. As the car came to a rest beside the curb, Freddie jumped out of the front seat to open the back door. "Jump in, Em. You must be freezing."

Before he could reach the handle, Vivi unlatched the door and pushed Emma through the opening, jumping in behind her.

"Drive us back to the house as soon as possible. We are both frozen."

Snow pounded the windshield, making it almost impossible to see the road. An uncomfortable silence reigned in the car as they made their way to his aunt's. As if no one wanted to be the first to broach the topic. Freddie unbuttoned his coat.

If only he could figure out what to say to Emma. He had to try to explain what happened. Jules was probably composing his apology to Vivi to make sure he got back into her good graces.

Freddie glanced into the back seat. Staring out the front window, Emma and Vivi huddled next to each other. He hoped they were getting warm back there. What was going through Em's head right now? Would she ever forgive him?

Jules finally broke the stillness. "What were you girls thinking, walking on such a cold night?"

Vivi spoke up first. "We were not thinking straight at the time. Emma simply needed to walk and could not go back into Harry's." Vivi blew on her hands. "I would like to know what took you guys so long."

Freddie finally found enough courage to turn around and face them. "I'm really sorry for messing up. Last time I was there it was a speakeasy, but it was different tonight. The other time, Harry didn't have any flappers dancing in the joint. I'll level with you. I shouldn't have gotten you into that sticky situation."

***

Emma gazed at Freddie. In the darkness, she couldn't read the look on his face, but he sounded sincere. Was sincerity enough to bridge the gap between them? Looking out the window, she made no comment as they drove the final blocks to the house.

Maybe her first reaction was a bit over the top. Since Freddie didn't know about the floor show, should it make a difference to her? He still had taken her into a speakeasy without informing her, or finding out what she would think about it. Her stomach was tied in knots, but she wasn't as angry as before. At this point, better to say nothing since she didn't know what to say.

A white blanket of snow spread before them by the time Jules parked the car in front of the house. Freddie jumped out and sprinted around to Emma's door before she could open it.

As she stepped out of the car, he grabbed her hand and pulled her up the stairs to the front door. "I need to talk to you." She barely heard him as he unlocked the door.

Emma didn't resist as he led her to a couch in the sunroom. Stroking Emma's hand with his thumb, he sat close and searched her eyes. "I meant what I said about feeling terrible. I wanted to take you into a nice quiet speakeasy to show you that they aren't so immoral, but instead we walked into a noisy joint."

"How could you imagine I would feel comfortable in any speakeasy?" Emma's look bore into Freddie. "Maybe they aren't all immoral, but they are all illegal—selling liquor like that."

"Yup, I messed up." Putting his arm around Emma's shoulder, Freddie held her gaze. "I'll never do anything so dumb again."

"I could never condone even a quiet one—if there is such a thing." She pulled her hand away from his grasp. "I'm a parochial school teacher after all."

Nodding, he stroked her cheek with his finger. "Em, can you ever forgive me? I don't want to ruin our weekend."

With tears welling up behind her eyelids, Emma swallowed. She tried to form words, but her mouth wouldn't cooperate. He said he was sorry and asked for forgiveness. Was it enough? Isn't that what love does—forgive as Jesus taught us? Wanting to believe him, she nodded.

Freddie blinked, his downturned lips curved in a half-smile. As he inched closer, Emma's lashes drifted shut, her heart pounding in her ears. He was going to kiss her. The tension in her shoulders melted away, like butter on a hot pancake, when his lips touched hers.

If only she could remember why she was mad at him. With heat spreading to her toes, Freddie wrapped her in his strong arms as the kiss deepened. Finally she drew back. "I'd better go to bed." She stood up, looking down at him. "We've had a very long night. I'll see you in the morning."

Emma dashed up the stairs. She needed time to think. How confusing this business of love was! At Harry's, an alarm bell went off in her head, but on the couch it turned into the beautiful song of a bird on a glorious summer morning. Was she giving in to him too easily?

Of course she should forgive him, but how long would it take to forget? She reached the bedroom as Vivi walked toward her from the bathroom.

"It looks to me like you and Freddie made up." Vivi's eyes twinkled as she smiled. "I walked past the sunroom door a while ago coming from the kitchen and saw what you two were doing."

Emma shook her head. "It's so easy to get caught up in a kiss, leaving all rational thoughts behind." Closing the door, she plopped on the bed. "When I'm up here with you, I'm still so confused about Freddie, but when he's kissing me, the confusion disappears immediately. The tingles run all the way down my leg. I'm not sure that's good."

She took off her shoes and stockings. She liked the attention of a boyfriend, but still something deep within her told her things weren't right with Freddie. "Did you and Jules get a chance to talk?"

"Yeah, he said he was sorry for tonight." Vivi crawled underneath the thick quilt. "I do not think either of them planned for that to happen."

"Right now I don't want to talk or think about it anymore." Emma slipped a nightgown over her head. "I'm so exhausted. I simply want to go to sleep."

"Absolutely." Vivi pulled the quilt up to her chin. "Let us see what tomorrow brings." They both turned toward the window as a gust rattled the pane. "I wonder how much snow we are going to get. It sounds like the wind is coming off the lake now."

Emma crawled in beside Vivi and snuggled under the warm blanket. "I hope it doesn't snow too much. I have to get home tomorrow and be ready for school on Monday."

It couldn't be worse than tonight, at least. Or could it?

Chapter 25

The blustery storm roused Emma from a deep sleep when tree branches rattled against the windowpane. Her eyes popped open to see the room drenched in whiteness. Throwing off the quilt, she raced to the window despite the freezing wooden floor. "Oh, no! It's really deep out there."

"Then the best thing to do is crawl back in bed and stay nice and warm." Pulling the blanket higher around her neck, Vivi snuggled deeper under the quilt. A second later she bolted upright with wide eyes. "What about church? It is Sunday today."

Emma tucked her hair behind her ear. "I completely forgot about that, too." Reacting to the cold floor, she tiptoed toward the bed. "How will I explain my absence?"

"Before we came, I made Jules promise he would get us back to Racine for the church today." Vivi lay back on her pillow. "Guess that is out of the question." She patted the bed. "You might as well stay warm in here for a while since we are not going anywhere soon."

After talking for half an hour, they jumped out of bed and hurried to dress. Heading down the stairs, Emma peered out the window. How much snow was already piled up? At least it wasn't coming down as hard. "Hope we can head back to Racine shortly. Looks like the snow has almost stopped. That'll be good since I need time to finish my work." The sound of sizzling reached Emma's ears as she entered the kitchen.

"Good morning, sleepyheads." Jules glanced their way. "We've been up for hours already." He pointed to a pan on the stove. "Are you hungry for a few scrambled eggs?"

"We were up an hour ago, also, but decided we might as well stay in the warm bed for a bit." Vivi walked toward the stove and stirred the eggs. "Where's Freddie?"

Jules put his arm around Vivi's waist. "He's outside checking on the snow situation."

"Will we be able to leave soon?" Emma opened the glass-door cabinet and retrieved several plates. "I need to get back as early as possible."

"Here he comes now. Let's see what's up."

Opening the back door, a cloud of snow escorted Freddie as he entered the house.

Jules pushed the door shut. "How does it look, man?"

"It's deep out there. Not safe for driving." Smiling, Freddie stamped his feet in the entrance.

"What?" Emma set the dishes on the table and stood with arms akimbo. Not this on top of everything else. "It has almost stopped snowing already, and it's not even noon." Glancing out the window, she wished for the tenth time she had stayed in Racine. "Can't we shovel out the car and go now?"

"If we put our nose to the grindstone, we could maybe make it, but it'd be tricky. It's pretty slick out there." Freddie looked at Jules. "Besides, who wants to work that hard?"

Were they in cahoots with one another? Emma pointed her finger at her chest. "I'm willing to go out there and shovel if it'll get me to Racine."

Vivi scooped the eggs into a bowl, the spoon clinking on the edge, and headed for the table. "There must be some way to get back."

"You slay me, Em." Freddie shook his head. "It's the perfect excuse to get a day off work, but you want to go out there and sweat today?"

"We can say we're snowed in up here. Our boss won't know how bad it is." Jules patted Freddie on the back. "I'm ready for a day off. He'd have to believe us since he's not here."

"You betcha." Freddie smiled.

"What about me?" Emma looked from one to the other. "There's school tomorrow. I have to be there." She paced across the kitchen floor. "Who would teach my class?"

"That's the principal's problem." Grabbing her hand, Freddie stopped her in her tracks. "There's a phone here. You can call him and tell him we're snowed in." His thumb stroked her palm. "I'm sure he wouldn't want you to drive on bad roads and get in an accident."

"But it's hardly even snowing right now." Fighting the tightness in her chest, she placed four forks next to the plates. The guys didn't understand. "I can't miss school."

"Let's forget about it for a while and play mahjong after breakfast. Then we can decide later this afternoon. I think Aunt Esther stores her set in the sunroom." Freddie pulled out a chair and sat down. "Don't get in a tizzy, Emma. Everything will turn out all right." The other three joined him at the table.

"Have you heard from her this morning?" Emma passed the bowl of eggs to Jules. She hadn't thought of the sick relative at all. "Is she going to be coming home in this weather? Maybe if she gets here and the roads aren't too bad, we could try to go home."

***

Swallowing twice, Freddie shook his head. "Oh . . . she called this morning. She said the snow's too deep, so she's staying there till tomorrow." Caught in the web again. At least he might as well use the web to strengthen his argument. "Aunt Esther knows how bad the driving is here, so I think we should follow her example."

"I'm not giving up hope yet." Emma's downturned lips made her look like her last friend had died. "We can check again later." She pushed her plate away.

"Great idea. Let's go look for the mahjong set." He shoveled a forkful of eggs into his mouth.

Vivi raised her coffee cup to her lips and took a sip. "Time passes quickly when we are playing mahjong."

"Right you are." Jules picked up his plate and took it to the sink. "Freddie and I will set up the game while you gals wash the dishes."

"Bingo. Nifty idea." Freddie followed Jules's example and headed for the sunroom.

An hour later, Freddie stood and stretched. "Em, you've been looking out the window every couple minutes. Are you bored with the game today?"

She turned toward him. "I'm checking on the snow. Just can't concentrate. Can we go home now? I think the snow's stopped entirely." She stood up and walked toward the window. "It doesn't look any deeper."

"That's for Jules to decide since it's his car." Freddie joined Emma at the window. Maybe this was his chance to accomplish what he couldn't do last night. He still hadn't had the time to snuggle up with her to make his move.

"He'll have to go out there and make a decision." Freddie put his arms around Emma's waist and pulled her back against his chest. He planted a kiss on her neck. "I'll go with him, and we'll talk about it."

Shivering in his embrace, she stepped away from him and rubbed her neck. "Terrific. Maybe it's not as deep as you think."

Ten minutes later, Freddie burst through the door with Jules right behind. His pulse racing, he couldn't hide the Cheshire-cat-like grin plastered on his face. "It's too treacherous for Jules's car to make it tonight. No plows are on the roads yet."

Emma cupped her head in her hands. "Are you sure?"

Freddie drew near Emma and clasped her hands. He knew this would be a sticky situation for her. "I'll help you call your principal to explain the problem. Then I'll call Ma to let her know about it."

"I don't know what to tell him." Emma tightened her hands into fists. "How can I explain I'm out of town with you and Jules, and now, snowed in?" Biting her lower lip, she ran a hand through her hair.

Freddie reached for her clammy hands, giving them a squeeze. "You worry too much, doll."

"But what about my job?"

Sauntering toward the telephone stand in the hallway, he reached for the handset. "I'll talk to him myself if need be." He picked up the phone, dialed zero, and spoke to the operator. "I need to make a long distance call." He cupped his hand over the mouthpiece. "I don't know the principal's name."

In a quiet tone, Emma responded. "Robert Dietz." Mumbling, she rubbed her hands up and down her arms. "Dear Lord, please help me know what to say to him."

When Freddie heard the phone ring on the other end, he handed it to Emma. "Hello, Mr. Dietz. This is Emma Ehlke. I'm afraid I have bad news."

"No, I'm fine. Nothing like that."

"I'm in Milwaukee with some friends, and it snowed up here something fierce. We can't make it back to Racine tonight."

Freddie smiled. She made her point very quickly. No beating around the bush.

"Yes, I understand. O.K." She turned to look at him.

"I'll get there as soon as I can. Thank you very much. Good-bye." Her shoulders slumped after she hung up the phone.

"See, that wasn't so hard."

"Wonder who he'll get to teach in my classroom until I can get back."

"Guess that's what he has to figure out." Freddie squeezed her hand.

***

Hours later the four were sitting around roaring flames in the fireplace.

"It's nice to see you so relaxed and smiling." Freddie gazed into Emma's nut-brown eyes. "Everything worked out just like I said." Pulling her close with his arm draped over her shoulder, he gave her a peck on the cheek.

She leaned her head against his arm. "It's surprising how calmly Mr. Dietz took the news." She turned toward Vivi, sitting on another couch next to Jules. "It'll be interesting to see who he'll get to substitute for me tomorrow. Maybe Elsie Schneider. She's a former teacher who got married a couple years ago."

"Well, at least, you do not have to think about it anymore." Looking out the window, Vivi sat cuddled into the curve of Jules's protective arm. "I am sure glad we did not have to drive tonight. It is nice to be in front of the cozy fire instead of driving through deep snow in the dark."

"We should be able to get going by ten or so tomorrow morning and be back around noon." Freddie squeezed Emma's shoulder. He'd better not push this any longer than necessary since she was so nervous about the whole thing.

"Yeah, I'm sure some of the snow will be plowed away in the morning." Jules smiled broadly. "My Tin Lizzie can get through all kinds of weather."

Emma shot up in her seat. "Then why didn't we try to go home this afternoon? Maybe it would have been easy for your 'Tin Lizzie.'"

"Don't fly off the handle, Em. We didn't go, and now it's too late." Freddie pulled her back into the curve of his arm. He only had a short time to take advantage of the situation here and wanted to get her alone. "Let's go into the sunroom and see if there are any good books to read."

"Why would we leave this nice toasty fire?" Emma leaned against Freddie. "If we have to stay here, I don't want to move an inch."

"I agree." Vivi smiled at Jules. "For all the twists and turns this weekend brought us, I am glad we came. Just this quiet time makes up for the rest of it."

Emma sighed. "Not quite, but it's a start."

Jules stood up and stretched. "Let's go for a walk, Viv." Pulling her up from the couch, he looked at Freddie and winked. "I feel like I need some fresh air."

"Are you crazy?"

"Just for a while." Jules folded his hands in front of him. "I'll explain in a minute."

"If you say so . . ." Vivi headed toward the front door, grabbing her coat off the hook.

Now was his chance. Good old Jules, going for a walk in such weather. Freddie's pulse raced as he tightened his arm around Em's shoulders.

She leaned forward and looked at him. "Why would they do that?"

"No idea." Shrugging, he gathered her into his embrace and brought his head close to hers. "You look dazzling tonight in the firelight." He whispered in her ear, lilac perfume tickling his nose.

He kissed her warm cheek and scattered tiny kisses on her face, moving ever closer to her soft lips. His heart beat double time, heat rushing through him. He couldn't get enough of her.

He forced himself to deny his craving and kissed her gently, moving toward the hollow of her neck. She melted against him, nestling into the crook of his arm. Now he was getting somewhere.

His lips sought out hers as he gently opened his mouth against hers. At first Emma returned his passion, but she stiffened against him as his kiss deepened. His arms tightened around her as she squirmed beneath them.

Putting her hands against his chest, she pushed him away. She drew in a deep breath and shook her head. "Freddie, we can't do this." She scooted toward the other end of the couch. "I feel as though I should be married before I do these things."

Freddie's breath caught in his throat. Just when he was getting somewhere. "I'm sorry, I didn't mean to get you upset."

"I think it's time I head for bed." She rose from the couch and started in the direction of the steps. "We'll have to get up early to get out of here anyway."

"Don't go." Rising, Freddie stepped toward her and clasped her hand. "I won't do that again. I'll behave." At least, he'd try.

"You're not whom I'm worried about." She looked over her shoulder and sent him a sad smile before ascending the stairs. "Goodnight."

"G'night." Watching her skirt swish to the rhythm of her hips, he nodded his head. He'd have to come up with another way to pursue this.

Chapter 26

Emma scurried toward the school as fast as her legs would take her. It was after one o'clock, the school day half gone. Her legs screamed at her, burning from the fast pace. She was almost there.

Freddie and Jules had worked hours to dig the car out of the snow. Emma had even helped with the shoveling to speed up the process. When they finally were able to get onto the open road, the slow trip back to Racine had lasted more than two hours. Watching the scenery creep by the window, Emma's fingers had clenched more with each passing mile. The snowbanks looked smaller and smaller the farther south they drove.

By the time they reached their destination, white patches lay here and there. Jules had commented that it must have been lake effect snow in Milwaukee but hadn't come this far south. Would Mr. Dietz believe her when she explained how bad it was up north?

When they'd reached her house, Emma had thrown off her traveling clothes and changed into her navy skirt and cream shirtwaist. The buttons refused to cooperate with her flying hands.

Now, her stomach tumbling in somersaults, she approached her classroom. Who would be teaching for her? How would the children react to having her walk into the room so late in the day? What would Mr. Dietz say after school? She quietly opened her classroom door to assess the situation.

The booming voice of Pastor Hannemann hit her like a wave as soon as the door cracked open. What was he doing here? She peered around the edge to see him standing up in front of class with a book in his hands. Marching back and forth, he explained how to multiply two numbers together. Pausing, he wrote several numbers on the blackboard, the chalk clicking against the black surface. Pastor was her substitute?

Emma swept the classroom with her eyes. First-graders Clara and Ella were sucking their thumbs—something both girls had quit doing the second week of school last fall. Why would they be doing that again? Some of the other younger children sat as if they were trying to make themselves invisible—their heads bent low, arms tucked close to their bodies. All forty children were bathed in silence. Not a peep, except for Pastor's deep voice. She slipped into the room.

As Emma closed the door with a loud click, forty-one pairs of eyes turned to stare at her. She had the impression that the entire room exhaled, including Pastor.

With eyes shining, his lips formed into a slow smile. She almost heard the relief his face was broadcasting.

Heat radiating through her chest, peace descended on her shoulders after the traumatic weekend. She was home again.

"Hello, children, I'm back, so I'll take over the arithmetic lesson." She swept up the aisle toward the front of the room, picked up her glasses from the desk, and placed them on her nose. The children sat up straighter, and Clara and Ella popped their thumbs out of their mouths simultaneously.

"I'm glad you're back safe." Looking heavenward, Pastor's smile spread across his face. As he approached her, he handed her the open book. "I was working with the fourth graders on their lesson." Their hands touched, sending a shock up her arm.

"I'll come in after school to fill you in on the rest of the day," he said to her in a quiet voice. "Good-bye, children." He headed between the desks toward the back of the room and disappeared out the door.

Emma flew from task to task the rest of the day. She hadn't had time the day before to finish preparing and now couldn't even pull her thoughts together. Not a good way to face a classroom of children for the afternoon.

Her mind couldn't get past the scene she'd encountered upon her arrival. Pastor teaching her students? How did he manage first graders? Why had they look so shell shocked when she had entered the room? Why had Mr. Dietz not chosen a different substitute? Would Pastor be upset with her as well as Mr. Dietz? With all those thoughts swirling through her head, she managed to finish teaching arithmetic before afternoon recess. She rode a perpetual roller coaster the rest of the day.

As the last child walked out the door, Mr. Dietz walked in. "Miss Ehlke, I'd like to speak with you for a moment." He sat on top of a small desk, glaring at her. "I am very disappointed in your actions yesterday and today."

Emma removed her glasses and laid them on the desk. "Mr. Dietz, I wanted to talk to you also . . . to apologize." Lowering her eyes, she sat with folded hands. "I'm very sorry I was not able to make it in this morning."

Mr. Dietz steepled his fingers in front of him. "What you did yesterday was incredibly unprofessional. A stunt like that might be expected from a college student, but a teacher should never miss school for that amount of snow."

Emma's mouth dropped open. Snapping it shut, she stared at him. Was he accusing her of lying? "It looks like it didn't snow too much down here, but I can assure you it snowed nine or ten inches in Milwaukee. It must have been lake effect snow." She swallowed. If only she could have persuaded Jules and Freddie to drive back yesterday afternoon. Now she was in trouble with the principal. "The person driving didn't want to chance it with the deep snow yesterday. I'm very sorry, but I couldn't do much about it."

"At any rate, I want you to understand you are a professional now and can't miss school for situations like this." He stood up. "Make sure it doesn't happen again." He headed for the door. "By the way, the money to pay Pastor for substituting today will come out of your paycheck because you weren't sick." With that, he left the room.

Astounded by his indictment, Emma sat frozen behind her desk, struggling to take a breath. She already felt guilty for not coming back yesterday, but how could she have changed anything? She had tried to persuade Freddie and Jules to come back. She didn't mind paying Pastor for helping her out, but did she really deserve such strong language?

Putting her head in her hands, she tried to sort out her feelings and get her thoughts together. No way would that happen again because she would never again go out of town with them. Oh, why had she let them persuade her to go on an adventure? It had been a disaster from the start. A stray tear trickled down her cheek. But it really had snowed.

***

Knocking on the doorjamb, Neil noticed Emma's dejected pose. What was wrong? His heart had turned a somersault when she had walked into the room to rescue him from his teaching duties earlier. He couldn't imagine what had happened in the short time since he'd left her.

She'd marched into the room and taken charge like nobody's business, yet now she appeared to be in abject misery. "Is it . . . all right for me . . . to come in?" His hands worked their way around the rim of his hat.

Emma's head popped up as she swiped her cheek. Looking toward the door, her shoulders sagged. "Yes, I mean . . . Sure. I was just trying to get my thoughts together." She combed her fingers through her hair. "Mr. Dietz left only a moment ago. Did you see him?"

"No. I wanted to talk to you about school." Neil took a deep breath. "I don't know where to start." He sat on a child-size desk.

How could he deal with the strong emotions he felt right now? The feelings had grown deep in his heart beginning late last year. Those Tuesday evening classes with Vivi hadn't helped either. Besides that, he had tried to avoid Emma as much as he could since he knew the feelings weren't returned.

"What do you mean?" Emma tilted her head to one side. She shuffled some papers on her desk, not looking directly at him.

"You . . .were amazing when you came in this afternoon." Neil followed the crown of his hat with his fingertip. He worked hard to hide his fondness for her below the surface.

Her eyes flew to his. "Amazing?"

"You took charge immediately—the children could feel the difference as soon as you walked in the door." Though he didn't move an inch, the pull between them was palpable. This was getting too intense for him. "You were a professional through and through."

"Oh, my!" Emma burst out laughing, breaking the spell.

"What's so funny?"

"Mr. Dietz just informed me of the opposite. He said I was unprofessional today by being snowbound in Milwaukee."

"How can you control the weather?" Neil crossed one knee over the other and shook his head. "And this makes you unprofessional?"

The ticking clock filled the silence.

Biting her lip, Emma fidgeted with her glasses. "I was, um, out of town over the weekend . . . with friends."

"Oh?" Neil folded his hands over his cocked knee. What wasn't she saying? By the blush in her cheeks, she looked as if she was guilty of something.

The story trickled out over several minutes until she stopped and looked into his eyes. "I felt terrible that we didn't come home yesterday. I tried to persuade Jules to at least attempt the trip, but he said the roads were closed in Milwaukee. Mr. Dietz called me 'unprofessional' because he thought I was just skipping school." She looked down at her folded hands.

"You weren't the one making decisions about trying to drive on the snow-covered roads." He stood and stepped toward her desk.

Emma shifted in her chair. Her pink cheeks made her look more appealing. "By the way, thank you for the compliment, but I don't feel very professional at the moment."

"It's true." Placing his hand on her desktop, he leaned closer. "I wasn't just saying that. I can't imagine how you do it every day. That was the longest morning of my life." Could he tell Emma he admired her? Was that too personal? He didn't want to come on too strong and scare her off.

Stepping off the platform, she walked around her desk to stand in front of him. "What happened? Did someone misbehave for you?"

Shaking his head, Neil rubbed the back of his neck. "When I walked in the door this morning and explained I would be teaching until you got here, half of the class burst out crying. I didn't know I was so scary."

The corner of Emma's lip tipped up in a smile. "I'm sure the little ones were just nervous. You're so much taller and louder than I am." She looked as if she was enjoying this. "Don't take it personally." She gazed into his eyes.

With heat rising up from under his collar, he struggled to keep his mind on the conversation.

"You have the patience of a saint in my book." Neil's throat constricted. Swallowing, he managed to continue, "You're an amazing teacher." He glanced down at his hands before looking at her.

***

Their eyes collided. Emma couldn't look away. She could barely squeak out, "Thank you." Neither of them moved.

Time was suspended, even though the world seemed to tilt. Her heart yearned to reach across the space toward him, but she had a boyfriend already. Besides, this was Pastor talking to her.

"Did—did Karl Piggott give you any grief?" Someone had to end the tension.

He cleared his throat. "He didn't do anything in front of me, but I could see in his eyes he was plotting something." He squinted, rubbing his hands together.

Emma could see the glint in Pastor's eyes. Was he teasing her? "I'm sure he was planning a revolt on the playground at recess." She gave him a half-smile.

"If you hadn't come in at just the right time, I was ready to sit on him to make him behave." Pastor grinned at her. "But I wouldn't have allowed a full-scale revolution, no matter what."

Emma's stomach performed a flip and then another, refusing to come to a complete standstill. Was this really Pastor talking to her? If only she'd known he was so witty. This was a new side for her to see, and she liked this side of him more than she thought possible.

"I knew my classroom was in good hands. That's why I stayed away so long." She couldn't stop the silly grin on her face.

Better to back out of this now. Freddie popped into her mind. He was still her boyfriend. "In all seriousness, I want to thank you immensely for helping out in my classroom today."

"I won't say it was my pleasure, but it sure was a good experience." As if a switch had turned off, his face changed into a solemn mask. "I now know, first hand, that teachers deserve a special blessing for facing a classroom of children day after day. I'll let you get back to your work." He turned toward the door.

Emma reached out and placed her hand on his arm. "Thank you so much again." The heat, spreading through her fingers and up her arm, took her by surprise. Had this ever happened with Freddie?

He covered her hand briefly with his. "You're welcome." He waved as he scooted out the door.

Her knees starting to buckle, she plopped onto a student desk. Rubbing her hand where his had been a moment before, she watched him leave. She had been depressed when he'd entered the room, but now felt more exuberant than ever before.

Had Pastor suddenly become more than her spiritual shepherd? She sighed. He seemed to understand her more than Freddie did. Warmth radiating from her, the smile on her face would not fade even after he was gone. *Lord, are you trying to tell me something? Help me understand this new friendship with the man who is also my pastor.*

Chapter 27

Freddie straightened his tie as he glanced in the mirror one last time before heading down the steps toward the living room. Finally, the time was right to put his plans into action. A nice dinner with Emma and a ride down by the lake should put her in the right frame of mind for his scheme to work.

Since they'd come back from the Milwaukee excursion, she'd been avoiding him. It sure seemed that way for the last three weeks. Did the ill-fated entrance into the speak-easy have something to do with her new attitude toward him? Didn't seem like it. She'd been fine the rest of that evening and most of the next day. Something had to have happened after their return to Racine to make her pull back.

But what?

Em had used the excuse of being too busy. Report cards were her stated reason. Did it take weeks to fill out the grades? He shook his head.

He hopped down the front steps and strolled across the lawn toward the Muellers' driveway. The hint of spring in the air this Friday evening lifted his spirits despite the long lonely weeks preceding.

At least, the night for the big date had arrived. He'd worked hard at persuading Em to take the time off tonight. He'd told her it was a special occasion. What an understatement.

After climbing the porch steps, he knocked on her door. Would he really be able to go through with the plan?

***

"Here we are." Freddie stopped the car on a bluff in the park overlooking Lake Michigan. The wide expanse of the deep blue water sparkled as the full moon rose off the eastern horizon. Her lilac perfume tantalizing him, he put his arm along the back of the seat and ran his finger along Emma's neck.

They had gone to a fancy restaurant in Kenosha for a nice quiet dinner. He'd led the conversation toward safe topics, not wanting to spring the surprise too early.

Was she ready for an explanation now?

Turning toward her, he grasped her hand. It was time. He'd planned this evening for weeks, even borrowing the family car from his father to make this happen. After the weekend in Milwaukee, Freddie knew he had to make a definitive move to win her over. He didn't want to wait around anymore. Time to take the plunge.

Jules had tried to dissuade him of this idea, but it was the only way Emma would come around. She had said so herself on the couch at his aunt's house. Now he was faced with the reality of saying all this out loud to her.

"What a wonderful view." Emma looked out across the lake in the dusky twilight.

"That's why I chose this place. You need something calm in your life right now."

He swallowed twice, spotting the blinking light of a ship far from shore. Up the coast he could see Wind Point Lighthouse silhouetted against the inky backdrop with the steady light flashing back and forth.

"You're right. I've been so busy lately." She laid her head against the back of the seat. "It's so beautiful I could relax here all night."

Freddie moved closer to Emma. It was now or never. Could he find the courage to say the right words? "You're beautiful tonight, doll."

Her eyes widening, Emma sat up and turned to him. "No one has ever said that to me before." She brushed her hair behind her ear. "Thank you."

"But it's true." Freddie leaned closer and touched his lips to hers. "Over the past weeks, I've come to realize I love you." He held his breath; his gaze burned into her. He'd debated long and hard if those three words needed to be said for this to work. His conclusion, yes they did. Those words had never before crossed his lips for any girl. If only he didn't feel as if he were hanging off the edge of a cliff, holding on by three fingers.

***

Emma sat in silence, except for the noisy pounding of her heart. What should she say? Love? She hadn't expected to hear that word from Freddie any time soon, especially not tonight. She hadn't even talked to him much the last three weeks.

Ever since her conversation with Pastor in her classroom, she found herself thinking about him several times a day, much of the time comparing him to Freddie. Why couldn't Freddie be more like him? Things would be perfect then.

She couldn't sit there without responding. "I . . . I . . . think . . . I love you, too." She had been telling herself this for months. It must be true. Now she said it. After all, that's why she had forgiven him so readily after the speakeasy incident. She enjoyed his company—he made her laugh. This had to be love.

And besides, his kisses were amazing.

She leaned toward him to put her words into actions, but deep within she heard her inner voice say, "What would Pastor think?"

Closing her eyes, Emma dismissed the disruption and concentrated on Freddie. When their lips met, Freddie enclosed her in his arms and deepened the kiss. She felt herself go limp against him. This just had to be love.

Wanting to hear those words from the love of her life, she had envisioned this moment for years. She had longed for a man she could look to for support and protection. Was Freddie the one for her?

He lifted his head. "Baby, I'm thrilled to hear you say that." He placed his hands on her shoulders. "I was afraid you wouldn't level with me—that you wouldn't feel the same way." He cupped her face in his hands and brought his lips to hers, gently opening his mouth over hers.

"Stop!" Putting her hands against his chest, she broke off the ardent passion. "I can't do this." Her insides rolling like a ship tossed at sea, she had to steady herself before looking into his eyes. "Freddie, not this way."

"You're right." Clearing his throat, he sat up straight and took a deep breath. "That's why I think we should, um, get hitched."

Gasping, her mouth fell open. She glanced down, studying her hands, as she tried to hide the shock surging through her veins. How could he suggest such a thing without even meeting her parents? What would she tell them? He was moving way too fast. "M . . . married? I . . . I don't think we're ready to talk about that yet." Emma brushed her hand through her hair. If only she could think clearly. "I'm just in my first year of teaching. I want to keep teaching for a while."

"I've thought of that." Freddie stared out the front window. "I know when women walk down the middle aisle, they have to resign from teaching. I don't understand the rule, but that's the way it is." He grasped her hands. "I wouldn't want you to quit teaching either."

What was he hinting at? She flicked a glance at him before staring out over the lake.

"I've been thinking of a solution to this situation. And, I've figured out a way around it." He plowed on. "We could go to Waukegan, Illinois to get hitched. No one would know about it here in Racine."

The world spinning around her, Emma stared at him in disbelief. She tried to open her mouth, but Freddie didn't give her a chance to speak.

"The North Shore Line at the Kenosha station would take us to Illinois. A train ticket doesn't cost too much dough. We could get a justice of the peace to marry us and be back here on Monday morning for school. That way we'd be married and wouldn't have to be careful about necking and such, and, like I said, you could still be a teacher."

Was he kidding?

Forcing herself to unclench her teeth, Emma couldn't believe he had planned all of this before he even mentioned the topic to her. Her heart pounded in her ears. What made him think she would ever elope? Didn't he want to get married in a church and have his wedding blessed by God? She would never consider starting a marriage any other way. "I—"

***

"No—" Freddie touched his fingertips to her lips. "Em, I know this plan of mine is all new to you. I don't want your first reaction, because I'm sure it's no." He ran a finger along her cheek. "Just think about it a while."

His finger ended under her chin, tipping it up so they were eye to eye. "Of course, when we are ready to make the marriage public, we can then have a church wedding to formalize our vows."

There it was—out in the open. He'd passed the point of no return.

Freddie had gone to the train station to check out the schedule. He'd even written a letter to a county clerk in Illinois finding how much the marriage license would cost. He'd covered all his bases before broaching this subject with her.

It was the only way he could get what he wanted from Emma—the pleasures of marriage without all the responsibility. He wasn't really ready to set up housekeeping with her, but this way he could have it all—Emma as his wife and still let her work.

Eventually, they would have to rent an apartment and live as man and wife in the open, but until she was ready to stop teaching, this temporary situation was perfect for him. He just hoped Jules could keep it under his hat as long as necessary.

"Freddie . . ."

"No." He reached toward her. "Let's not beat our gums about it anymore tonight." Freddie started up the engine and put the car in reverse. "After you sleep on it, we'll talk more."

Silence reigned during the ride back to his house. Relieved to have it out in the open, he was sure he'd have to do some more persuading tomorrow. All the arguments were lined up in his mind, ready to be brought out as she laid the opposing points on the table. It was the only way to solve his problem with her.

***

Emma sat beside him not moving an inch. Her brain scrambled to find any logic to all this. She was positive "sleeping on it" would not change her answer at all, but he refused to even talk about it tonight.

Was she so wrong about him? Freddie didn't seem to respect her at all to suggest they elope, just so they could sleep together. At least, that's what it sounded like to her.

He had never even asked for her opinion. He hadn't really proposed to her. That hurt. Why hadn't he consulted her?

Pinching her lips tight so she wouldn't explode, she glared straight out the window.

That was not love by any standard and definitely not the Christian love that a man and woman brought to marriage. The longer she thought about it the more her jaw ached.

Unshed tears burning her eyes, she refused to let them fall in front of him. She was thankful when they arrived on their street. She couldn't wait to get away and be by herself.

As soon as the car stopped in front of Freddie's garage, Emma jumped out without a word and headed toward her house.

"Yoo-hoo!" His mother called from the front porch.

Emma halted in midstride and glanced over her shoulder. Terrific. Not what she needed right now.

"I saw the car drive in and wanted to catch you. I haven't had a chance to talk to you lately." She beckoned Emma to come back to their house.

Sighing, Emma trudged in that direction.

"Why don't you and Freddie come in for a cup of hot chocolate before you head home? We could catch up on the latest news."

What could Emma do? She couldn't offend Mrs. Neumann, but having a cup of hot cocoa was about the last thing she wanted to do right now. "Sure."

In an instant, Freddie was at her side, grasping her hand. She tugged to free herself, but he held tight. She couldn't very well make a scene.

"Swell idea." Putting his arm around her waist, he drew her closer. "We got cold sitting in the jalopy jabbering at the park. Hot chocolate would hit the spot right now."

Was he going to pretend that it never happened? Emma stiffened against Freddie's arm as he led her toward his house. She didn't even want him to touch her.

How was she going to be pleasant through a cup of hot cocoa when she was boiling already? She plastered a smile onto her face as she got closer to the front door. If only she could concentrate on talking to Mrs. Neumann and avoid Freddie as much as possible. Could she pull off this charade?

She followed Mrs. Neumann into the kitchen and sat in the chair Freddie's mother indicated. Taking off her coat, she draped it across her lap since she wouldn't be staying long.

"I'm so glad I saw you coming." Agnes turned back to the stove. "I haven't seen you much lately. How is school going?" She busied herself with the cocoa, the sweet scent of chocolate filling the kitchen.

Emma's mind was so numb she had a hard time concentrating. "The children are looking forward to Easter vacation, so they're getting wiggly these days."

Mrs. Neumann laughed. "They're like calves in spring, ready to bust outside." She handed a cup of cocoa to Emma. Looking at Freddie, she handed him his cup. "By the way, I got a phone call from Aunt Esther today saying they got home from Florida all safe and sound."

Freddie's head jerked away as he glanced as his mother. "Great." His face matched the cherry-colored couch in the living room. "How's Uncle Irvin doing?"

Ignoring his question, Emma peered at his mother. "Isn't Aunt Esther the one that lives in Milwaukee?"

"Why, yes." Mrs. Neumann answered her instead of Freddie. "You four went to her house a few weeks ago."

Freddie pulled at the collar of his shirt. "I'm glad she's back now." He hurried on, "This hot cocoa is perfect, isn't it Em?" He raised his cup toward her.

Turning back to Mrs. Neumann, Emma's brows furrowed. "She must have had a short trip to Florida if she's back already." She grasped her cup in both hands.

"Oh no, my dear." Mrs. Neumann looked at Freddie, who was shaking his head vigorously. What was going on with him?

Emma turned her attention back to his mother.

"She and her husband left for Florida the first week of January." Mrs. Neumann took a sip of cocoa. "They wanted to get out of the cold weather for a change and had the money to do it this winter."

Heat exploded onto Emma's cheeks. "They were gone while we were up at their house?" She glared at Freddie.

"Well, sure, they were gone." Mrs. Neumann glanced from Emma to Freddie. "That's why Freddie had to go up there. He had to pick up the mail and bring it back down here."

Emma couldn't believe what she was hearing. Freddie had told her an outright lie when they were in Milwaukee. He had declared his love to her not more than an hour ago and asked, no, told her, that they were going to elope and now she finds out he had lied straight to her face weeks earlier. Her stomach almost in her throat, Emma struggled into her coat sleeves.

"I . . . I'm sorry. I have to leave now, Mrs. Neumann. Thanks for the hot cocoa." She stumbled toward the door.

Chapter 28

"No, wait!" Freddie stepped between Emma and the door. Now he was in big trouble. Hoping to steer the conversation on a different path, he had done his best to change the subject. It hadn't worked. He hadn't wanted the truth to come out like that. How would he explain it to Emma?

"Is everything all right, dear?" Mrs. Neumann's widened eyes glanced from Emma to him and back again. He ignored her question.

Slipping past him, Emma flew out the door. "How dare you!" she threw over her shoulder.

He charged after her, the door slamming shut with a bang. "Em, wait!"

Whirling around as she reached the edge of the porch, she planted her feet apart and jabbed her finger in his chest.

"Let me ex—"

"How dare you . . . declare your love to me when you knew!" She swung around and took off down the steps

"C'mon, don't just walk off. Please." Freddie hurried after her, catapulting down the stairs. "Calm down and let me explain." He put a hand on her arm. How could he get out of the mess this time?

"How can you possibly expect me to do that?" Emma pulled her arm away from his grasp. "I just found out you lied to me when we were in Milwaukee, and not an hour ago, you told me you loved me. And I'm supposed to calm down?" She stormed off.

"I know it's all balled up. Look, I'm sorry. I'm really sorry." Would she even listen to him anymore?

"Sorry doesn't cut it tonight. I'll never believe another word from you." She froze in the middle of the sidewalk and turned back to him. "And I don't need to Sleep. On. It. The answer to your proposal is no."

***

Taking deep breaths, Emma put one foot in front of the other and stumbled down the sidewalk. Torn between rage and embarrassment, she didn't want to face anyone at the moment. She'd trusted Freddie for months. How could she have been so wrong about him?

God, what should I do now? Her head felt like Mount Vesuvius sitting next to Pompeii. Tears burned behind her eyelids, but she had to compose herself so she could think clearly.

She kept walking. One step at a time. It was no use. The tears, refusing to stay in check, streamed down her cheeks. There was no way to stop their course at this point. With blurred vision, she found herself hurrying toward school. Maybe that was where she should go. No one would be there on a Friday evening—the perfect place to be alone. No one would bother her there.

When she reached her classroom, she sagged into her chair. At least, she'd be able to vent her feelings of betrayal to this empty room. Her anger, however, escaped in loud sobs.

How could he have lied to her? She'd thought she loved him for months. He'd been fun to be with. Maybe there were more important things in life than fun. Would she be able to trust her feelings ever again? She laid her head on her arms and gave in to her sobs.

***

Neil turned off the switch in his study before heading up to bed. As he glanced out the window, he noticed light showing from Emma's classroom. Why was that? Maybe she'd forgotten to turn them off when she left in the afternoon. He'd seen her hurry home about five o'clock.

Grabbing his coat, he headed toward school to take care of it.

The last time he'd been in her classroom was three weeks ago—the day he taught her class. Good thing she wouldn't be there tonight. He'd let his guard down that day, allowing her to read his feelings for her. At least he thought so. He wanted to kick himself for letting it happen. Never again, but it was becoming so hard to hide what he felt.

Unlocking the door, he slipped inside. What was the noise he heard upstairs? He crept up the stairs with both ears tuned in, listening to the rustling. Was someone in Emma's room stealing something? As he got closer, the noise became more distinct.

Crying. Was Emma here at this hour? Why would she be here now? Was she hurt? He skipped up the last few steps.

Emma's door stood open. Peering around the corner to assess the situation, he saw her sitting with her head in her arms. Her shoulders shook with each sob.

He stifled the urge to sprint to her side. What had happened to her? Something dreadful, no doubt. *Lord, show me how to help her. Only You can give me the right words.*

Clearing his throat, Neil stepped into her room. "Emma, what's wrong?"

Her head shot up as she faced the door. Her reddened eyes and tear-stained cheeks told him she had a serious problem.

Throat aching, his heart went out to her. Masking his feelings, he steered toward her desk. "Have you heard bad news? Something from home?"

Swiping her cheeks, Emma shook her head. She slumped against the back of her chair. "N . . . No." Blowing her nose on a hankie, she wiped the traces of tears off her cheeks. "Why are you here?"

"I saw your light on and came to turn it off, not realizing you were in the room." He took off his hat, setting it on her desk. "Are you all right? Would you like to tell me what happened?"

"It's a long story." Emma hiccupped and let her breath out.

Smiling at her, he sat on one of the child-size desks. "That's O.K. I have all night." If only she would return his smile.

"This is hard to admit. I . . ." She glanced down, twisting the damp hankie in her lap. "I found out Freddie was lying to me tonight."

Neil's hands balled into fists. So, this was about that Freddie character. Having known this would happen someday, he'd have to be very careful not to let anger cloud his judgment.

"I'm sorry to hear that." He rubbed his hands together to keep the tension from showing. "I'll be glad to listen if you want to tell me. Sometimes that helps." He longed to touch her, but that wouldn't do right now. "Remember I'm your friend, as well as your pastor."

Emma's eyes filled with tears again. She blinked several times. "A friend is what I need tonight." Her mouth turned up at the edges.

"I'll always be here for you . . . because we're friends." Neil filled the silence by running his fingers down the crease in his trousers. Waiting for her to open up took all the patience he could muster.

Emma stood and walked toward the window. She stared into the blackness. "Pastor, this is . . ."

He interrupted her. "Emma, since we said we're friends, don't you think you should call me Neil?" Walking toward the window, he stood just behind her. He kept his arms at his side, resisting the urge to hold her.

Emma turned to look up at him. "I'll try." She swiveled back again toward the window. "This is hard for me to say. I don't know where to start." A flush crept up her cheeks as she shook her head.

"Just start at the beginning." Neil shifted his feet. "It'll be easier after you get going." What was she about to tell him? This must be earth shattering.

"Tonight Freddie told me we should get married." Her cheeks turned a deeper shade of red.

"And?" His heart raced, nearly exploding, as he waited for her to continue. Had he already lost her to Freddie? But if that were so, she wouldn't be here crying, would she? "Wait. He told you—not asked you?"

"Let me finish first." She took a long slow breath and brushed her hair behind her ear. "He planned for us to go to Illinois next weekend to get married secretly. He said that then

I could keep teaching and no one would know we were married." Her words a mere whisper.

Neil could see her blushing face in profile as she stared out the window. "Wh—?" Silence reigned as he continued to gaze at her. "Why would he suggest such a thing?"

Emma didn't respond at first. "Because I wouldn't . . . with him." She buried her face in her hands.

He rested his hands on her shoulders and slowly turned her toward him. Tears streaming down her cheeks, she stared at his shoes.

"Oh, Emma." He put a finger under her chin, raising her head until he made eye contact. "You didn't do anything wrong." His pulse racing, warmth spread up his arm. He was her pastor. He couldn't let his heart rule the situation. "You shouldn't be embarrassed about this at all."

"It's hard not to be." Her brown eyes avoided his.

"You did the right thing by stopping his advances. It's what God wants you to do." He could see her shoulders relaxing.

"Why would he do that to me?" Their eyes made contact. "He didn't even ask what I wanted. He told me he loved me, but then told me what we should do." Her words faded away.

"What Freddie did to you was wrong." Neil swallowed his anger. "He was thinking only of himself and going after what he wants in life."

***

Emma reflected on the past several months—the dances, the gambling while playing mahjong, and especially the weekend in Milwaukee. She swallowed past the lump in her throat. "How come I didn't realize it long ago?"

"There are more important questions to ask, Emma." Neil dropped his hands and stepped back.

"What do you mean?" Emma's breath caught in her throat.

"Where's Jesus?"

"I don't understand." Emma's mind raced.

"Where's Jesus in your life?"

Emma studied his black shoes. She hadn't asked herself that question very much lately. She walked to a student desk and sat down.

Neil sat on the desk next to her and glanced her way. "Since you love God, Christ should shine in your life."

Emma's pulse raced. "Guess that hasn't happened much lately."

"His life is our life whether we're thinking about Him or not." Neil smiled. "Because of His death on the cross, God comes first in our lives as we live our lives according to His choices." Neil ducked his head. "Sorry, I didn't mean to give you a sermon tonight."

Emma couldn't look him in the eye. "I understand what you mean. Things like going dancing?"

Neil crossed his legs at the ankle. "That would be one example. Dancing in itself is not wrong, but it can lead people down the wrong path. Christ's love motivates us to stay away from things that are tempting."

Gathering courage, Emma glanced sideways at him. "I left home to experience life, have fun. I didn't think about the temptations I was facing."

"Most people don't. Freddie wasn't either."

She swallowed hard before proceeding. "We should have had this talk a couple months ago." Emma stood up and peered out the window again. "I've been having fun with Freddie, but sometimes my conscience bothered me."

"God was calling you back to Him."

Returning to her seat, Emma turned to look into Neil's eyes. "I didn't listen very well, then."

"You can start right now."

His gaze burned into her as if he had more to say. What was he trying to tell her?

Rubbing her temple, Emma tried to clear her mind. So much emotional turmoil in the last couple hours. "Yeah, I need to put Christ first in my life." Sitting next to Neil, she leaned forward, bracing herself on her arms.

His hand covered hers, lying between them. "But don't you see? He has loved you through all of this. I'm sure you're hurting and confused now, but I'm also certain God has been guiding you every day. Guiding you on the path to your heavenly home."

Looking down at their hands, she had no words to answer him.

"But now, I think it's time you went home. It's been a long day for you." He patted her hand. "In fact, I'm going to walk you back to the Muellers' house. I don't want you to be out alone after what you've been through."

"You don't have to do that." Emma stood to retrieve her coat.

"Yeah, I do."

They headed down the steps and into the cool evening air. As they reached the sidewalk, Pastor grasped her hand, laying it in the crook of his arm. Heat spread up her arm as his hand rested on hers. This had never occurred with Freddie. Should she pull her hand away?

He didn't break the connection between them, instead rubbing his thumb across her knuckles. "You never told me how Freddie lied to you." He cut his eyes sideways at her.

Emma glanced at their hands as they walked. "Three weeks ago, Vivi and I went up to Milwaukee with Freddie and Jules. The day you had to teach in my classroom. I now know it was wrong to do this. Before we left, Freddie told me we were staying at his aunt's house. With his aunt as chaperone, I thought it would be fine."

She looked up into his face. "The whole weekend he lied to me. He came up with reasons why his aunt wasn't home. She never showed at all. Now I know why. She was in Florida the entire time. I would never have gone up there if I had known no chaperone would be in the house."

"There again, Freddie was showing he wanted his fun and accomplished this by lying to you." Neil shook his head. "This is his problem, not yours."

Stopping close to a street lamp, Emma pulled her hand from his arm. "I trusted Freddie. I believed everything he told me." She hesitated. "How will I ever be able to trust another man?"

"Think what you're saying." Neil clasped her shoulders. "There are many good men that you can trust." He held her eyes in his gaze. "Trust me. I won't ever lie to you." They were standing only inches apart.

Emma searched his face, her head cautioning her to be careful, her heart telling her to trust him. "Neil . . ." His name rolled off her tongue. "I do trust you . . . as my pastor." Her heart fluttered in her chest.

Neil clasped her hands and whispered. "But, Emma, I'm also a man, a man you can trust."

Emma wanted to. With her whole being she longed for more. "I know you would never lie to me."

"Um, I . . ." He linked her hand on his arm again and continued down the street. Silence stretched between them as he held her hand. With dogs barking in the background, their feet clicked on the sidewalk marking the passage of time. What was he struggling to say?

"Since you know I would never lie to you, I have a confession to make." His breath tickled her cheek as he glanced sideways at her. "I've loved you from afar for months. Because of Freddie, I was afraid to tell you." He stopped at the end of the Muellers' driveway and clasped both her hands. "I'm hoping now it's our turn." In the dim light, she could see his mouth turn up in a half-smile.

Her heart froze. Could it be true? Relaxing for the first time all night, a smile crept across her face. For three weeks, she had been thinking of Neil in a new light. Not only was he her pastor, but he was also a man—a man she was falling in love with. Had she secretly been hoping things would turn out like this? Dreaming these very words would one day be spoken by Neil? It was as if she were now awakening from the dream. Before her mouth could form any words, she held her breath and nodded.

Cupping her face in his hands, he brought his lips slowly to hers in a gentle kiss. Backing away, she started to breathe again.

In the next instant, she found herself moving the short distance toward him. He met her halfway as their lips touched again. His arms slowly encircled her waist as the kiss lingered.

Her heart soaring, she pulled back and grinned into his warm eyes. "I could get used to this."

God had finally guided her home.

Epilogue

Her wedding day. Emma couldn't quite get used to the fact. Her stomach fluttering, she patted her curls. "Do I look O.K.?" As she stood in her childhood bedroom, she connected with Vivi's eyes in the mirror.

"You look beautiful, as all brides should." Vivi hugged her.

"Thanks. I'm glad you've finally finished working on my hair."

Vivi held a tube in her hand. "I am not used to styling hair without all my stuff around me. At least I brought my gel. The result is *superbe.* What is the word? Stunning."

"It was worth it then?" Emma chuckled.

"It certainly was. Pastor will not know what hit him when he sees you."

"I still can't believe the big day is finally here." Placing her hand on her midsection, Emma tried to stop the jitters. Was a gymnast performing a routine in there?

She looked at herself in the mirror. Running a hand down her ankle-length dress, she smoothed out the wrinkles as best she could. With alternating panels of ivory silk and tulle extending from her waist down to the hem, the dress made her feel like a queen. The high neckline of the silk bodice, covered in matching tulle netting, drew her eyes toward her face. Good thing her lacy sleeves covered her arms. She'd be warm enough this cool June day. The floor-length veil would be set in place when they arrived at the church.

"My mom did a wonderful job sewing my dress in such a short time."

"That is certain—seven weeks. I still cannot figure out how you planned your wedding so quickly." Vivi shook her head. "But what a blessing you will be to Pastor as he carries out God's work. He is the very lucky man."

"No, Vivi. I'm the one who's blessed. I thank God every day for opening my eyes and turning me toward Neil. He's so much more than I deserve."

"Even if he is so particular about how organized and perfect everything is in his life?" Vivi placed her hand in front of her mouth as a giggle escaped her lips.

Emma joined Vivi in the laugh. "You should have been here yesterday when he was cleaning his car to get it ready for the wedding. I would have been done in half the time it took him. He made sure every nook and cranny was spotless before he was finished. At least I know we'll have a clean house all the time. And that makes me love him all the more."

Neil was the man she loved, the man she'd been searching for her whole life. As she'd spent more time with him, she could see God's guiding hand in her life, a totally different direction than she had expected. Now she was getting married to this man who had become her support and protector.

Emma clasped Vivi's hands in hers. In her peach-colored bridesmaid dress and coiffed hair, she was the epitome of a French beauty. "I can't begin to thank you for being part of my wedding."

"That is what best friends are for."

Swallowing past the lump in her throat, Emma could manage little more than a whisper. "It means so much to me."

"Thanks be to God you learned the truth about Freddie before it was too late."

Was it only three months since her world had turned upside down? Since she had learned the truth about him?

Vivi stepped back. "I tried talking to Jules about Freddie, but he would not listen to me." Tears glistened in her eyes.

Emma searched Vivi's face. "I'm so sorry things didn't work out between you and Jules." They were so perfect for each other. Emma enfolded her in a hug. "It's hard for me to be so happy when I know you are alone again."

***

"Not to worry about me. I do not want to ruin your wedding." Being careful not to crush Emma's dress, Vivi returned her hug. "I think I am better off without Jules if I am honest." She swallowed. Her heart didn't like listening to her brain all the time, however. "I cannot be in a relationship with someone who does not share my belief in God." On that, her heart and head agreed.

"I'll pray that God helps you find your other half, as I found mine." Emma's smile lit up her face.

Vivi smiled. If only that prayer were answered, and soon. What would it feel like to be a bride? Emma looked so happy. Practically glowing. Someday. Vivi sighed. "Enough chatter. We better go down, or you will be late for your own wedding."

"Don't want that to happen."

Vivi accompanied Emma down the stairs to the living room. "Careful now. Cannot ruin anything this late in the day." They reached the last step. "Now we are ready when your brother gets here."

"Where is he?" Emma pulled on her gloves and paced between the window and door. "Danny should have been here long ago." She glanced at the clock. "I'll be late."

Vivi clucked her tongue. "Calm down, Em." If pacing would make Danny come quicker, he'd be here in no time.

"I'm trying."

"He has made several trips to church already with your ma and the rest of the family."

"It's a good thing Pa was able to buy his car this spring. I can't imagine going in a wagon dressed like this." Giggling, Emma ran her hand down her skirt.

"You are right there. He will be back soon." Vivi peered out the window. "Besides we want to be the last ones to arrive at church before you walk down the aisle."

"Never thought of that." Glancing in the mirror, Emma patted her curls.

Vivi spotted the car coming up the driveway. "Here he comes now."

"Finally."

Vivi opened the front door and headed out to the porch. "It is about time you got back. We have been waiting for hours." She crossed her arms, but the smile on her face belied her harsh words. On this beautiful day, she couldn't be irritated with anyone.

Exiting the car, Danny glanced toward the porch. He whistled, his smile rivaling the sparkle in his brown eyes. "Wow, very cute in your new dress." As soon as the words left his mouth, color blossomed on his cheeks.

Heat climbed Vivi's face in response. Hers probably matched his, but the grin didn't fade from her lips. So handsome with his square jaw and hair dipping across his forehead, Vivi swallowed as her heart fluttered. Was the excitement of the wedding causing her giddiness?

He cleared his throat. "As for your comment about being late, you can quit acting like the big cheese here." He climbed the steps to stand beside her. "I hurried back as fast as I could. Where's the bride?"

"Pacing in the front room." Glancing over her shoulder, Vivi headed back into the house. She pointed toward the long veil and headpiece draped over the couch. "We need to load her veil into the back seat before she gets in the car. I do not want her dress to wrinkle too much. Can you please help me, so it does not touch the ground?"

"I'm at your command." Looking spiffy in his black suit, he bowed at the waist. His right arm swept sideways. "What else would you like, m'lady?"

"Oh, do not tease." She ducked her head.

Winking, he picked up the lacy fabric and draped it over his arms. "I'll be able to handle it from here." He held it above his head as he walked down the porch steps.

Vivi couldn't wipe the smile off her face as she concentrated on getting the veil placed in the car. "Lay it out like this." Vivi's hand touched Danny's arm as he tried to untangle his hands from the midst of all the lace. Feeling a shock streak up her arm, she yanked her hand from the fluffy fabric.

When they got the veil spread out, she turned her attention to Emma. "Em, maybe you can sit next to the veil? I am afraid your dress will get all rumpled if we all try to sit in the front." Vivi helped her climb in the back and got her situated as best she could.

"Perfect." Danny hurried around the car to open the door for Vivi. "You can share the front seat with me." His eyes danced as she approached the open door.

***

Smiling, Emma leaned against the back seat. Terrific. Vivi and Danny were engrossed in a conversation all their own. It looked like a spark was igniting between them.

As she watched hayfields fly past her window, Emma thought back on her whirlwind romance with Neil. It hadn't taken long for their friendship to turn into something much stronger.

During her Easter vacation, Emma had taken him home to meet her family. They had gotten on famously with Neil, and now, according to her mother, loved him like their own son. He'd told her he felt at home, having grown up on a farm in Wisconsin. Helping out with the milking and other farm chores, he fit right in.

By the end of April, Neil had proposed, making Emma's heart overflow with joy, a much-improved affair after her experience with Freddie. He'd planned a lovely evening—dinner in a nice restaurant and a walk along the lake.

When the sun dipped slowly over the horizon, he'd turned toward her and grasped her hands. "I'm—I need—I'm not very good at coming up with the right words at a time like this." Glancing up, he'd finally managed to look into her eyes. "I've learned to love you more every day. I've seen your love for others and your strong Christian faith. Those are qualities that I need by my side every day for the rest of my life as I do God's work. Will you marry me and become my helpmeet?"

She'd been expecting these words during the last couple days since Neil had hinted of a special event occurring soon. "I love you, too." With tears streaming down her cheeks, she'd whispered, "Yes, I'll marry you."

She sighed. Had they gotten engaged less than two months ago? So much had happened since then. The month of May had flown by with Emma still teaching and trying to plan a wedding at the same time. Her mother had been delighted to step in where Emma couldn't, since the wedding would take place in her home congregation. Neil continued to be the steady rock she had learned to love and depend on. And now the long-awaited day was finally here.

She glanced out the window, spotting calves romping in the fields. This time when she left Juneau, it would be permanent.

Of course, she'd occasionally return for visits, but never again would this be home. She blinked away a threatening tear.

The car pulled to a stop in front of the church. Danny glanced at his watch. "We'd better hurry, or they'll start without you." He winked at Vivi.

The gymnast routine inside her started acting up again.

"Sit tight, Em. I will help you." Vivi scurried to open Emma's door. "Danny, can you deal with the veil? Or do you need someone to help?"

"Don't let it touch the ground." Emma stepped out of the car, keeping an eye on her brother.

"I know, I know. I'll figure it out somehow." He singlehandedly removed it from the back of the car and, following after them, managed to get it into the narthex.

Emma put a hand on her abdomen. Must be somersaults in there now.

Ma and Maggie greeted them at the door. "Thanks, son." Ma kissed Danny on the cheek. "Now you get yourself up to the sacristy. I'm sure Neil and the rest are waiting to hear all the girls are set to go."

Her mother placed the Juliet cap on Emma. "Girl, you look beautiful." She hugged her. "I think everything's all ready now."

Arranging the veil's length down Emma's back, Vivi nodded. "You're right, Mrs. Ehlke. She is beautiful."

Maggie embraced her sister. "Wonder if I'll ever be a bride as pretty as you are today."

"Your day will come." Emma returned the hug.

Emma and her father waited for their turn to walk down the aisle. The gymnasts were now acrobats in her midsection. If only they would settle down.

She tucked her hand into the crook of Pa's arm and squeezed. He glanced at her. "Even though you'll be leaving your mother and me, you'll always be our little girl." His eyes glistened with unshed tears as he kissed her cheek. "We love both of you very much."

"Thanks, Pa." Her throat closed. No more would come out.

Emma's eyes filled with tears. They were next in line. Blinking several times, she took her first steps down the aisle at her father's side. Her vision cleared in time to see Neil waiting in front of church. Her breath caught.

Everything melted away, leaving him standing alone at the head of the aisle. Swallowing past the lump in her throat, she put one foot in front of the other. She was going home.

Acknowledgment

There are so many people to thank for helping me get this book published. My critique partners at Writer's Block and ACFW Scribes 218 were very patient as I learned the craft of writing. Dr. Lorna Weidman and Marie Poppe, my beta readers, pointed out the areas that needed rewrites. Many thanks to Liz Tolsma and Belinda Cortright, my editors. They helped me to wordsmith my story and turn it into the novel it is today. I send my sincere thanks to my book designer Lisa Hainline, who created my wonderful cover. A special thank you to Janet Ransdell for a fun photo shoot. Most of all, my heartfelt thanks goes to my husband and family for being so supportive through all these many years. I couldn't have accomplished this without all this help.

Above all, to God be the glory for His many blessings.

About The Author

Connie Cortright has been a history buff all her life, reading biographies and history since grade school. Naturally, when she considered writing a story, her first thoughts turned toward historical fiction. Her novels are set in America's Midwest and reflect her own Wisconsin farming roots.

Her life has been the fulfillment of her girlhood dreams: becoming a Lutheran school teacher, marrying a pastor, and having lots of children. Her life has taken her to both coasts (California and New Jersey) as she followed her pastor-husband in his service to various churches with their four sons.

She and her husband now live in Wauwatosa, Wisconsin. Their four sons are married to wonderful Christian women, with eight grandchildren scattered from California to Washington to British Columbia to Missouri. They try to see most of them at least once a year and are very thankful for Skype!

Connie loves reading books (especially historical romance) and now writing her own stories. Her book is available on Amazon.com. She can be contacted at Facebook or www.conniecortright.com. You can find her weekly blog at www.throughthemilkdoor.blogspot.com.

Made in the USA
Middletown, DE
02 December 2015